Lola's SUPER CLUB

"My Substitute Teacher is a Witch"

PAPERCUT^Z

NEW YORK

MORE GREAT GRAPHIC NOVEL SERIES AVAILABLE FROM PAPERCUTZ™

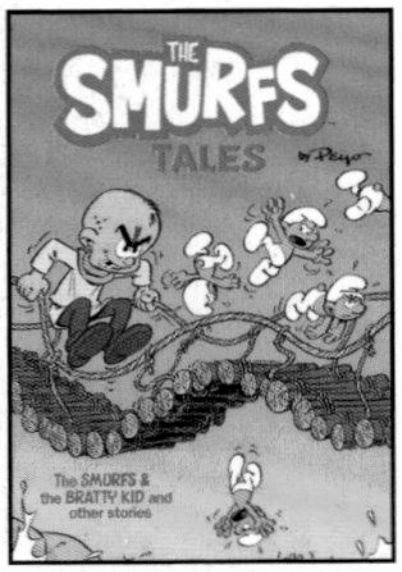
THE SMURFS TALES
The SMURFS & the BRATTY KID and other stories

THE SMURFS TALES

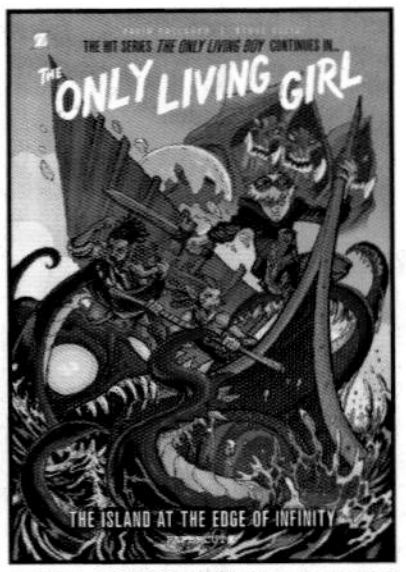
THE ONLY LIVING GIRL
THE ISLAND AT THE EDGE OF INFINITY

THE ONLY LIVING GIRL

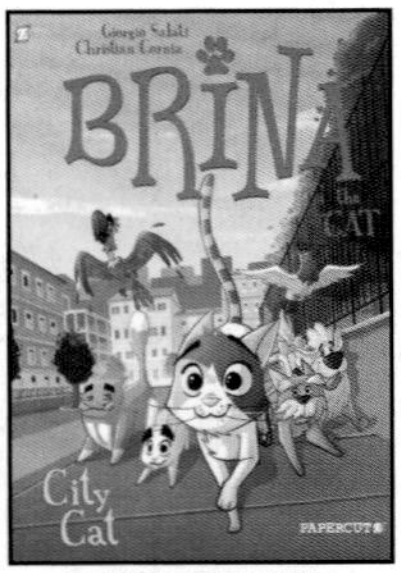
BRINA
City Cat

BRINA THE CAT

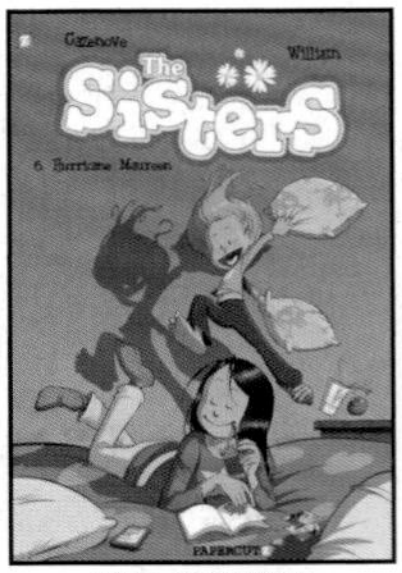
The Sisters

THE SISTERS

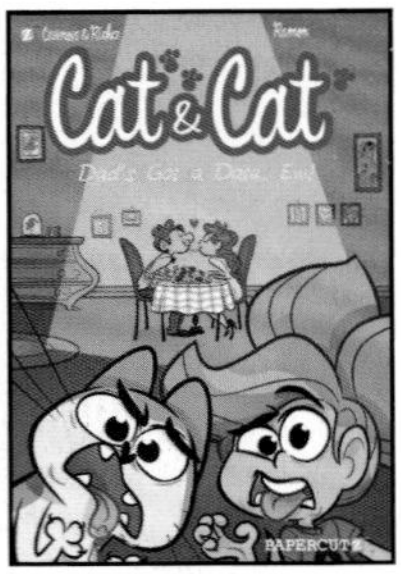
Cat & Cat

CAT & CAT

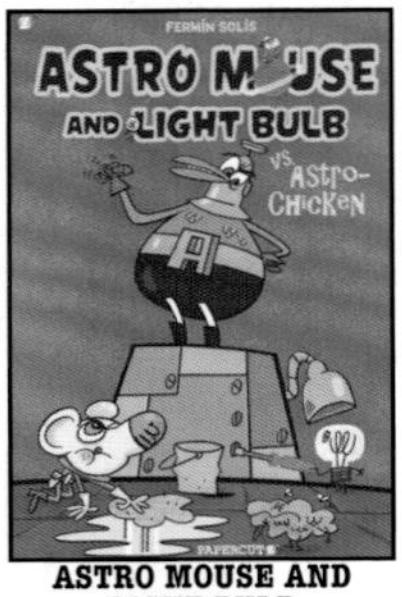
ASTRO MOUSE AND LIGHT BULB
VS ASTRO-CHICKEN

ASTRO MOUSE AND LIGHT BULB

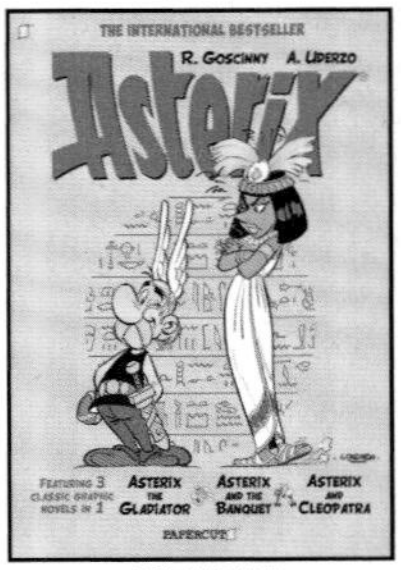
THE INTERNATIONAL BESTSELLER
R. GOSCINNY A. UDERZO
Asterix
ASTERIX THE GLADIATOR
ASTERIX AND THE BANQUET
ASTERIX AND CLEOPATRA

ASTERIX

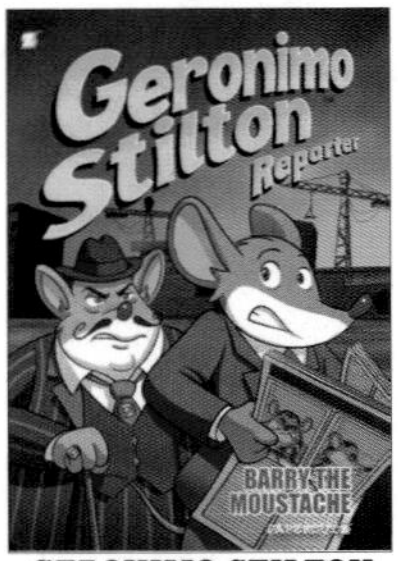
Geronimo Stilton Reporter
BARRY THE MOUSTACHE

GERONIMO STILTON REPORTER

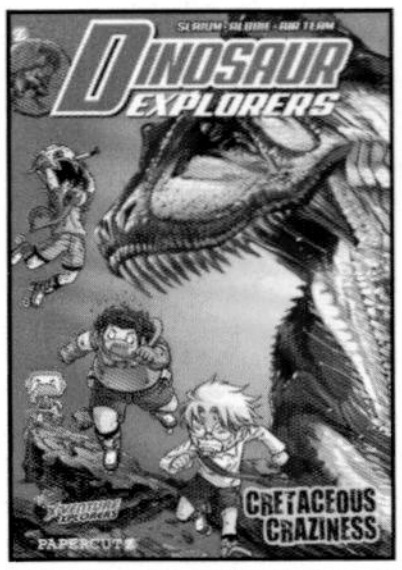
DINOSAUR EXPLORERS
CRETACEOUS CRAZINESS

DINOSAUR EXPLORERS

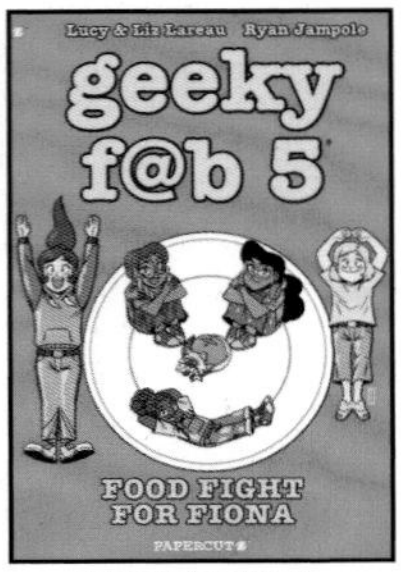
Lucy & Liz Lareau Ryan Jampole
geeky f@b 5
FOOD FIGHT FOR FIONA

GEEKY FAB 5

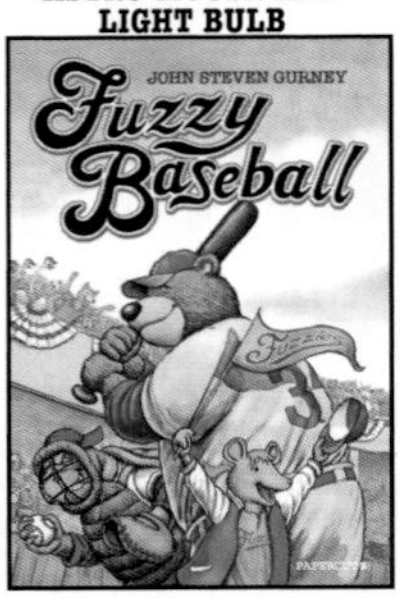
JOHN STEVEN GURNEY
Fuzzy Baseball

FUZZY BASEBALL

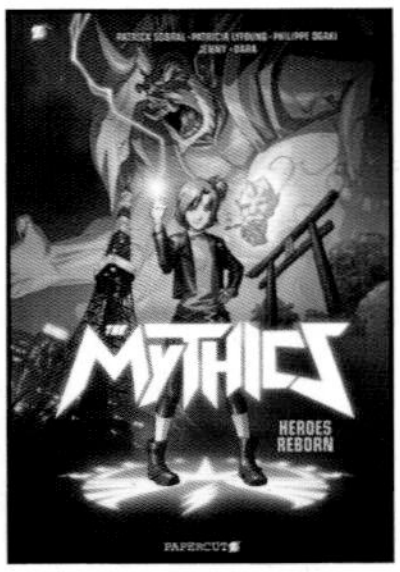
MYTHICS
HEROES REBORN

THE MYTHICS

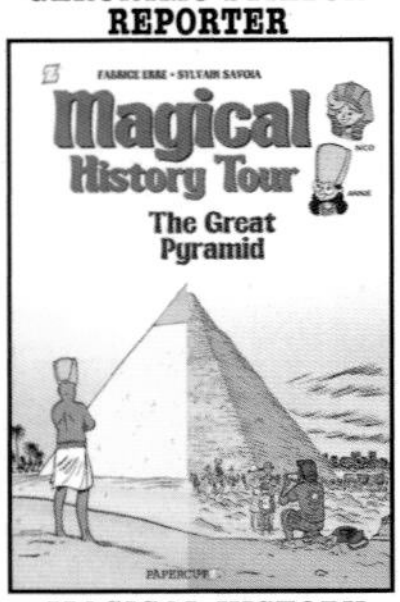
Magical History Tour
The Great Pyramid

MAGICAL HISTORY TOUR

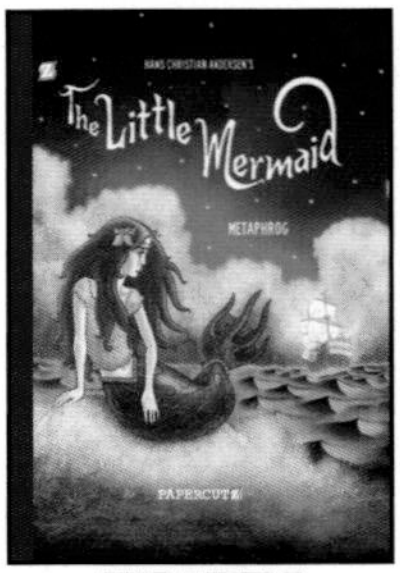
The Little Mermaid
METAPHROG

THE LITTLE MERMAID

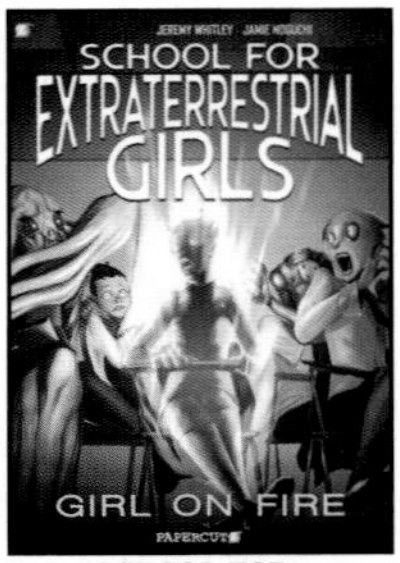
SCHOOL FOR EXTRATERRESTRIAL GIRLS
GIRL ON FIRE

SCHOOL FOR EXTRATERRESTRIAL GIRLS

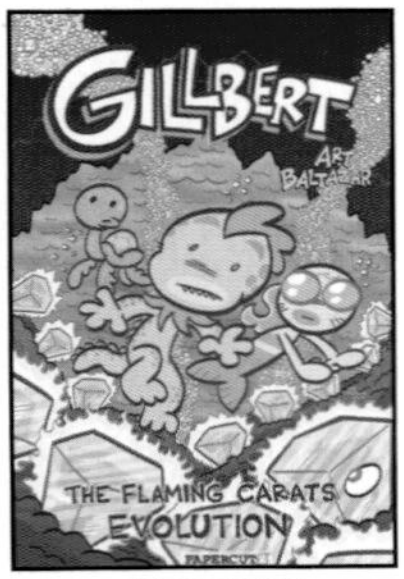
GILLBERT
ART BALTAZAR
THE FLAMING CARATS EVOLUTION

GILLBERT

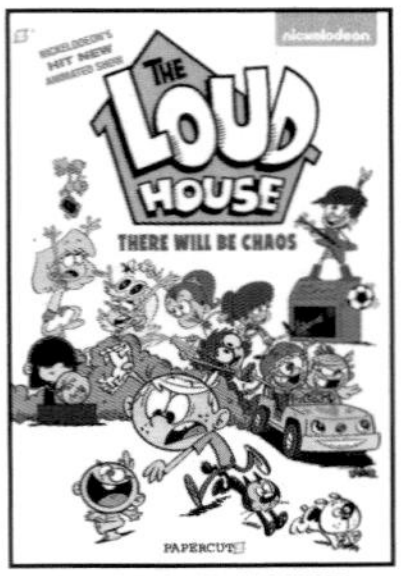
nickelodeon
THE LOUD HOUSE
THERE WILL BE CHAOS

THE LOUD HOUSE

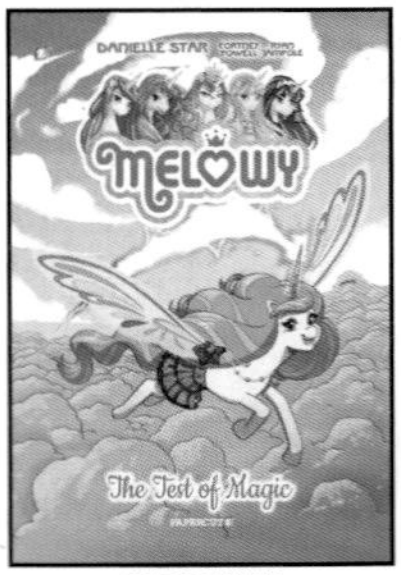
DANIELLE STAR
MELOWY
The Test of Magic

MELOWY

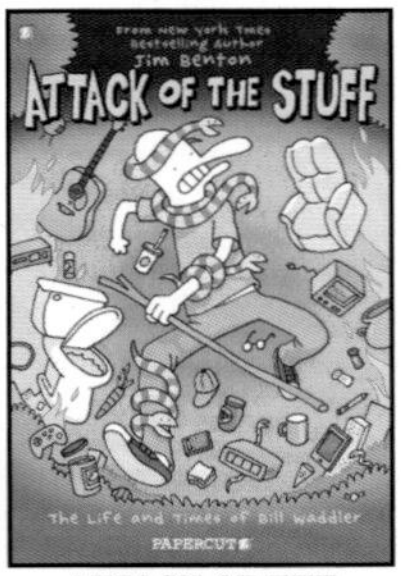
from new york times bestselling author Jim Benton
ATTACK OF THE STUFF
The Life and Times of Bill Waddler

ATTACK OF THE STUFF

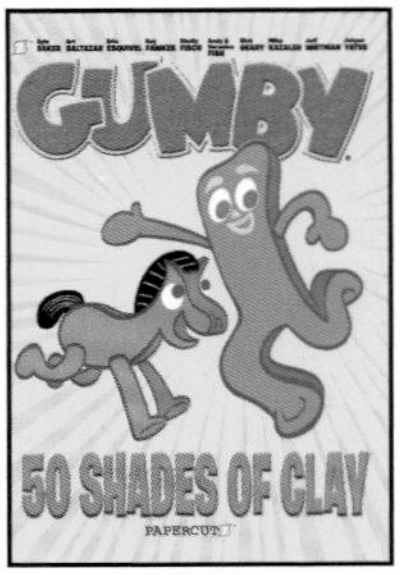
GUMBY
50 SHADES OF CLAY

GUMBY

papercutz.com

Also available as ebooks wherever ebooks are sold.

Lola's SUPER CLUB

2 - "MY SUBSTITUTE TEACHER IS A WITCH"

Script and art

Christine Beigel + Pierre Fouillet

Original editors

Maxi Luchini + Ed

Original designer

Immaculada Bordell

Paperback ISBN: 978-1-5458-0636-4
Hardcover ISBN: 978-1-5458-0635-7

Special thanks to Stephanie Barrouillet, Xavier Belltrán,
and Patricia Montalbán

Papercutz books may be purchased for business or promotional use.
For information on bulk purchases please contact
Macmillan Corporate and Premium Sales Department at
(800) 221-795 x5442.

Jeff Whitman – Translator, Letterer, Production, Editor
Jim Salicrup
Editor-in-Chief

Printed in China
August 2021

First Papercutz Printing
Distributed by Macmillan

PREVIOUSLY IN LOLA'S SUPER CLUB, LOLA (IN HER TUTU) AND HER SUPER CLUB, HER STUFFED DINO WITH A GROWTH SPURT PROBLEM, JAMES (IN UNDIES) AND HER CAT HOT DOG (IN DENIAL), HAD TO RESCUE HER HAPLESS DAD -- WHO IS ALSO SUPER SECRET AGENT JAMES BLOND -- FROM MAX IMUM AND HIS HENCH-DOGS ZERO + ZERO.

ALONG THE WAY, OUR HEROES MET THE SHAPE-CHANGING SCRIBBLE MONSTER MOMINA, A LIVELY SKELETON COUPLE WHO WERE ONCE SPIES, A SUPER-SHARK, AND A CROC WHO THINKS NOTHING IS FAIR. NOT TO MENTION THE FABLED PIRATE CAPTAIN RAIN-BEARD, THE VINE-SWINGING JUNGLOR, AND THE HIGH-FLYING SUPER HERO MOD MAN! TRULY A SUPER CLUB!

BUT MAX IMUM HAS MAXIMUM HELP TOO FROM HIS FAMILY, THE WICKED SPELL-CASTER MINI MUM AND HER RICH (BUT FORGETTABLE) LOVER, PRINCE GUINEMO, SORRY, GUILLERMO, (HIS NAME IS SO FORGETTABLE). WITH THE TWO CLUBS FORMED, IT'S UP TO LOLA'S SUPER CLUB TO SAVE HER HOMETOWN OF FRIENDLY FALLS AND EVERYONE IN IT... ONE ADVENTURE AT A TIME!

Lola's SUPER CLUB

"MY SUBSTITUTE TEACHER IS A WITCH"

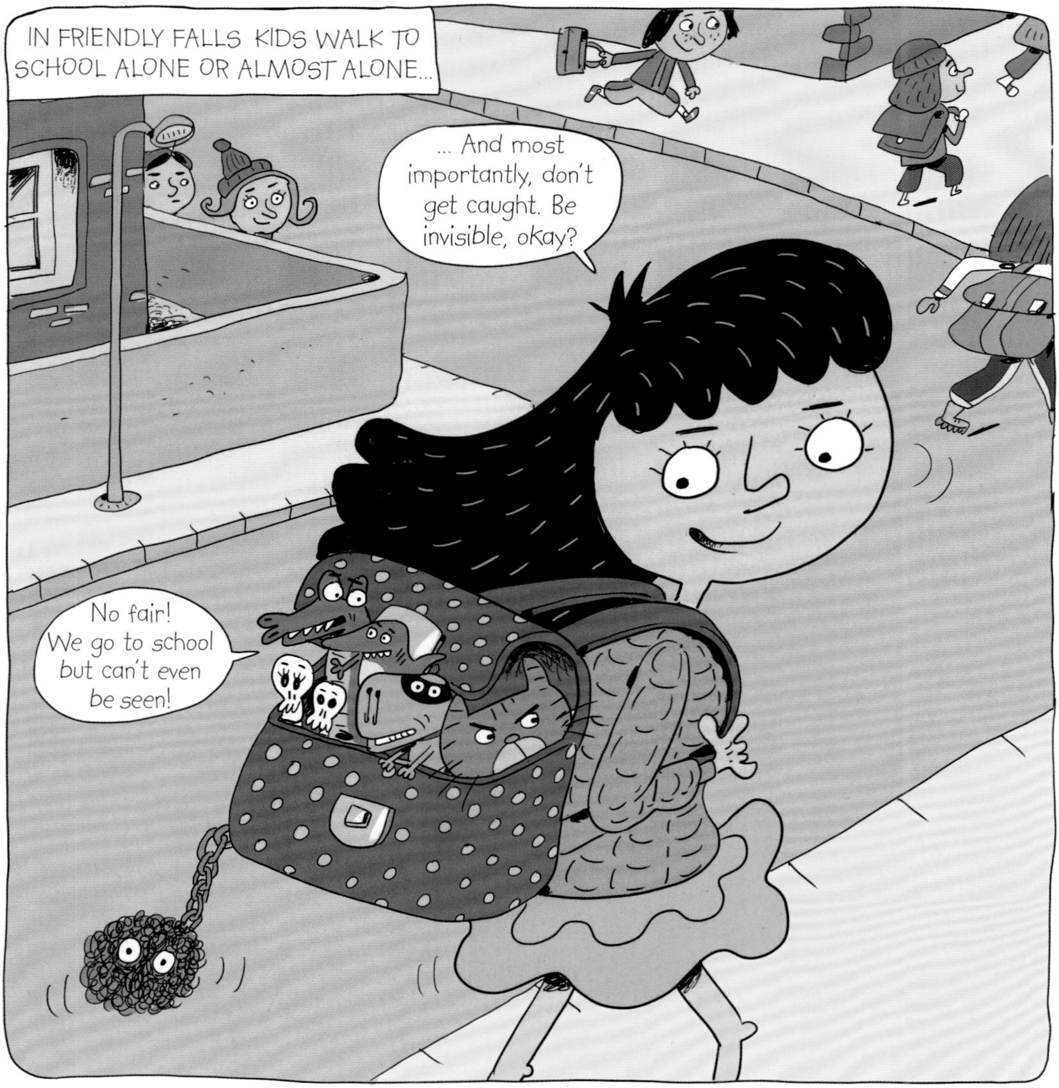
IN FRIENDLY FALLS KIDS WALK TO SCHOOL ALONE OR ALMOST ALONE...
... And most importantly, don't get caught. Be invisible, okay?
No fair! We go to school but can't even be seen!

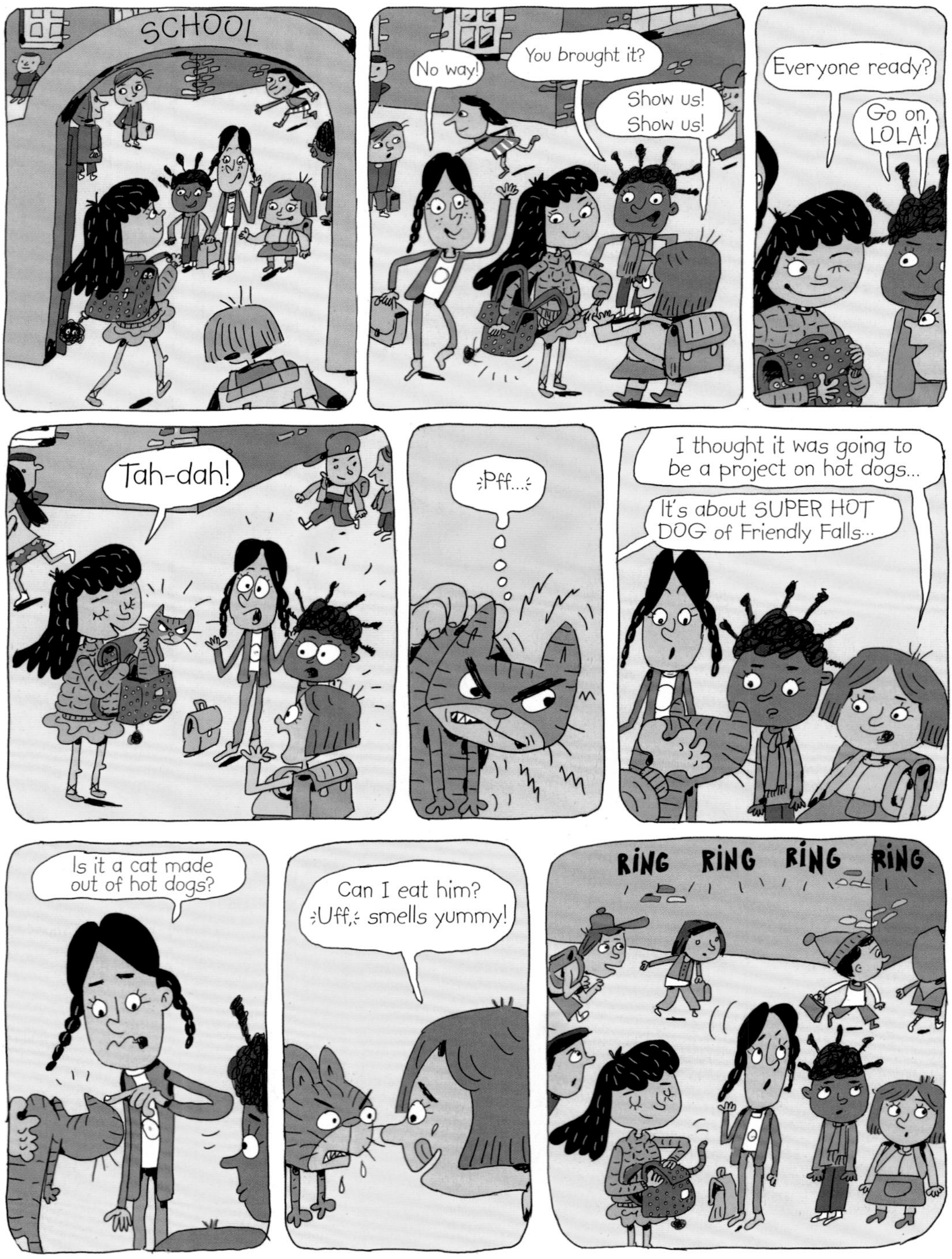
SCHOOL
No way!
You brought it?
Show us! Show us!
Everyone ready?
Go on, LOLA!
Tah-dah!
Pff...
I thought it was going to be a project on hot dogs...
It's about SUPER HOT DOG of Friendly Falls...
Is it a cat made out of hot dogs?
Can I eat him? Uff, smells yummy!
RING RING RING RING

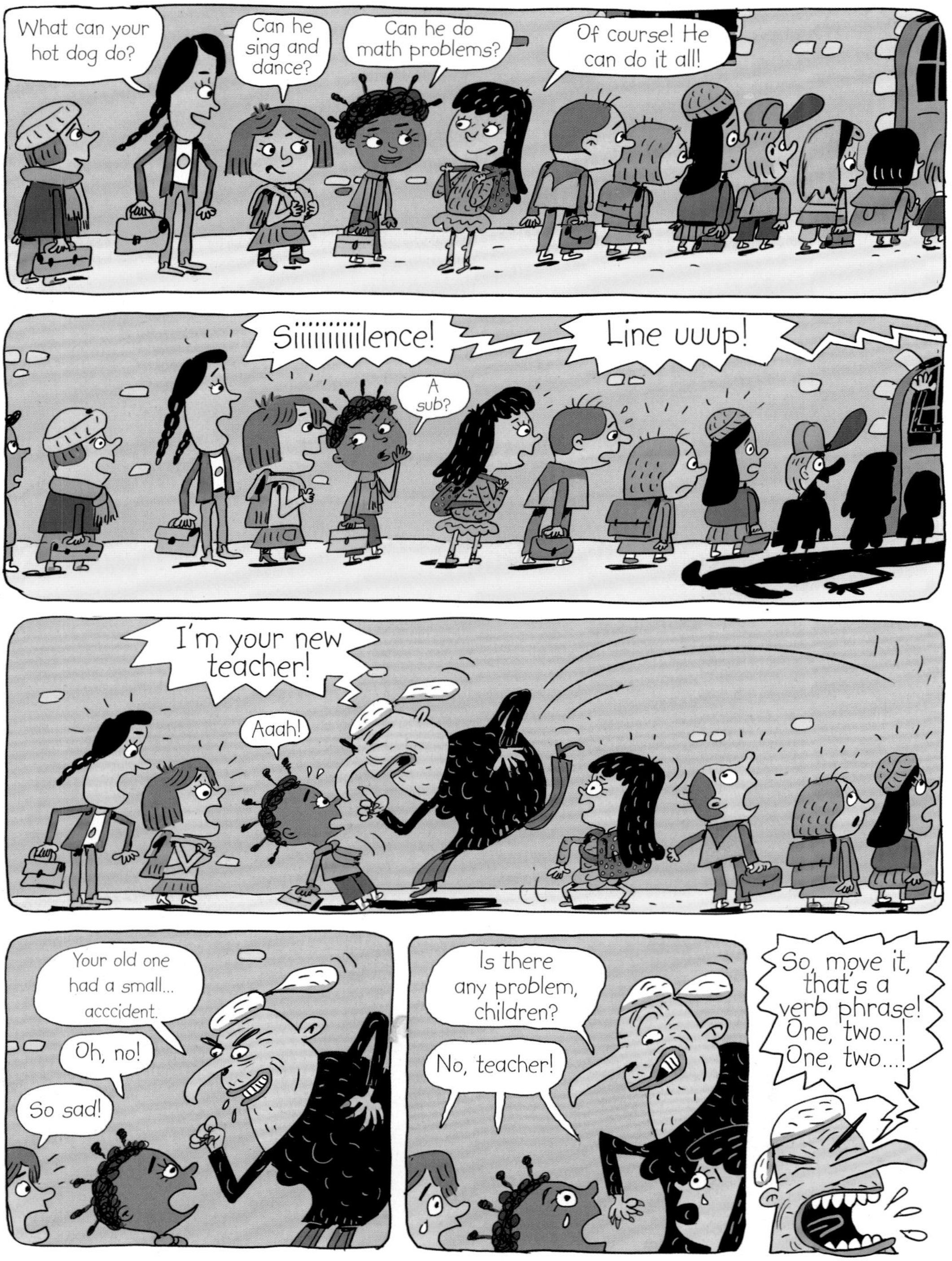
What can your hot dog do?
Can he sing and dance?
Can he do math problems?
Of course! He can do it all!
Siiiiiiiiiiilence!
Line uuup!
A sub?
I'm your new teacher!
Aaah!
Your old one had a small... acccident.
Oh, no!
So sad!
Is there any problem, children?
No, teacher!
So, move it, that's a verb phrase! One, two...! One, two...!

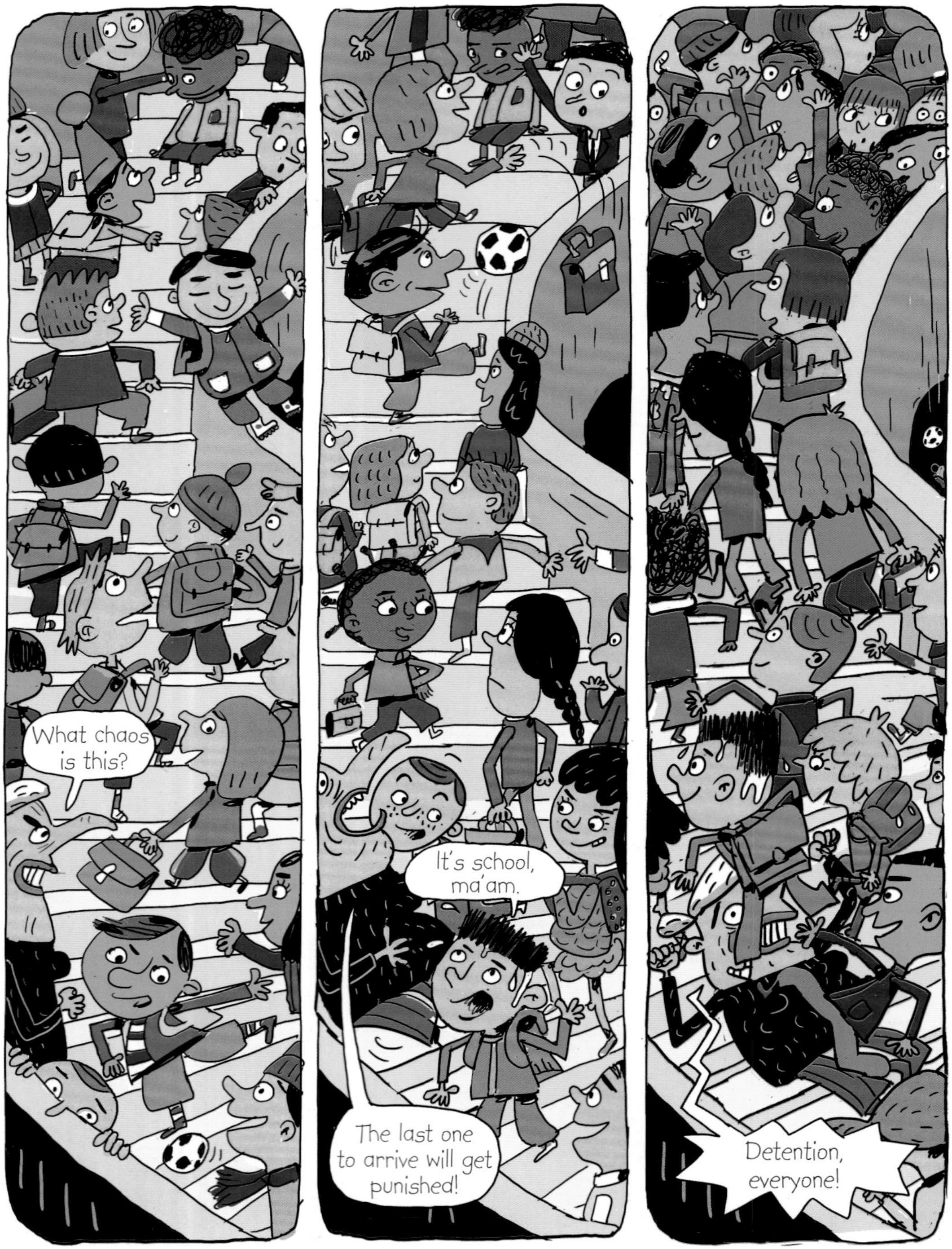
What chaos is this?
It's school, ma'am.
The last one to arrive will get punished!
Detention, everyone!

Coats on their hooks!

I don't have a coat, what do I do, ma'am?

INSIDE NOW! LET'S GO! Huh? How? What's on your head?

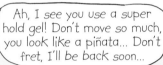

Ah, I see you use a super hold gel! Don't move so much, you look like a piñata... Don't fret, I'll be back soon...

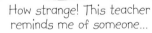
SPLOSH

TO YOUR SEATS! And siiiiiiiiiiiiiiiilence!

If you continue behaving like this, I'll be forced to punish you. Nyuk nyuk...

How strange! This teacher reminds me of someone...

POP QUIZ!

Knock Knock Knock

9

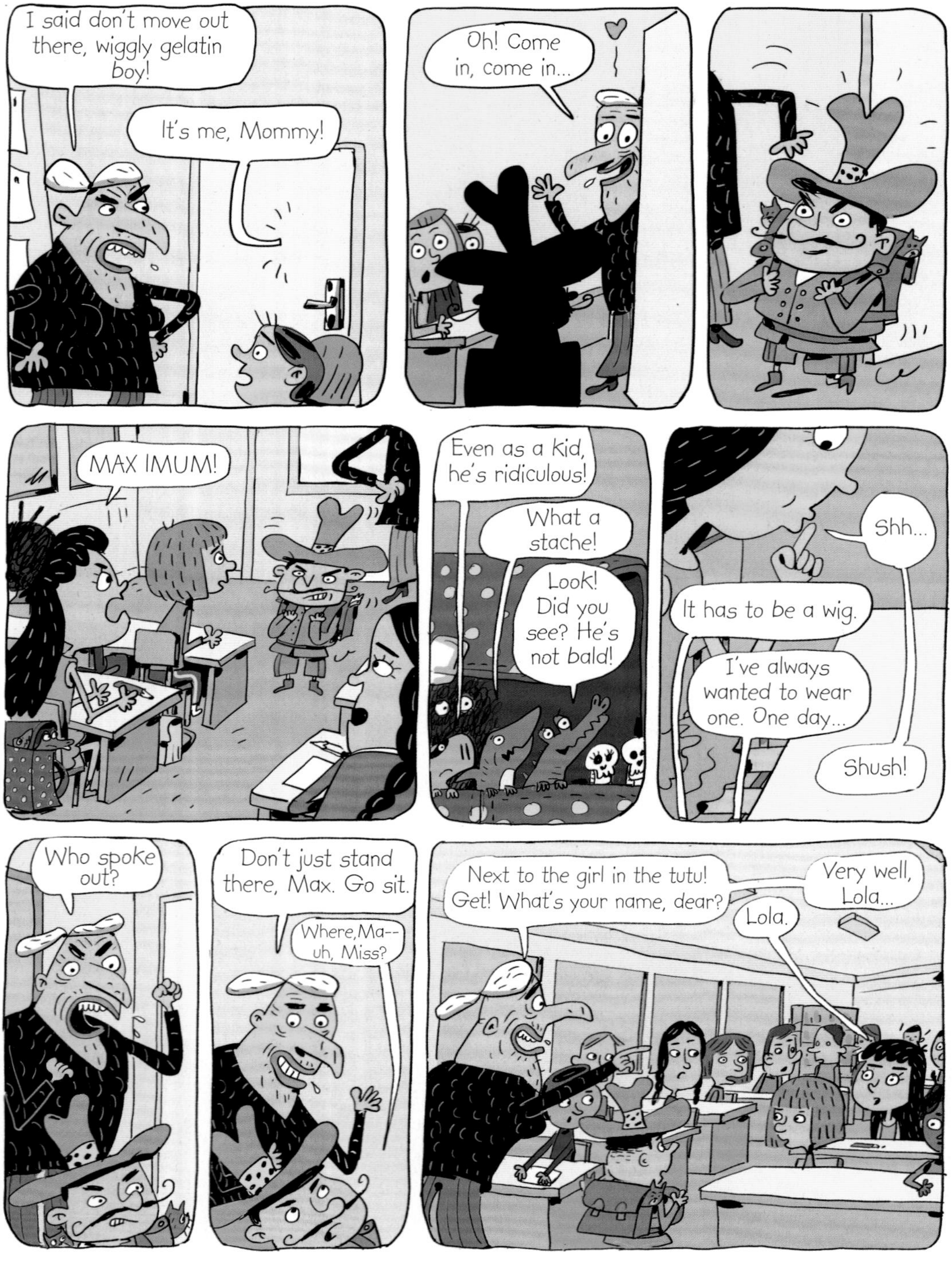
I said don't move out there, wiggly gelatin boy!
It's me, Mommy!
Oh! Come in, come in...
MAX IMUM!
Even as a kid, he's ridiculous!
What a stache!
Look! Did you see? He's not bald!
Shh...
It has to be a wig.
I've always wanted to wear one. One day...
Shush!
Who spoke out?
Don't just stand there, Max. Go sit.
Where, Ma-- uh, Miss?
Next to the girl in the tutu! Get! What's your name, dear?
Lola.
Very well, Lola...

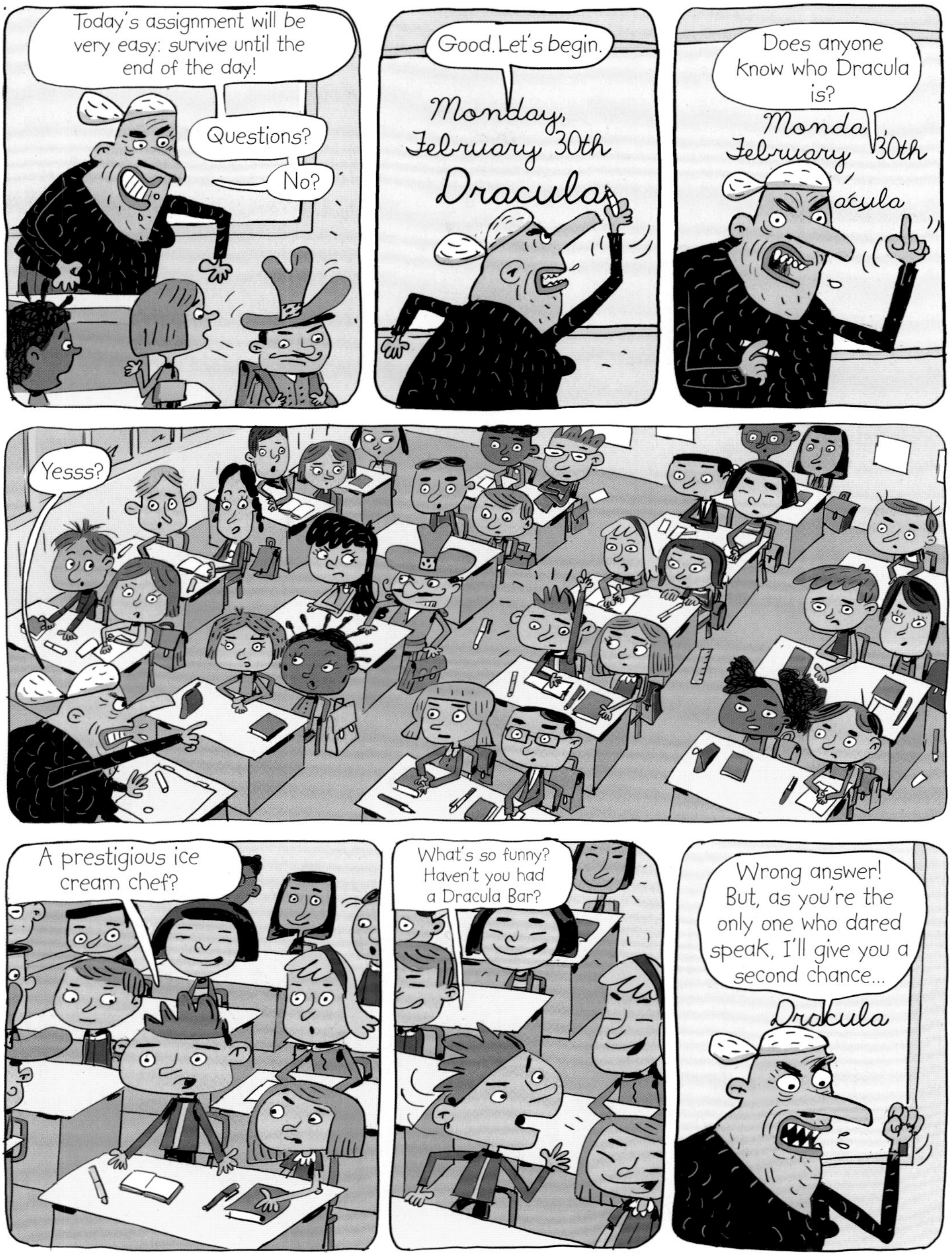
Today's assignment will be very easy: survive until the end of the day!
Questions?
No?
Good. Let's begin.
Monday, February 30th
Dracula
Does anyone know who Dracula is?
Yesss?
A prestigious ice cream chef?
What's so funny? Haven't you had a Dracula Bar?
Wrong answer! But, as you're the only one who dared speak, I'll give you a second chance...
Drakula

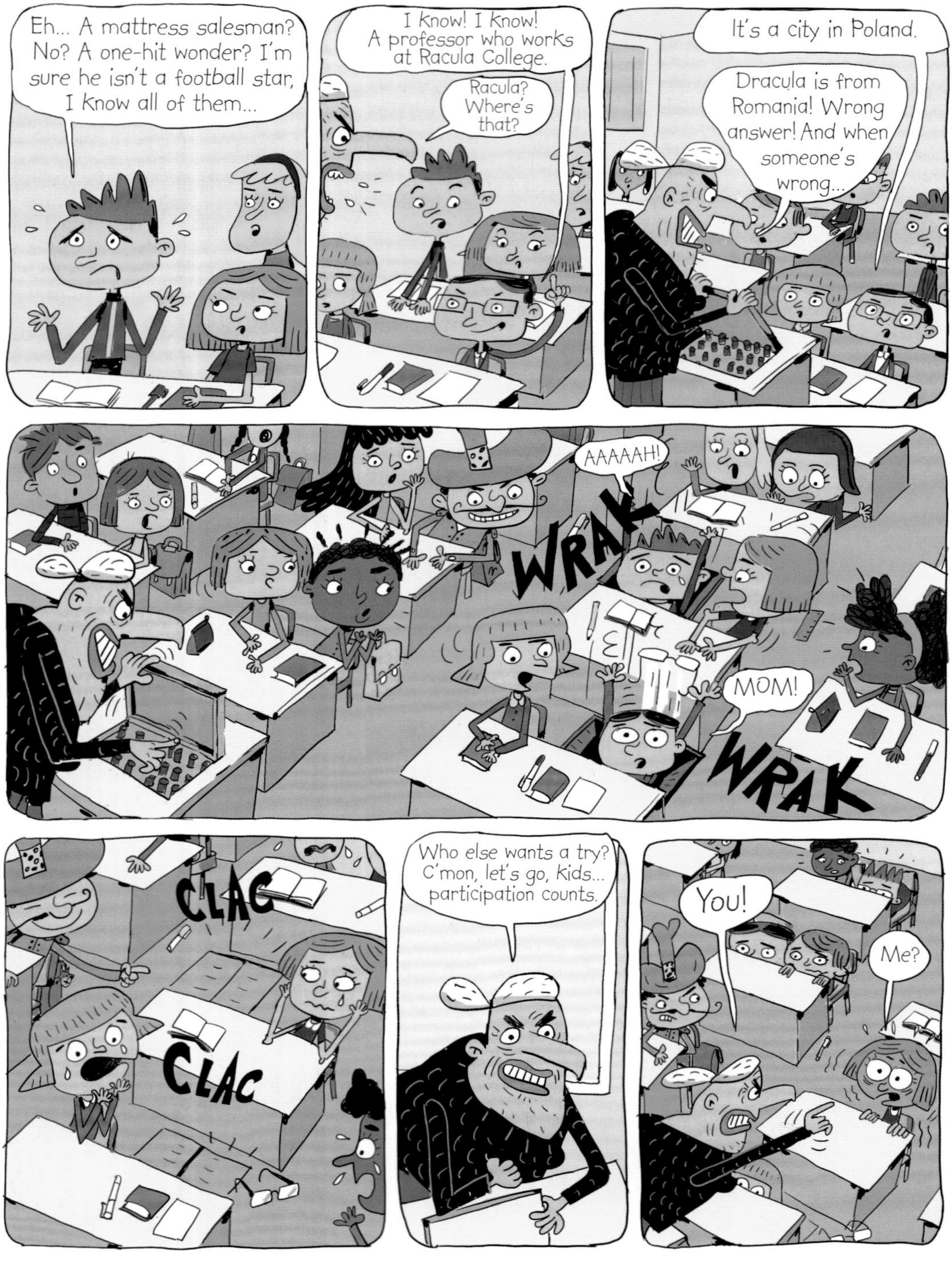
Eh... A mattress salesman? No? A one-hit wonder? I'm sure he isn't a football star, I know all of them...
I know! I know! A professor who works at Racula College.
Racula? Where's that?
It's a city in Poland.
Dracula is from Romania! Wrong answer! And when someone's wrong...
AAAAAH!
WRAK
MOM!
WRAK
CLAC
CLAC
Who else wants a try? C'mon, let's go, kids... participation counts.
You!
Me?

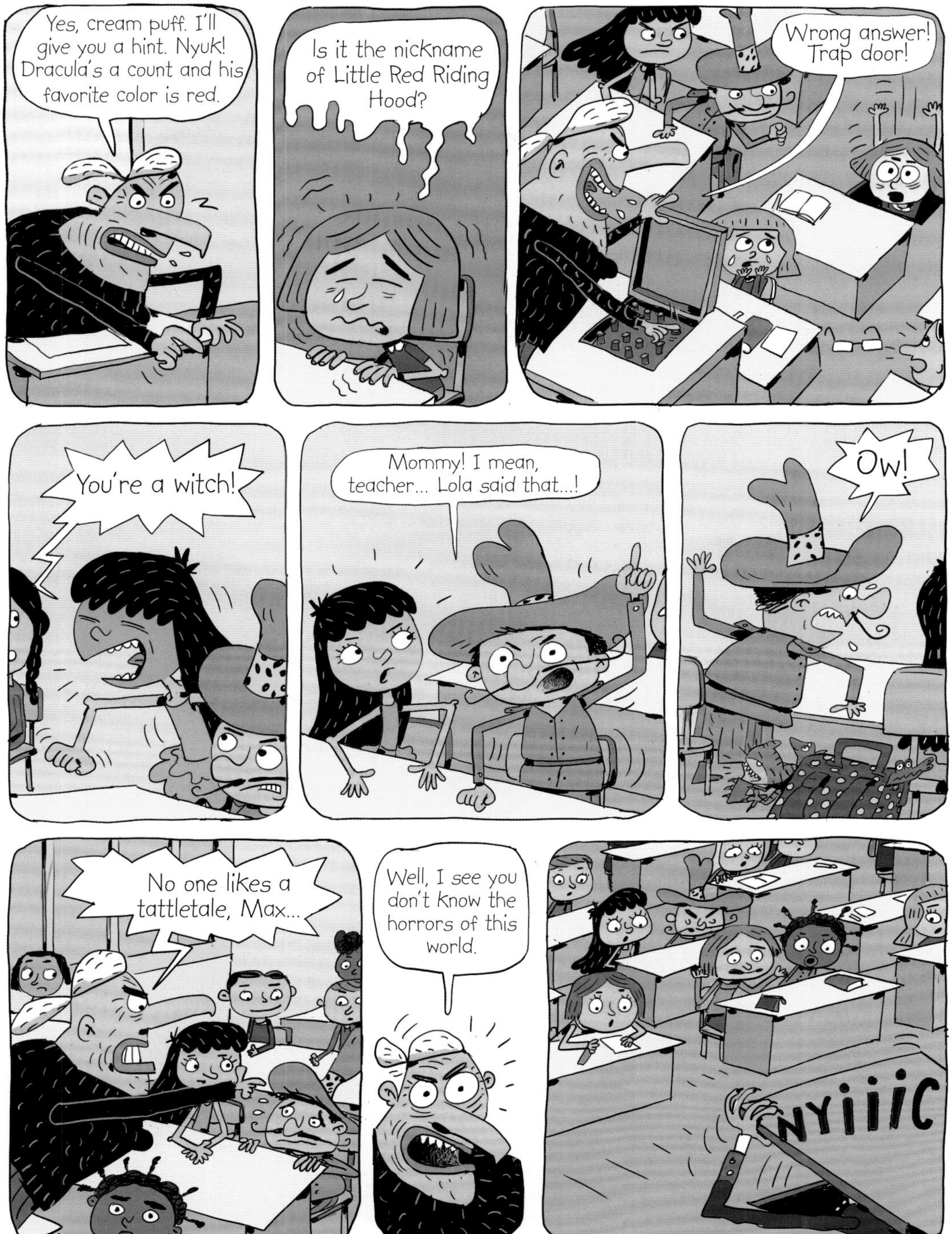
Yes, cream puff. I'll give you a hint. Nyuk! Dracula's a count and his favorite color is red.
Is it the nickname of Little Red Riding Hood?
Wrong answer! Trap door!
You're a witch!
Mommy! I mean, teacher... Lola said that...!
Ow!
No one likes a tattletale, Max...
Well, I see you don't know the horrors of this world.
NYiiiC

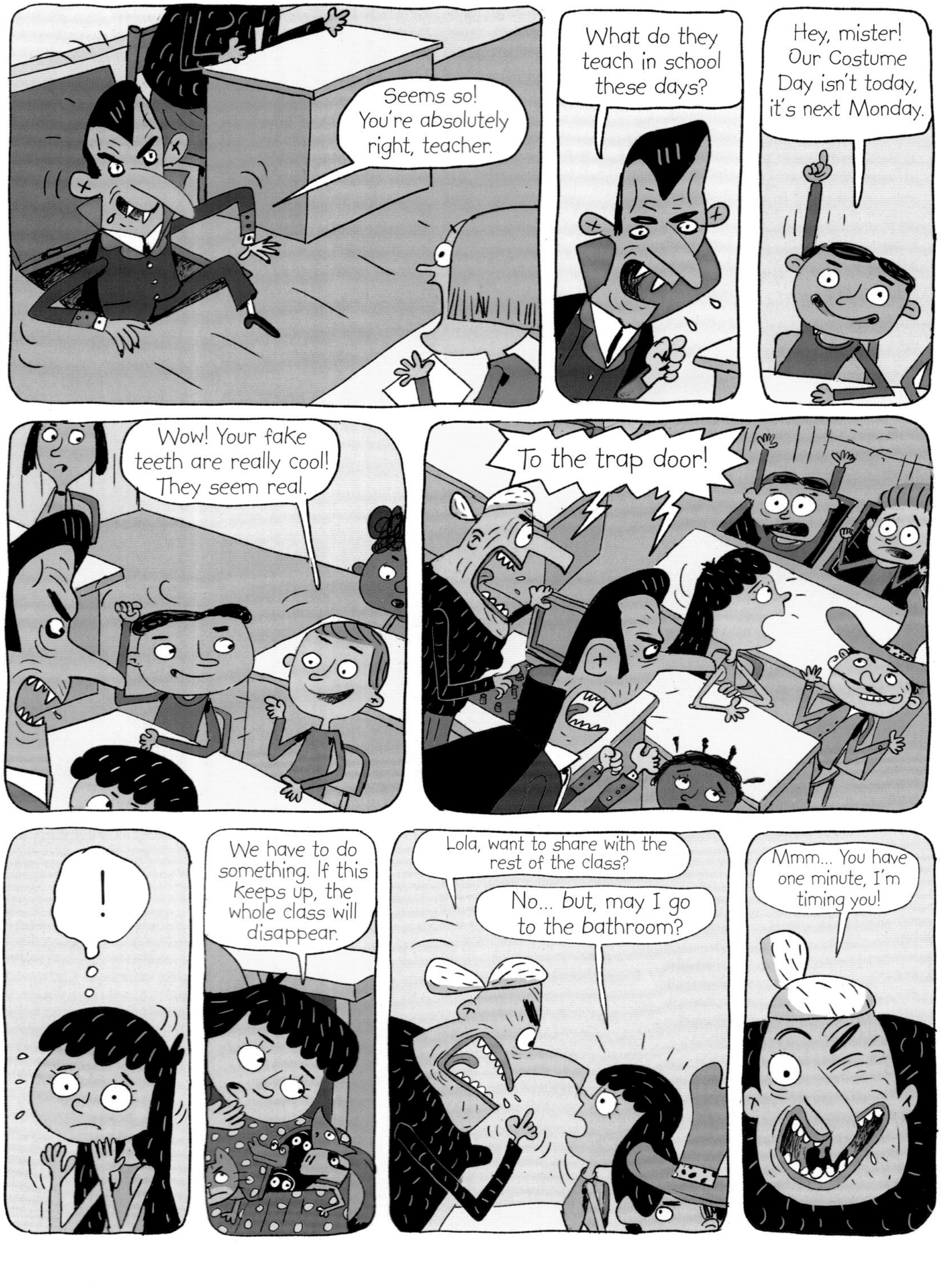
Seems so! You're absolutely right, teacher.
What do they teach in school these days?
Hey, mister! Our Costume Day isn't today, it's next Monday.
Wow! Your fake teeth are really cool! They seem real.
To the trap door!
!
We have to do something. If this keeps up, the whole class will disappear.
Lola, want to share with the rest of the class?
No... but, may I go to the bathroom?
Mmm... You have one minute, I'm timing you!

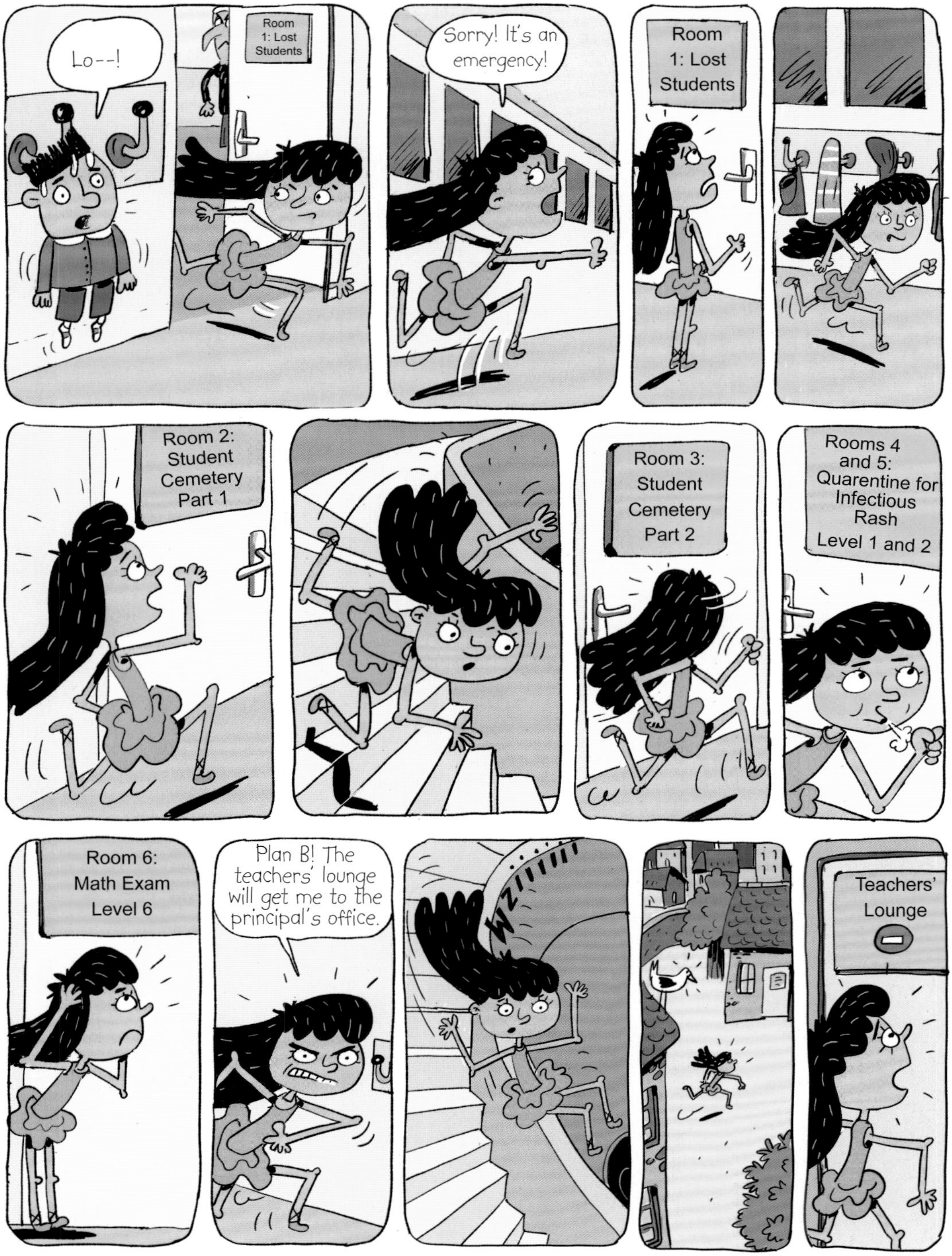

Lo--!
Room 1: Lost Students
Sorry! It's an emergency!
Room 1: Lost Students
Room 2: Student Cemetery Part 1
Room 3: Student Cemetery Part 2
Rooms 4 and 5: Quarentine for Infectious Rash Level 1 and 2
Room 6: Math Exam Level 6
Plan B! The teachers' lounge will get me to the principal's office.
WZ
Teachers' Lounge

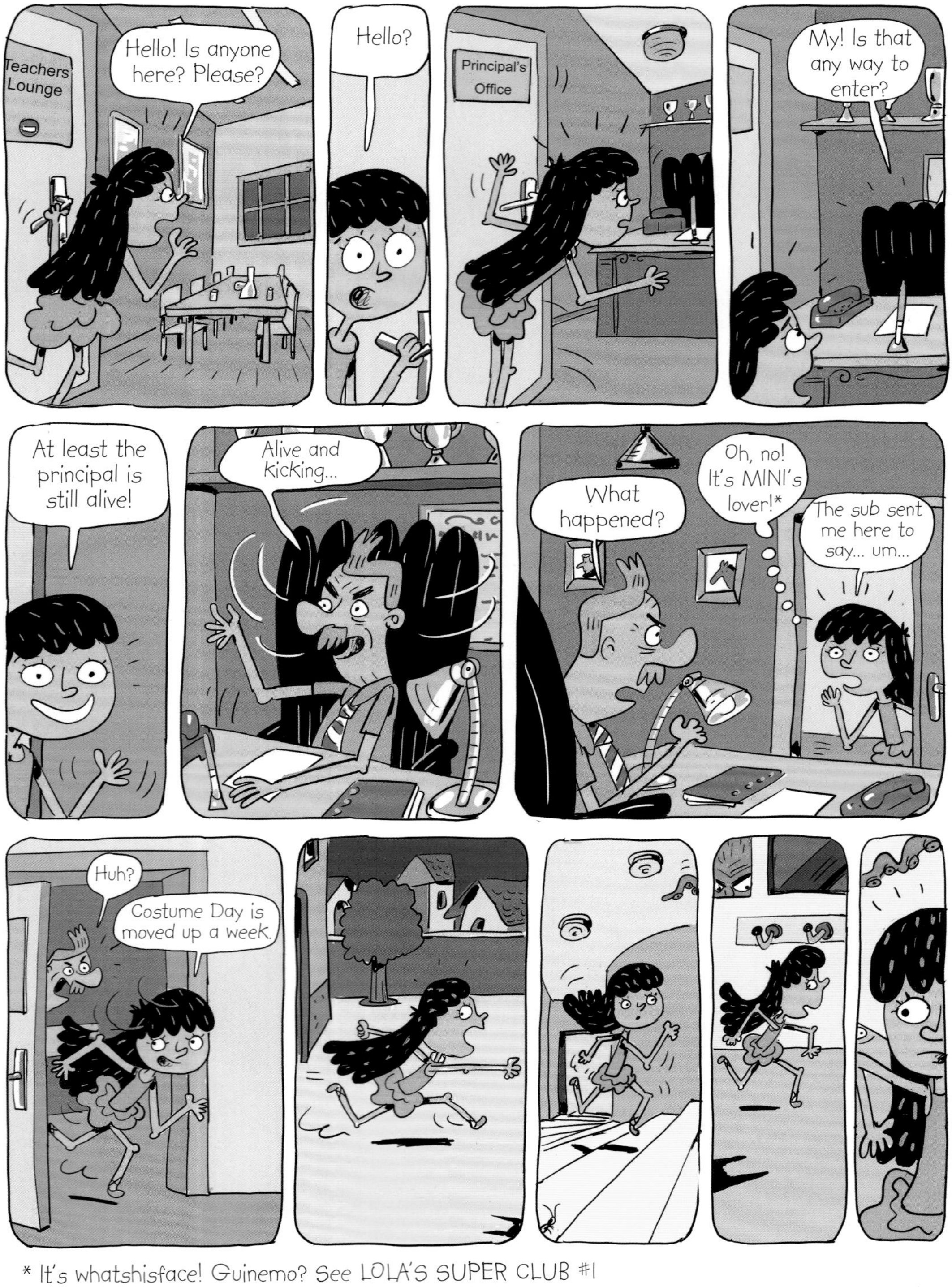
Teachers' Lounge
Hello! Is anyone here? Please?
Hello?
Principal's Office
My! Is that any way to enter?
At least the principal is still alive!
Alive and kicking...
What happened?
Oh, no! It's MINI's lover!*
The sub sent me here to say... um...
Huh?
Costume Day is moved up a week.

* It's whatshisface! Guinemo? See LOLA'S SUPER CLUB #1

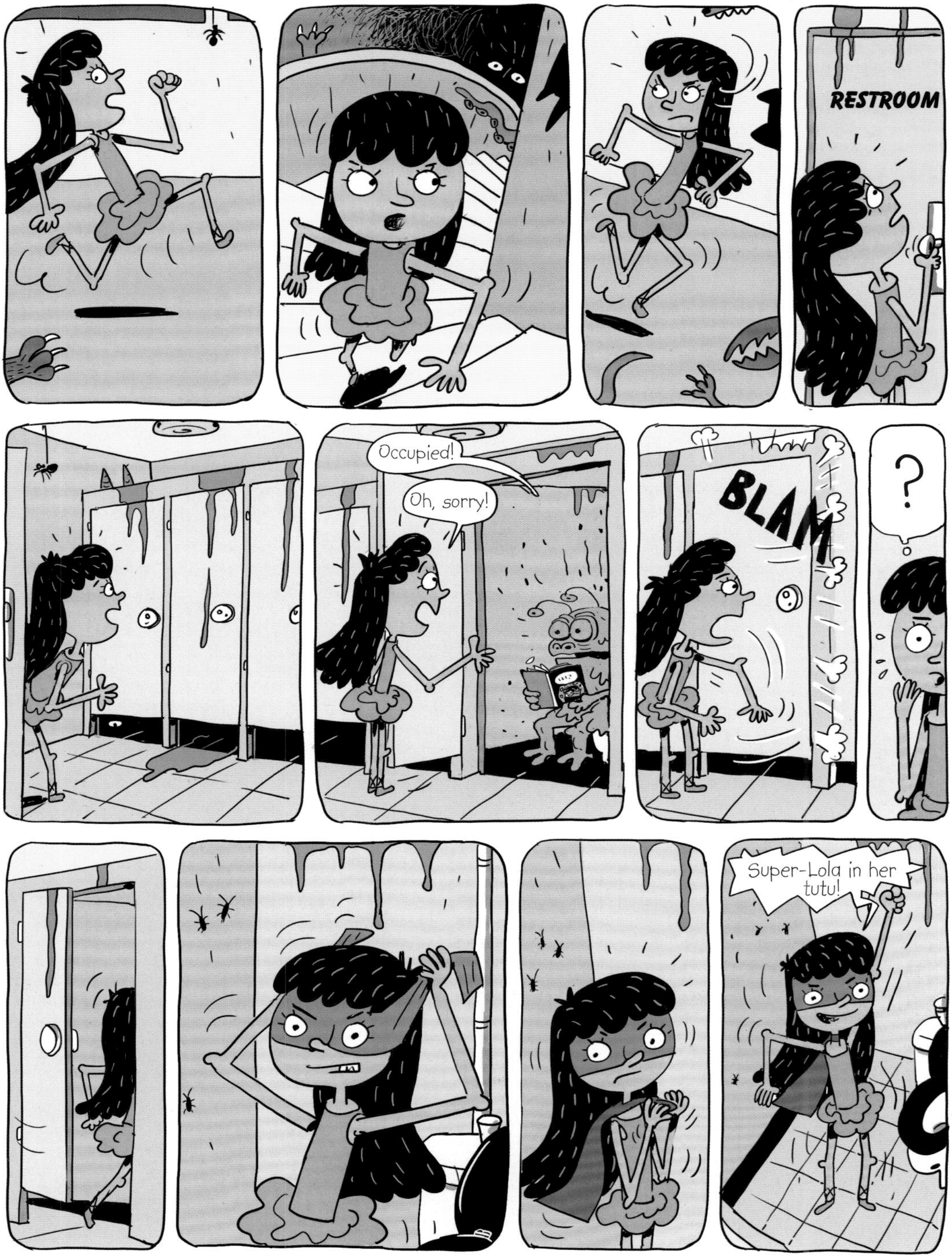
RESTROOM
Occupied!
Oh, sorry!
BLAM
?
Super-Lola in her tutu!

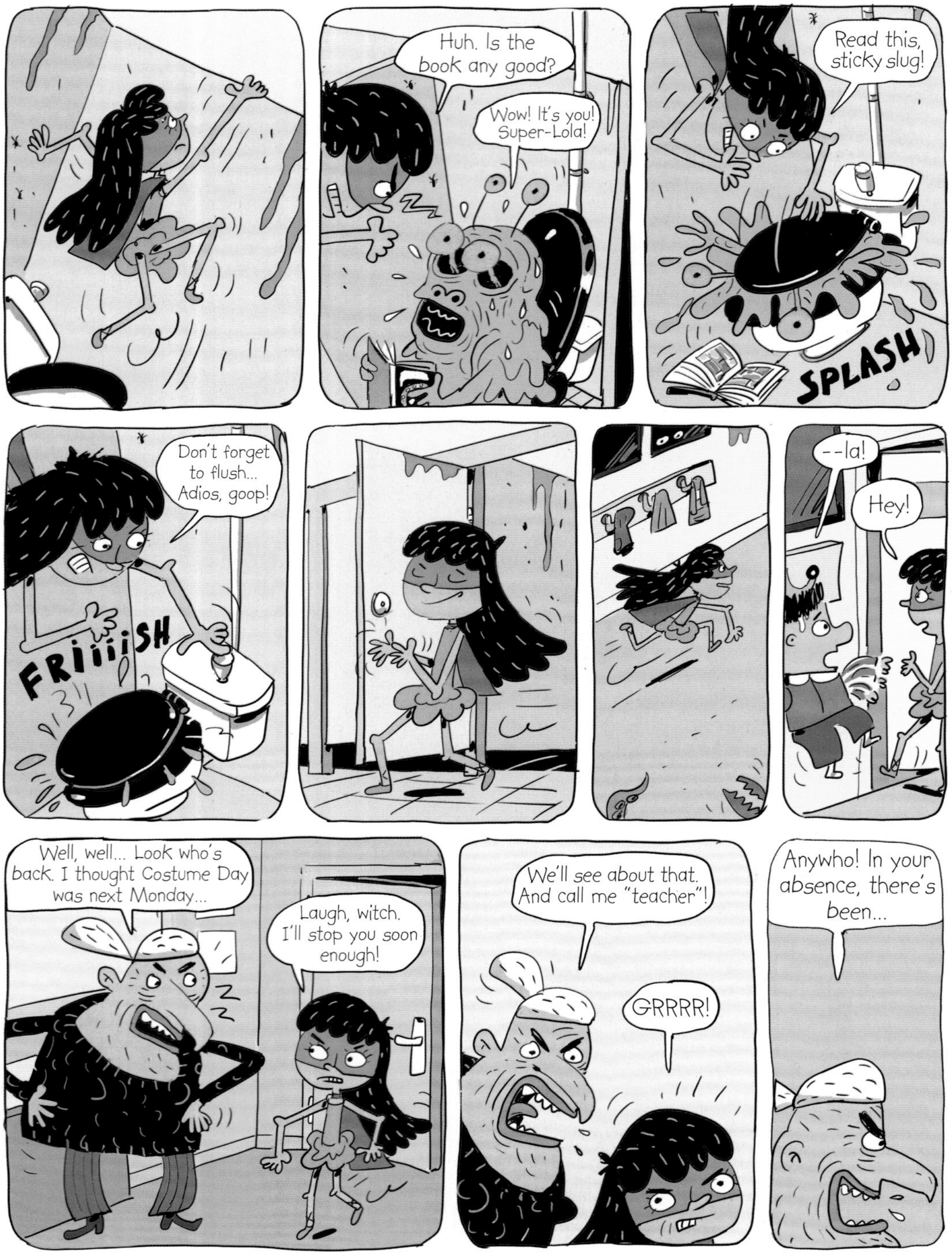
Huh. Is the book any good?
Wow! It's you! Super-Lola!
Read this, sticky slug!
SPLASH
Don't forget to flush... Adios, goop!
FRiiiiSH
--la!
Hey!
Well, well... Look who's back. I thought Costume Day was next Monday...
Laugh, witch. I'll stop you soon enough!
We'll see about that. And call me "teacher"!
GRRRR!
Anywho! In your absence, there's been...

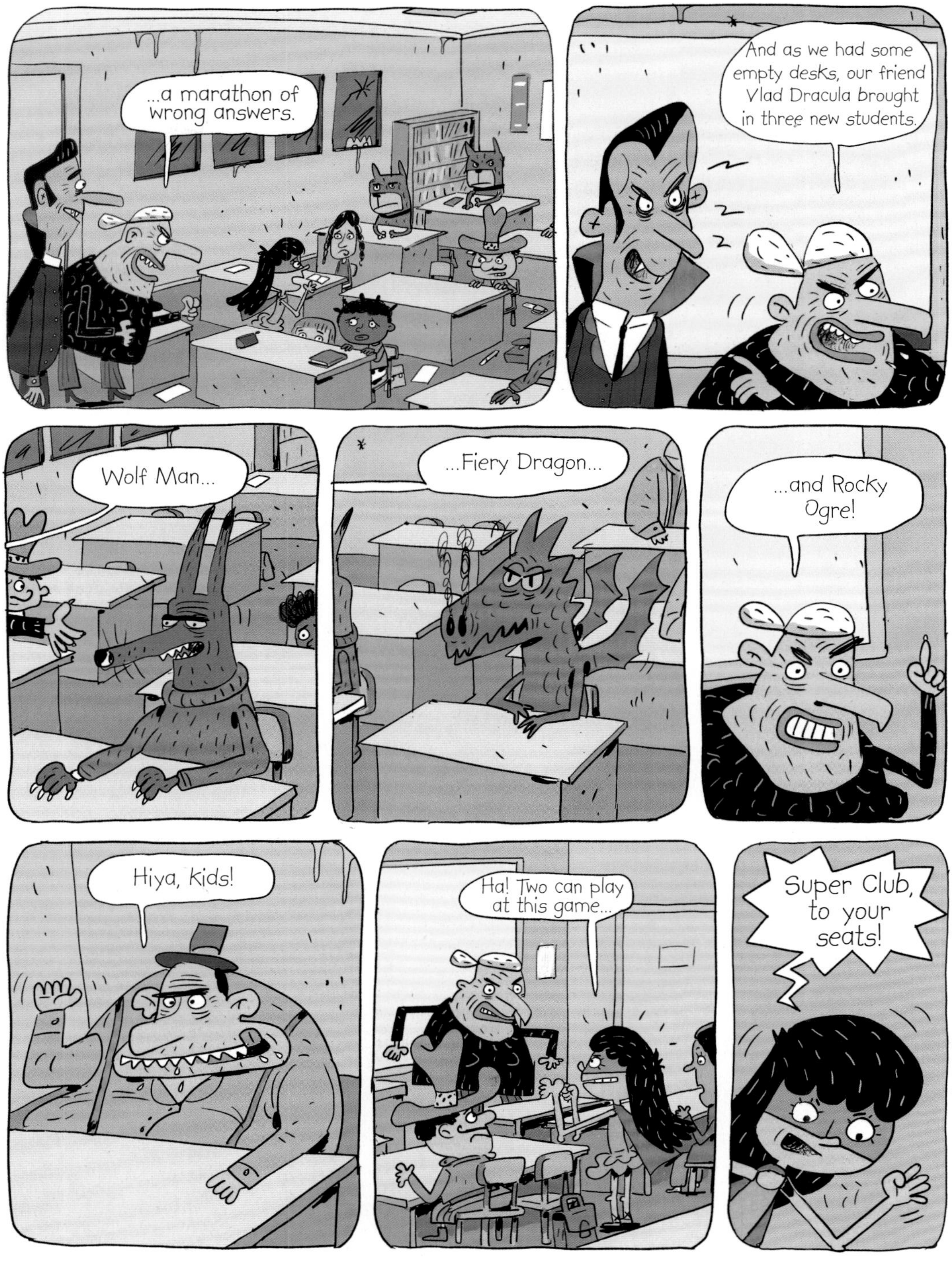
...a marathon of wrong answers.
And as we had some empty desks, our friend Vlad Dracula brought in three new students.
Wolf Man...
...Fiery Dragon...
...and Rocky Ogre!
Hiya, kids!
Ha! Two can play at this game...
Super Club, to your seats!

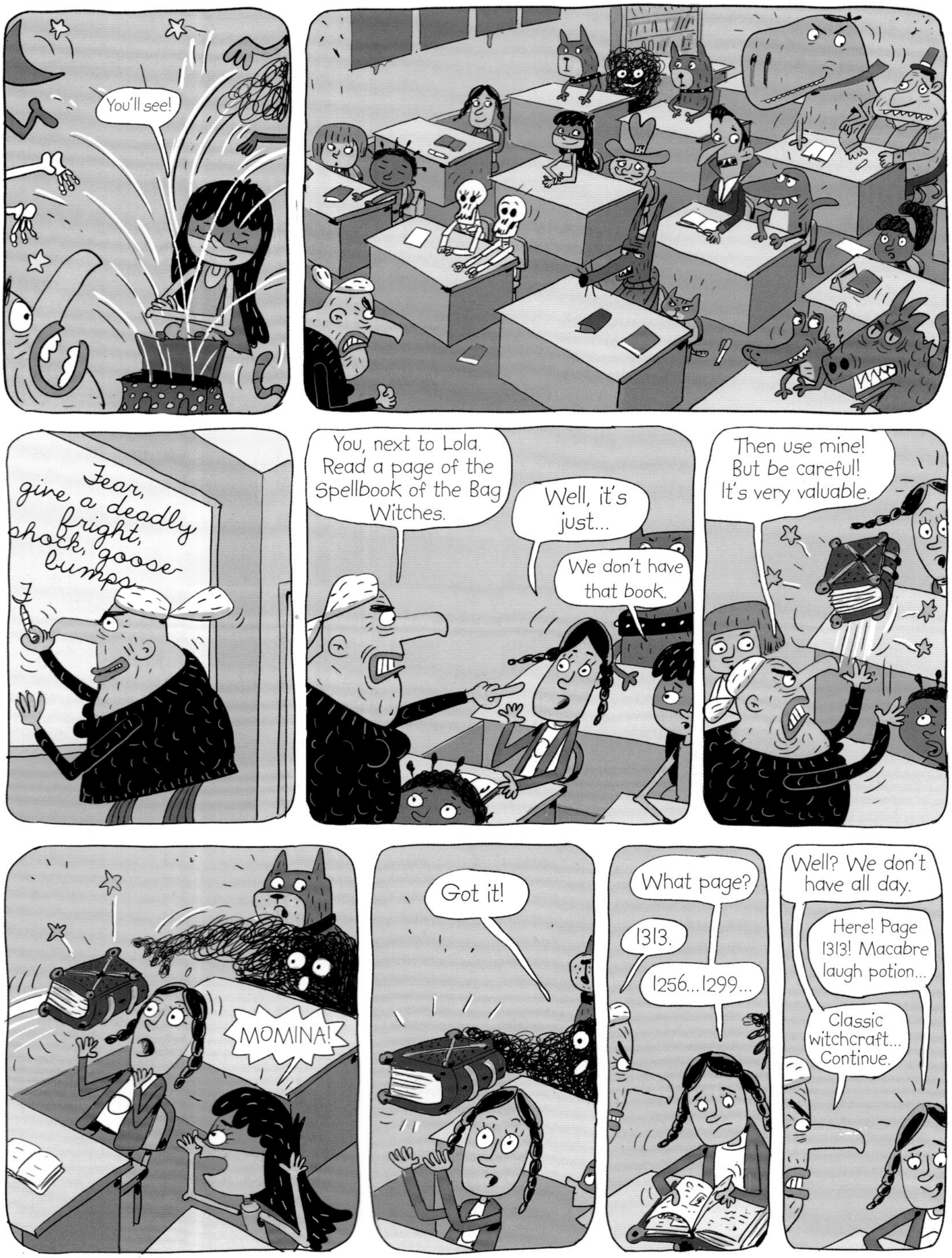
You'll see!
You, next to Lola. Read a page of the Spellbook of the Bag Witches.
Well, it's just...
We don't have that book.
Fear, give a deadly fright, shock, goose-bumps
Then use mine! But be careful! It's very valuable.
MOMINA!
Got it!
What page?
1313.
1256...1299...
Well? We don't have all day.
Here! Page 1313! Macabre laugh potion...
Classic witchcraft... Continue.

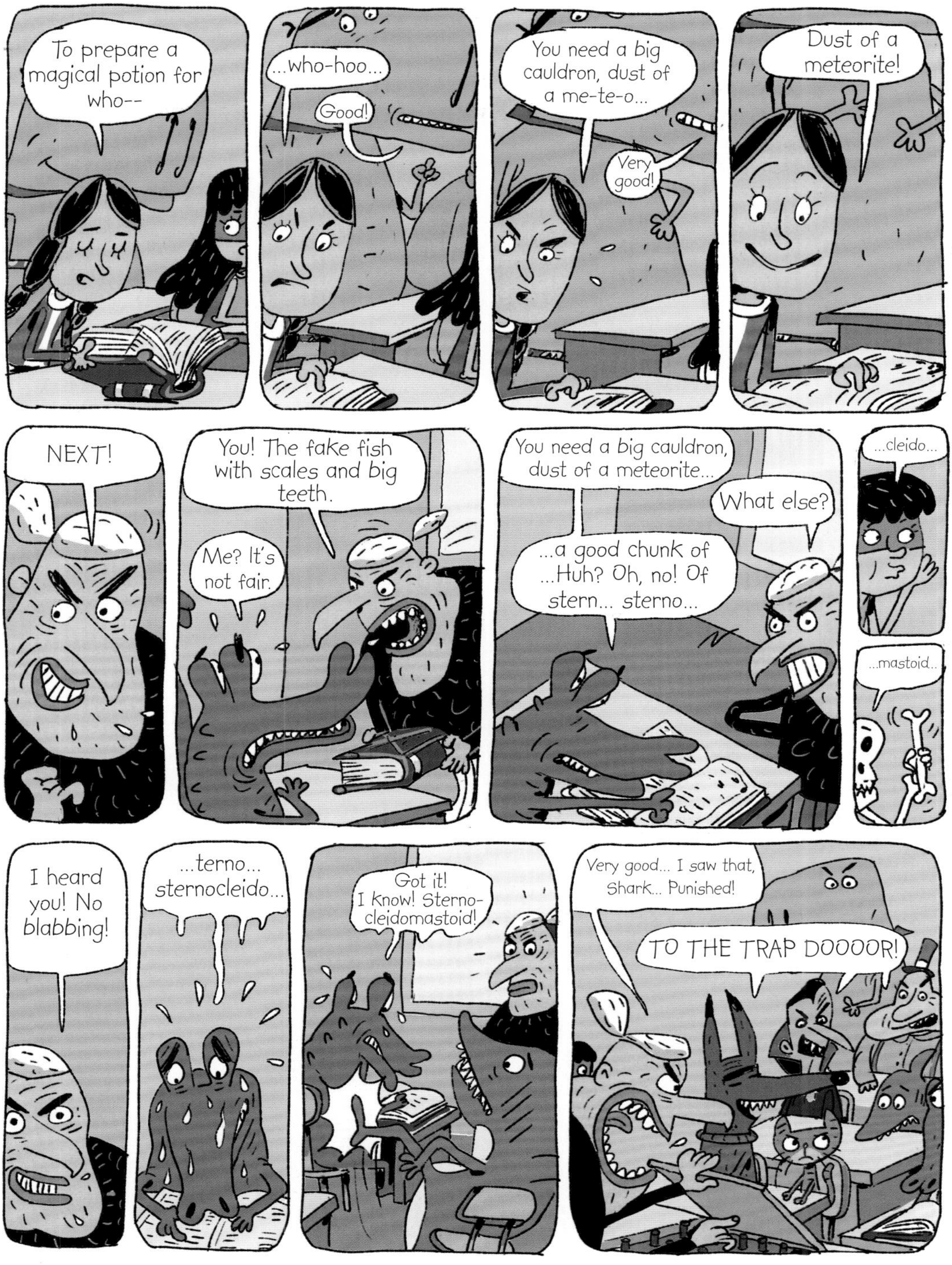
To prepare a magical potion for who--
...who-hoo...
Good!
You need a big cauldron, dust of a me-te-o...
Very good!
Dust of a meteorite!
NEXT!
You! The fake fish with scales and big teeth.
Me? It's not fair.
You need a big cauldron, dust of a meteorite...
What else?
...a good chunk of ...Huh? Oh, no! Of stern... sterno...
...cleido...
...mastoid...
I heard you! No blabbing!
...terno... sternocleido...
Got it! I know! Sterno-cleidomastoid!
Very good... I saw that, Shark... Punished!
TO THE TRAP DOOOOR!

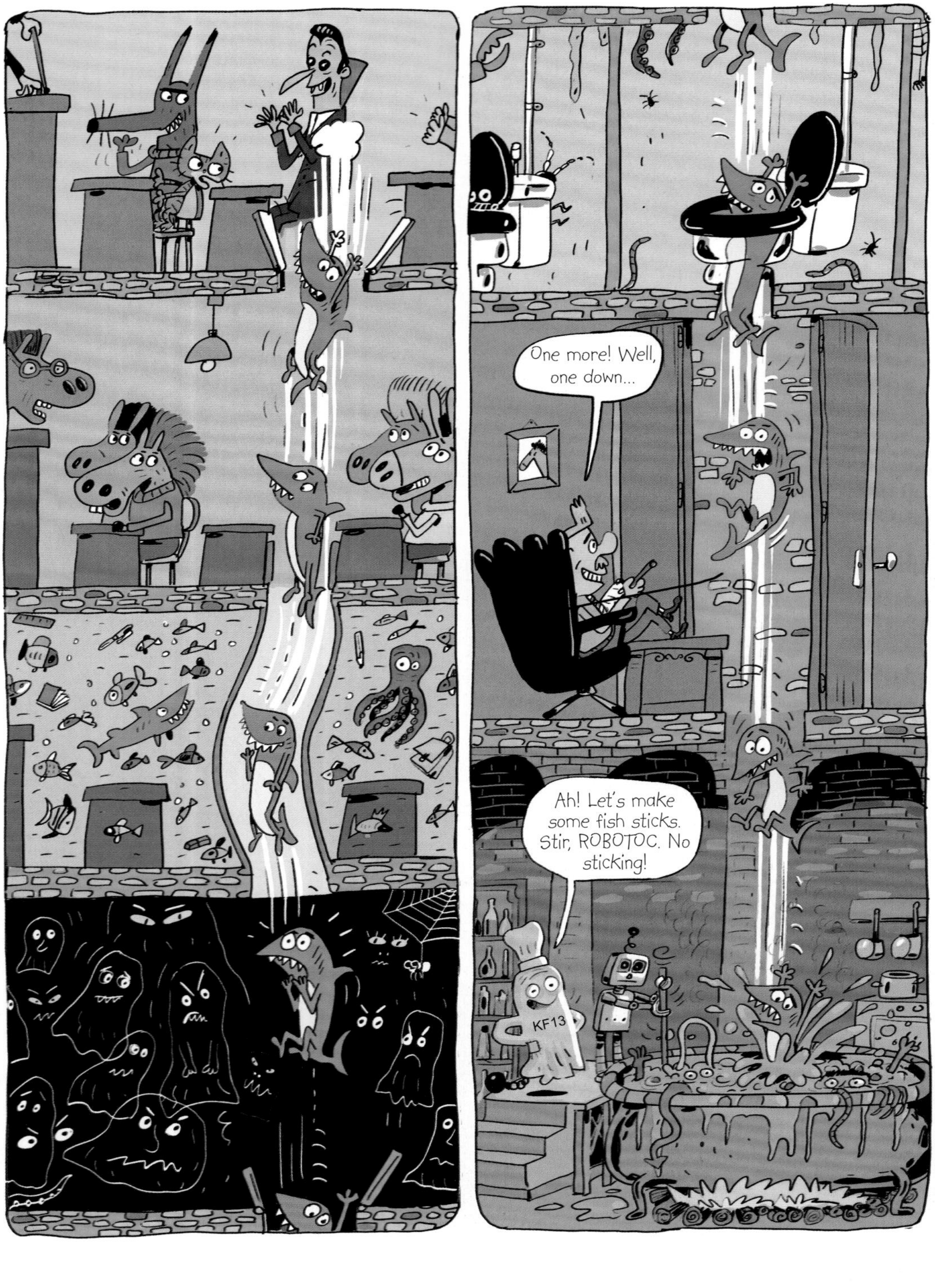
One more! Well, one down...
Ah! Let's make some fish sticks. Stir, ROBOTOC. No sticking!
KF13

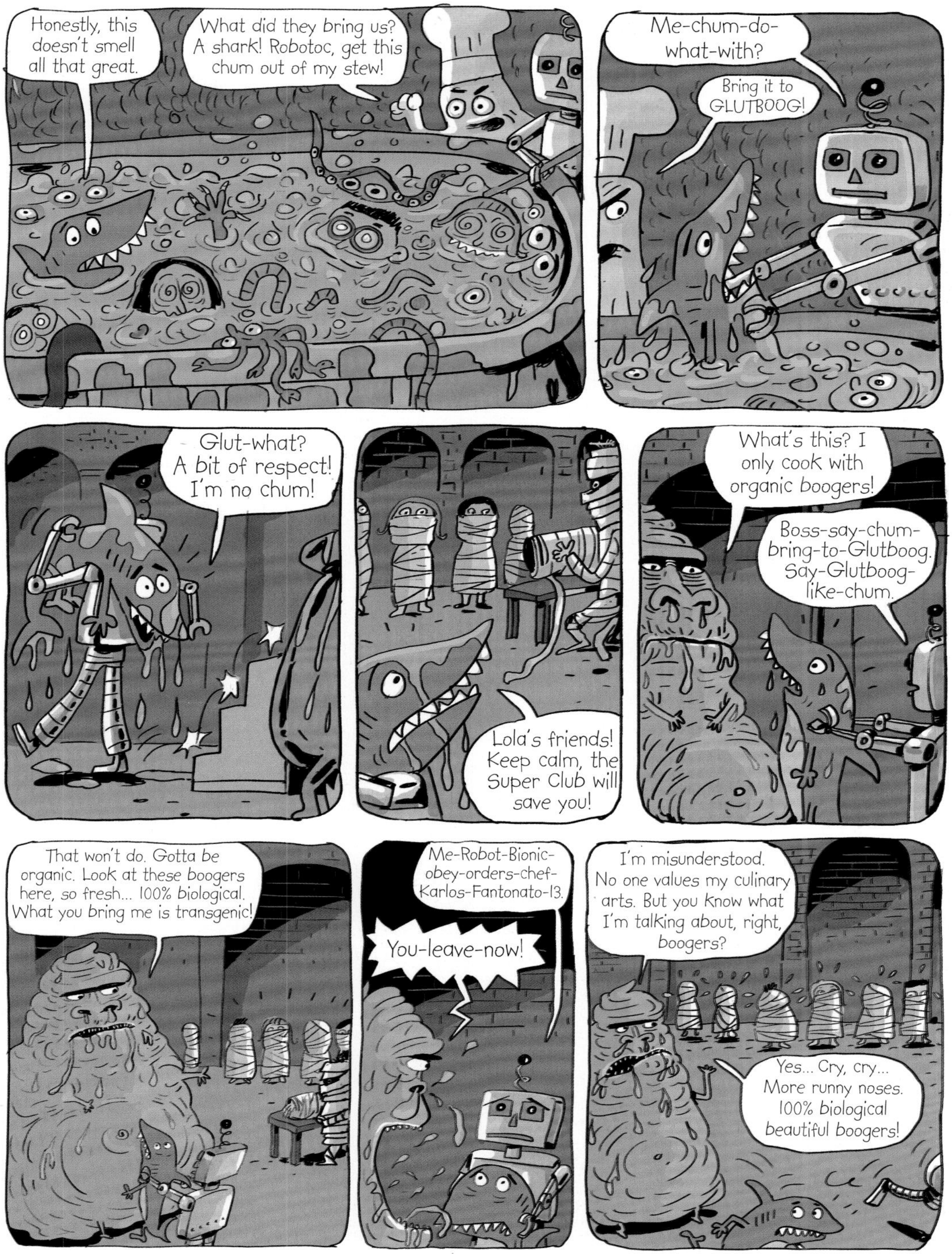

Honestly, this doesn't smell all that great.
What did they bring us? A shark! Robotoc, get this chum out of my stew!
Me-chum-do-what-with?
Bring it to GLUTBOOG!
Glut-what? A bit of respect! I'm no chum!
Lola's friends! Keep calm, the Super Club will save you!
What's this? I only cook with organic boogers!
Boss-say-chum-bring-to-Glutboog. Say-Glutboog-like-chum.
That won't do. Gotta be organic. Look at these boogers here, so fresh... 100% biological. What you bring me is transgenic!
Me-Robot-Bionic-obey-orders-chef-Karlos-Fantonato-13.
You-leave-now!
I'm misunderstood. No one values my culinary arts. But you know what I'm talking about, right, boogers?
Yes... Cry, cry... More runny noses. 100% biological beautiful boogers!

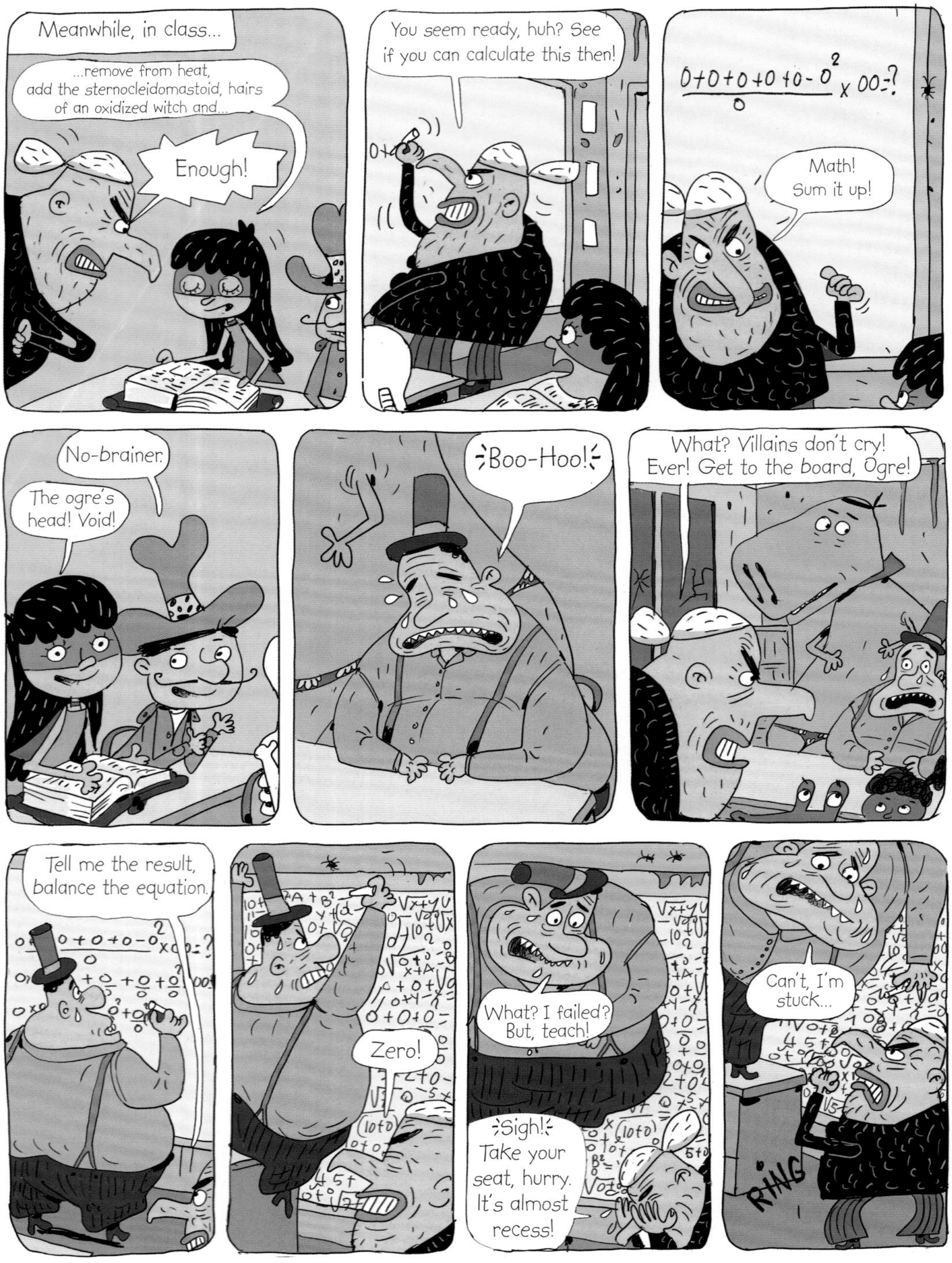
Meanwhile, in class...
...remove from heat, add the sternocleidomastoid, hairs of an oxidized witch and...
Enough!
You seem ready, huh? See if you can calculate this then!
0+0+0+0+0-0² x 00=?
Math! Sum it up!
No-brainer.
The ogre's head! Void!
Boo-Hoo!
What? Villains don't cry! Ever! Get to the board, Ogre!
Tell me the result, balance the equation.
Zero!
What? I failed? But, teach!
Sigh! Take your seat, hurry. It's almost recess!
Can't, I'm stuck...
RING

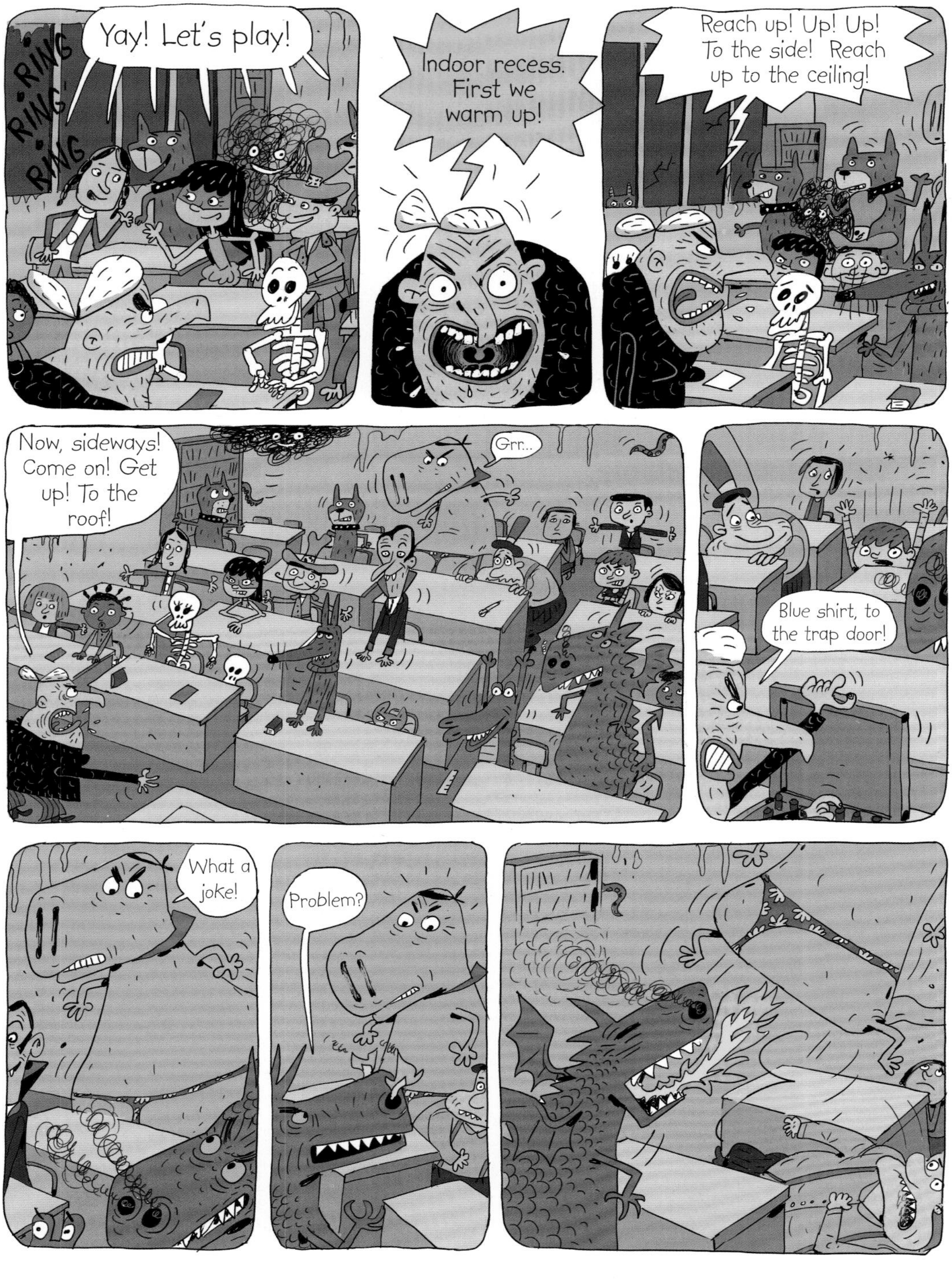
RING RING RING
Yay! Let's play!
Indoor recess. First we warm up!
Reach up! Up! Up! To the side! Reach up to the ceiling!
Now, sideways! Come on! Get up! To the roof!
Grr...
Blue shirt, to the trap door!
What a joke!
Problem?

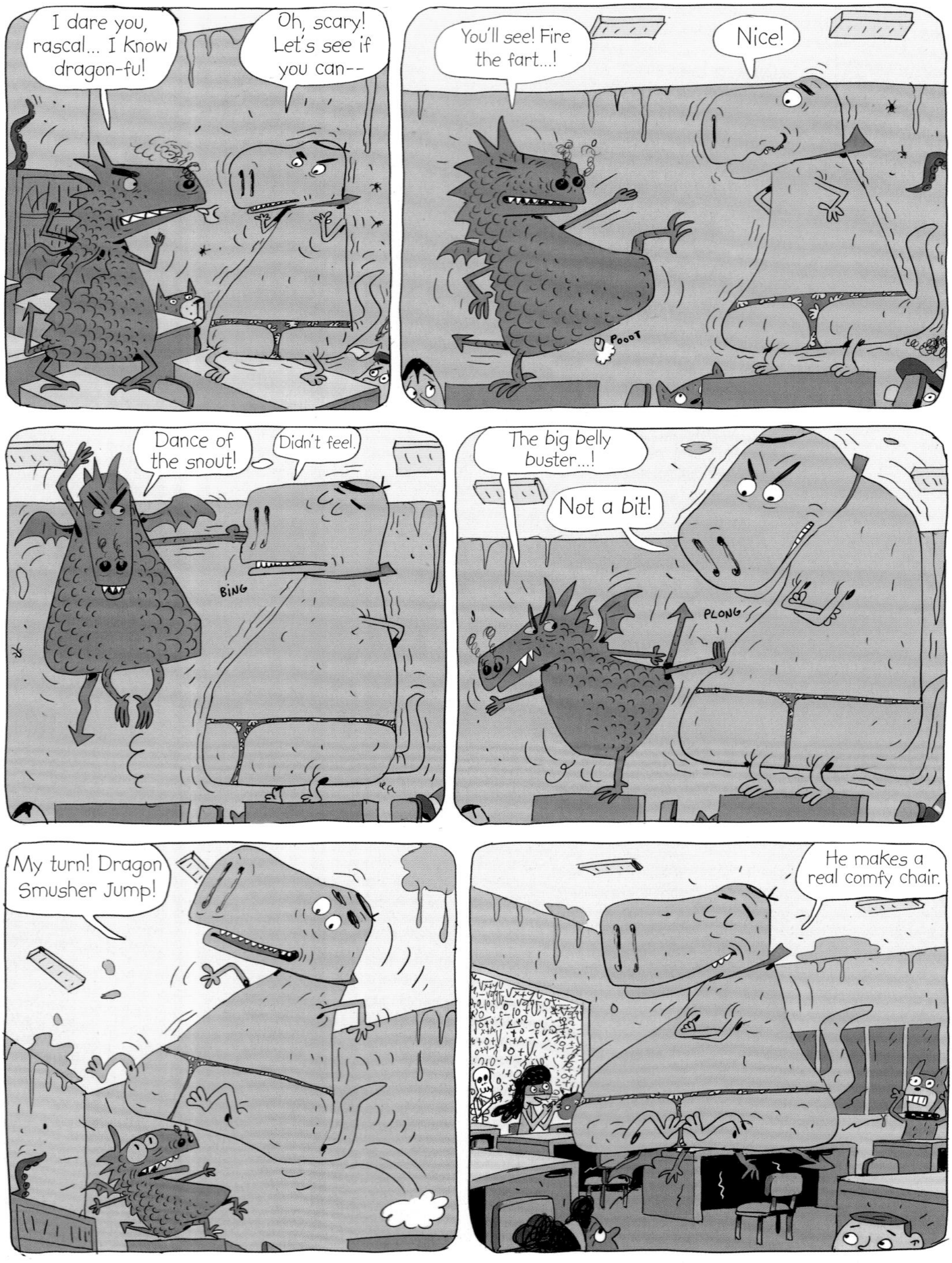
I dare you, rascal... I know dragon-fu!
Oh, scary! Let's see if you can--
You'll see! Fire the fart...!
POOOT
Nice!
Dance of the snout!
BING
Didn't feel.
The big belly buster...!
PLONG
Not a bit!
My turn! Dragon Smusher Jump!
He makes a real comfy chair.

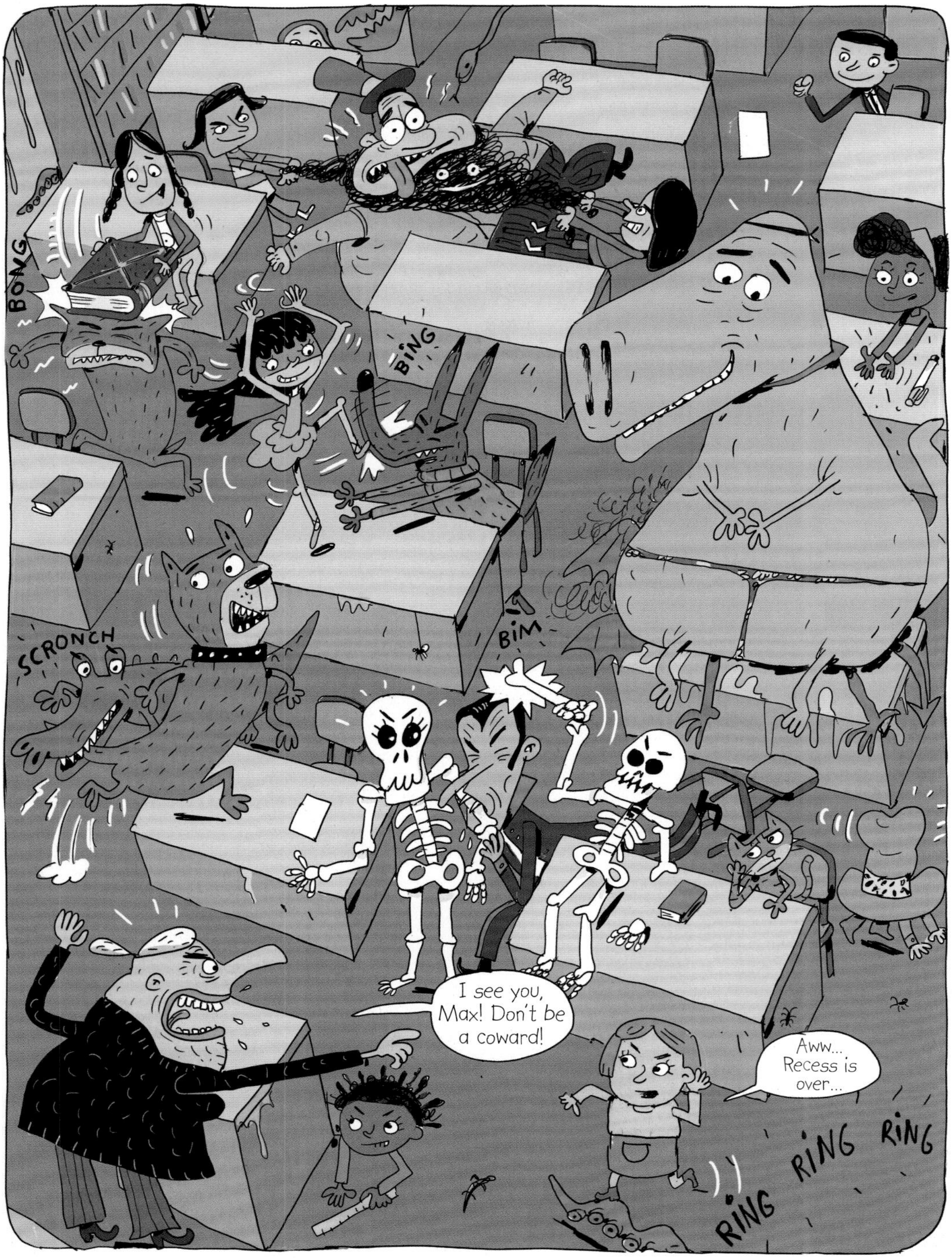
BONG
BING
SCRONCH
BIM
I see you, Max! Don't be a coward!
Aww... Recess is over...
RING RING RING RING

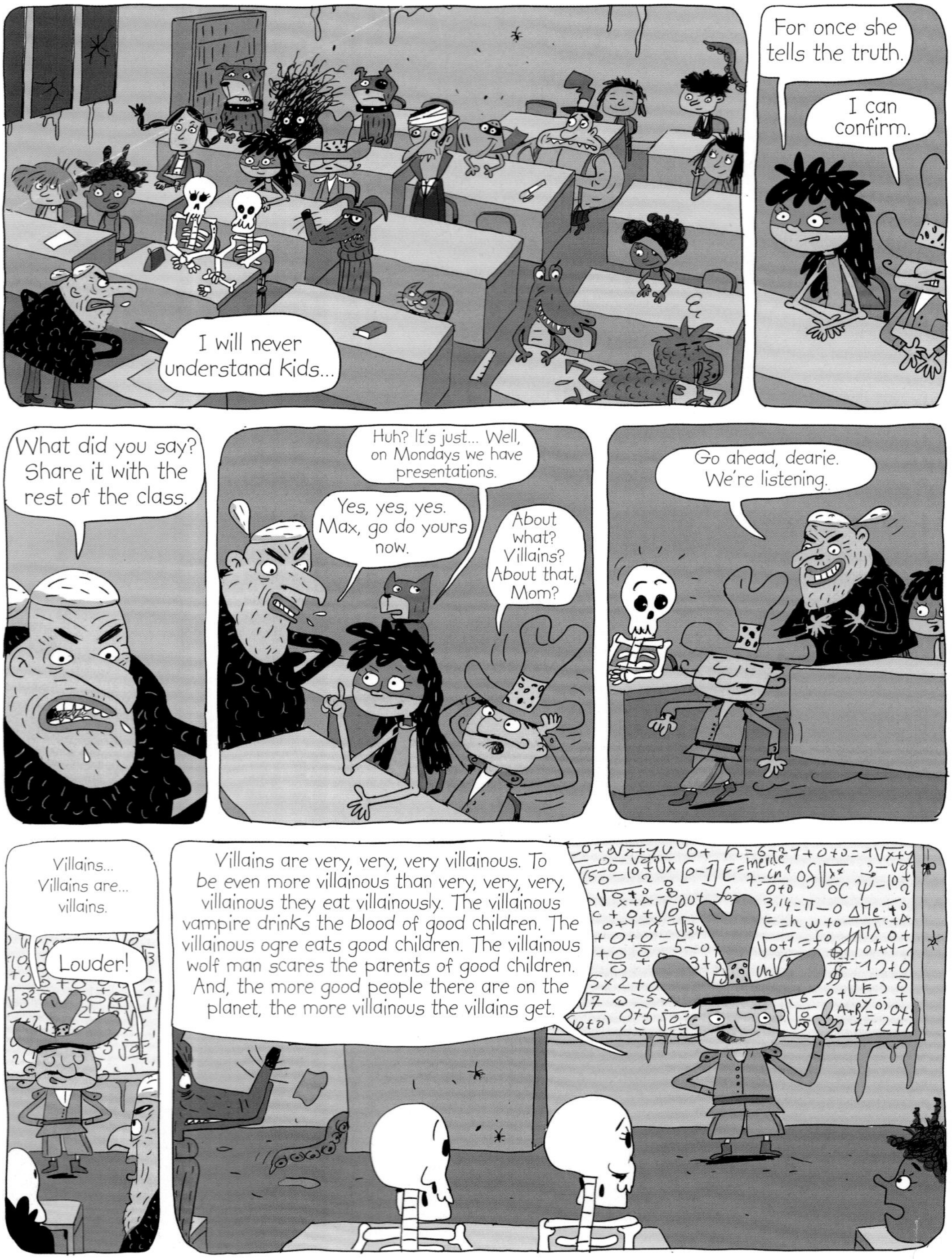
I will never understand kids...
For once she tells the truth.
I can confirm.
What did you say? Share it with the rest of the class.
Huh? It's just... Well, on Mondays we have presentations.
Yes, yes, yes. Max, go do yours now.
About what? Villains? About that, Mom?
Go ahead, dearie. We're listening.
Villains... Villains are... villains.
Louder!
Villains are very, very, very villainous. To be even more villainous than very, very, very, villainous they eat villainously. The villainous vampire drinks the blood of good children. The villainous ogre eats good children. The villainous wolf man scares the parents of good children. And, the more good people there are on the planet, the more villainous the villains get.

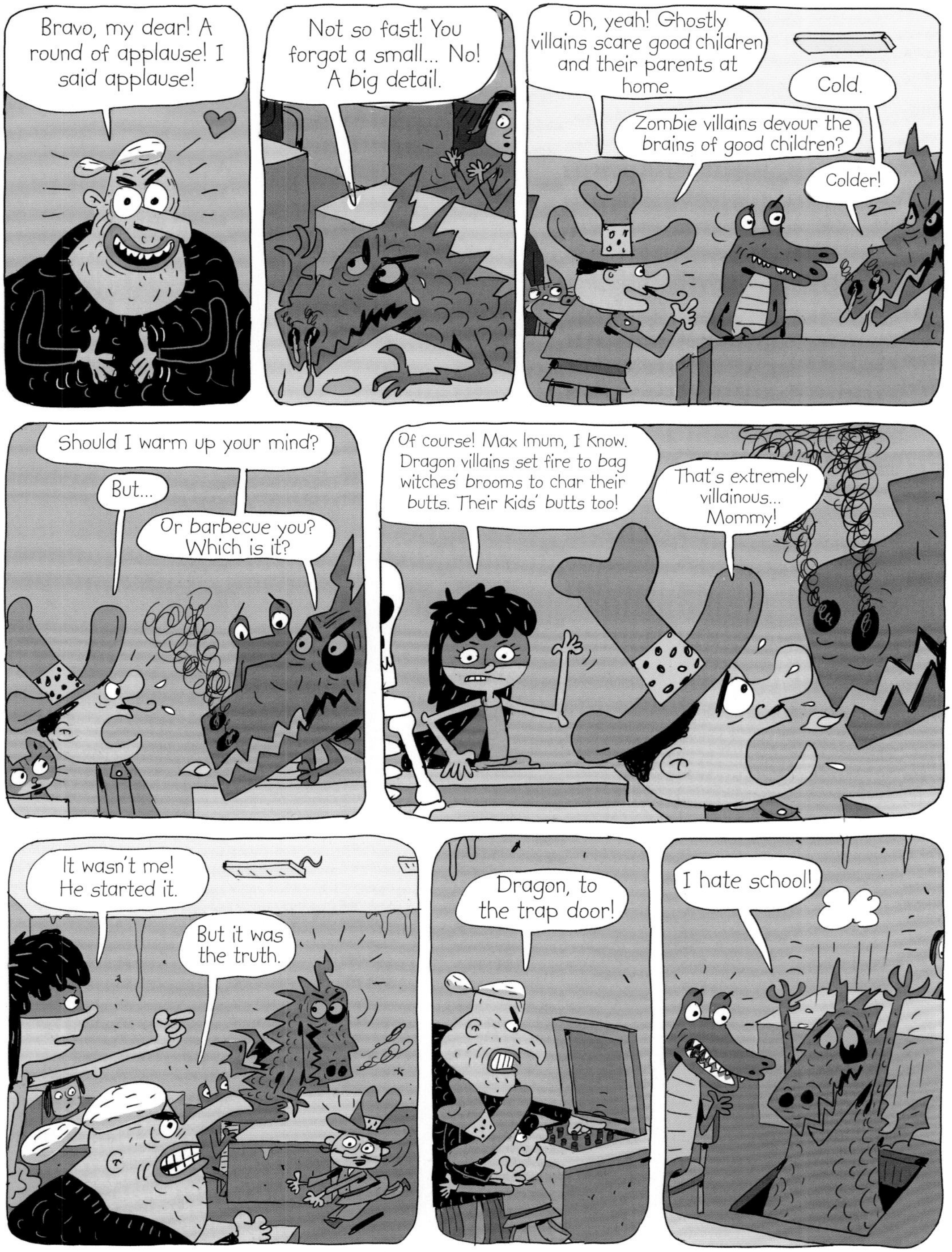
Bravo, my dear! A round of applause! I said applause!
Not so fast! You forgot a small... No! A big detail.
Oh, yeah! Ghostly villains scare good children and their parents at home.
Cold.
Zombie villains devour the brains of good children?
Colder!
Should I warm up your mind?
But...
Or barbecue you? Which is it?
Of course! Max Imum, I know. Dragon villains set fire to bag witches' brooms to char their butts. Their kids' butts too!
That's extremely villainous... Mommy!
It wasn't me! He started it.
But it was the truth.
Dragon, to the trap door!
I hate school!

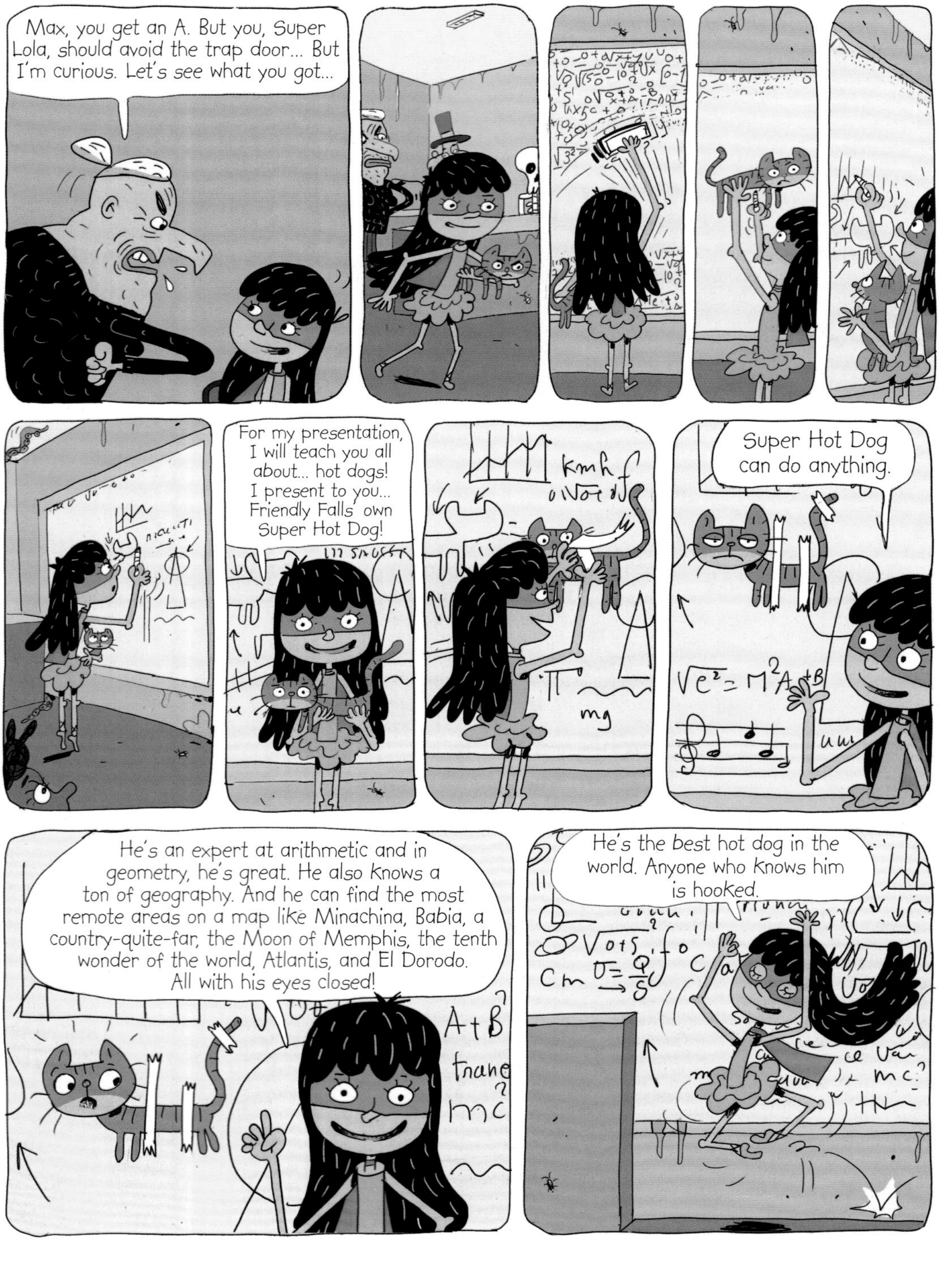
Max, you get an A. But you, Super Lola, should avoid the trap door... But I'm curious. Let's see what you got...
For my presentation, I will teach you all about... hot dogs! I present to you... Friendly Falls' own Super Hot Dog!
Super Hot Dog can do anything.
He's an expert at arithmetic and in geometry, he's great. He also knows a ton of geography. And he can find the most remote areas on a map like Minachina, Babia, a country-quite-far, the Moon of Memphis, the tenth wonder of the world, Atlantis, and El Dorodo. All with his eyes closed!
He's the best hot dog in the world. Anyone who knows him is hooked.

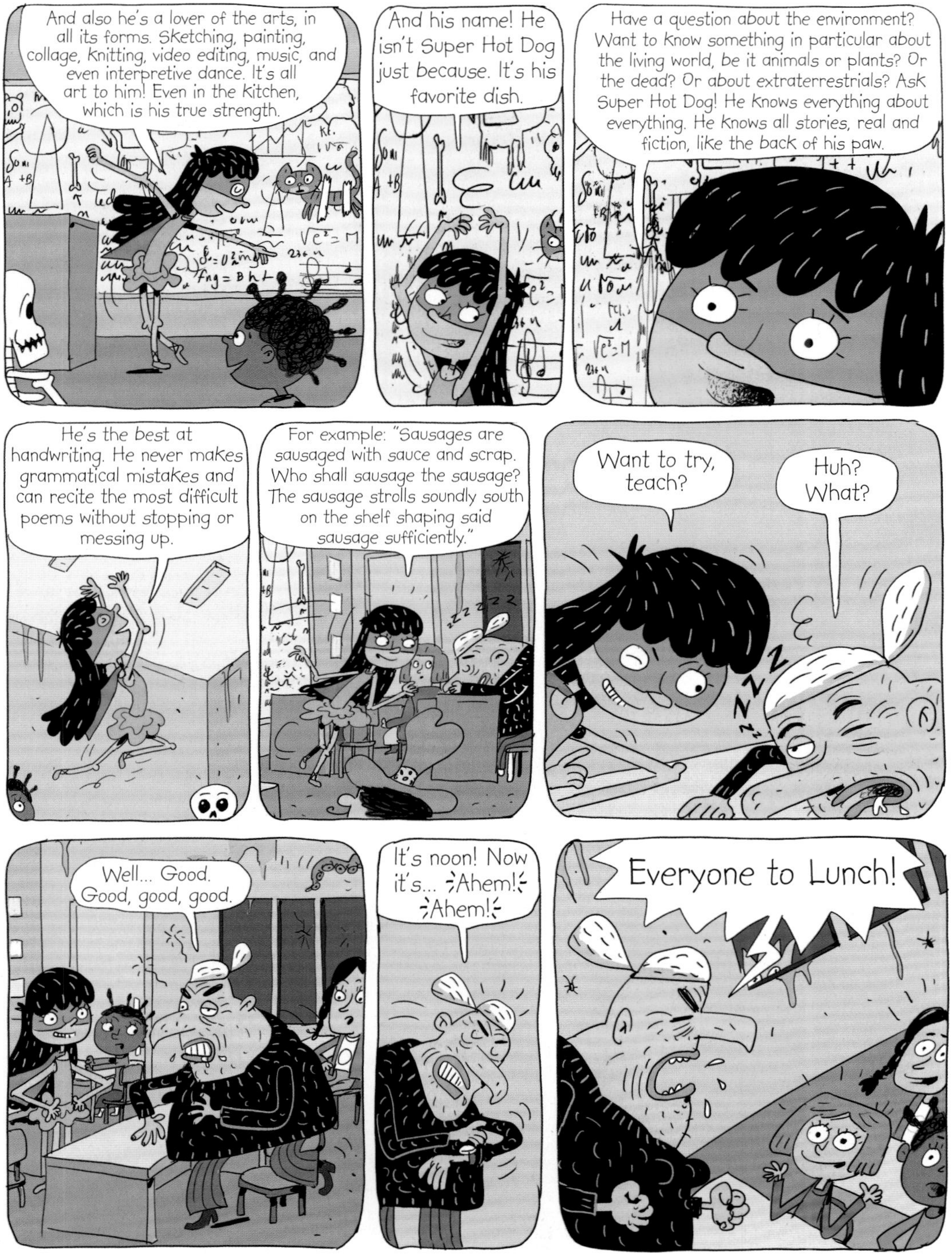
And also he's a lover of the arts, in all its forms. Sketching, painting, collage, knitting, video editing, music, and even interpretive dance. It's all art to him! Even in the kitchen, which is his true strength.
And his name! He isn't Super Hot Dog just because. It's his favorite dish.
Have a question about the environment? Want to know something in particular about the living world, be it animals or plants? Or the dead? Or about extraterrestrials? Ask Super Hot Dog! He knows everything about everything. He knows all stories, real and fiction, like the back of his paw.
He's the best at handwriting. He never makes grammatical mistakes and can recite the most difficult poems without stopping or messing up.
For example: "Sausages are sausaged with sauce and scrap. Who shall sausage the sausage? The sausage strolls soundly south on the shelf shaping said sausage sufficiently."
Want to try, teach?
Huh? What?
Well... Good. Good, good, good.
It's noon! Now it's... Ahem! Ahem!
Everyone to Lunch!

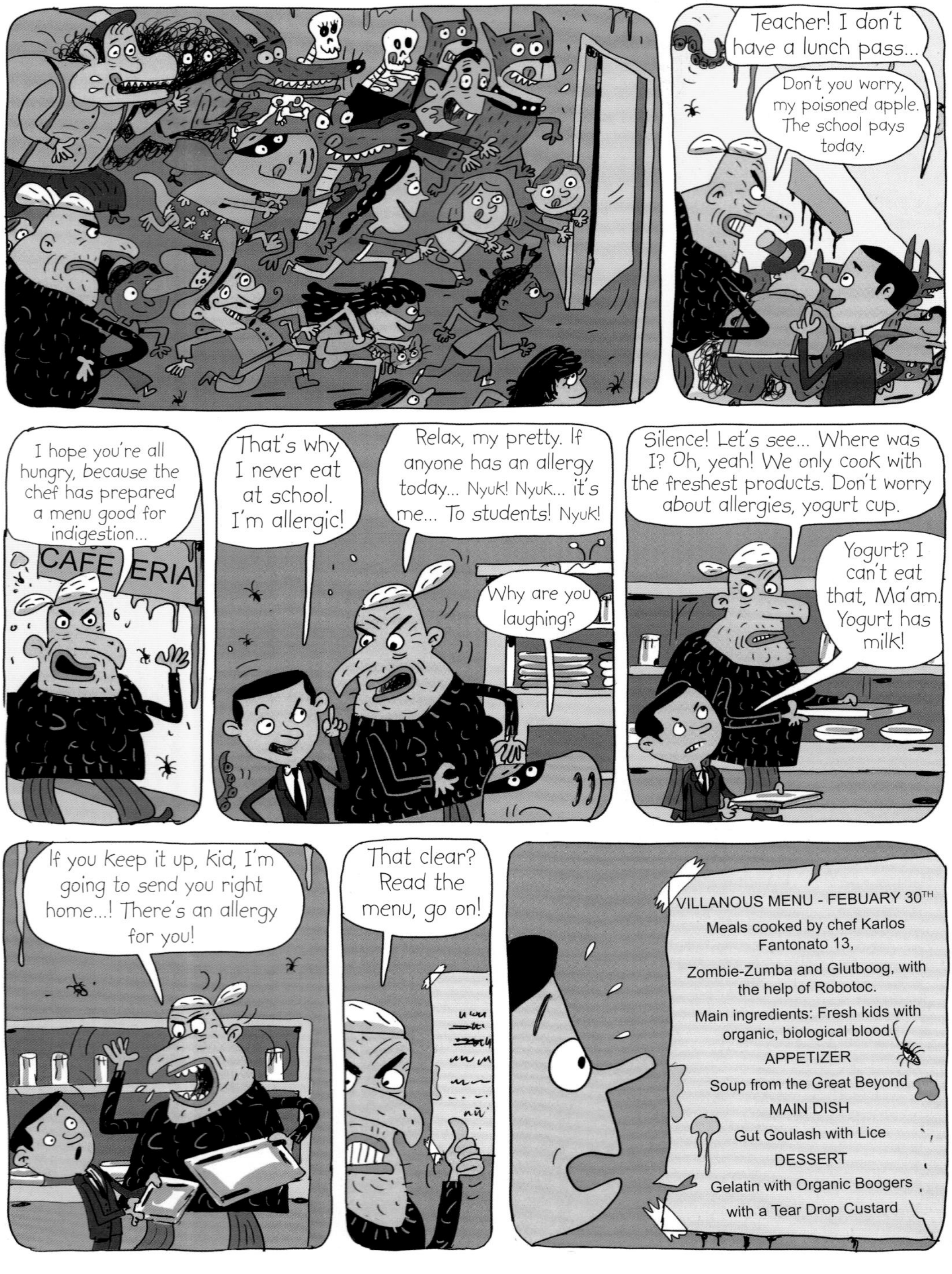
Teacher! I don't have a lunch pass...
Don't you worry, my poisoned apple. The school pays today.
CAFE ERIA
I hope you're all hungry, because the chef has prepared a menu good for indigestion...
That's why I never eat at school. I'm allergic!
Relax, my pretty. If anyone has an allergy today... Nyuk! Nyuk... it's me... To students! Nyuk!
Why are you laughing?
Silence! Let's see... Where was I? Oh, yeah! We only cook with the freshest products. Don't worry about allergies, yogurt cup.
Yogurt? I can't eat that, Ma'am. Yogurt has milk!
If you keep it up, kid, I'm going to send you right home...! There's an allergy for you!
That clear? Read the menu, go on!
VILLANOUS MENU - FEBUARY 30TH
Meals cooked by chef Karlos Fantonato 13,
Zombie-Zumba and Glutboog, with the help of Robotoc.
Main ingredients: Fresh kids with organic, biological blood.
APPETIZER
Soup from the Great Beyond
MAIN DISH
Gut Goulash with Lice
DESSERT
Gelatin with Organic Boogers with a Tear Drop Custard

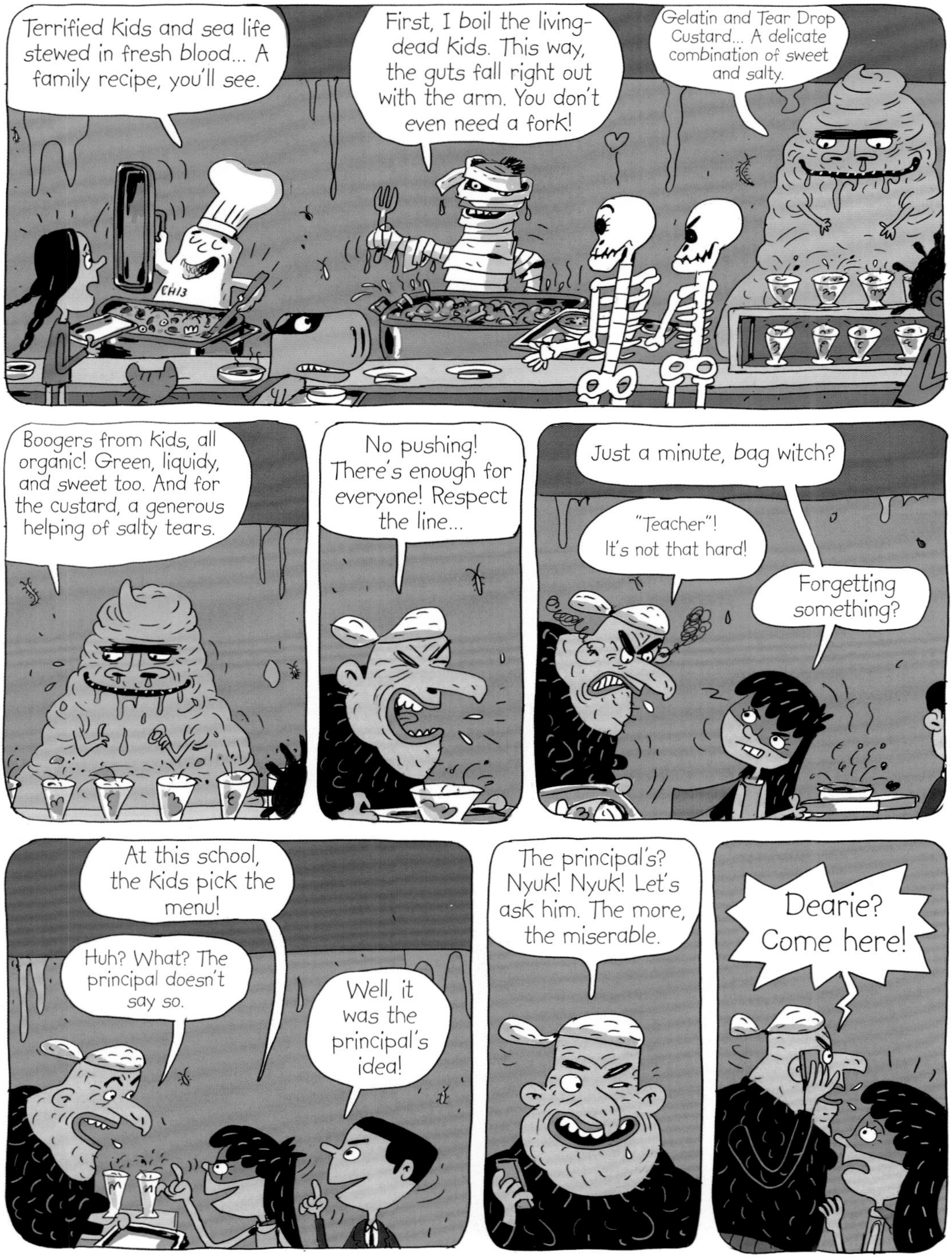
Terrified kids and sea life stewed in fresh blood... A family recipe, you'll see.
First, I boil the living-dead kids. This way, the guts fall right out with the arm. You don't even need a fork!
Gelatin and Tear Drop Custard... A delicate combination of sweet and salty.
CHI3
Boogers from kids, all organic! Green, liquidy, and sweet too. And for the custard, a generous helping of salty tears.
No pushing! There's enough for everyone! Respect the line...
Just a minute, bag witch?
"Teacher"! It's not that hard!
Forgetting something?
At this school, the kids pick the menu!
Huh? What? The principal doesn't say so.
Well, it was the principal's idea!
The principal's? Nyuk! Nyuk! Let's ask him. The more, the miserable.
Dearie? Come here!

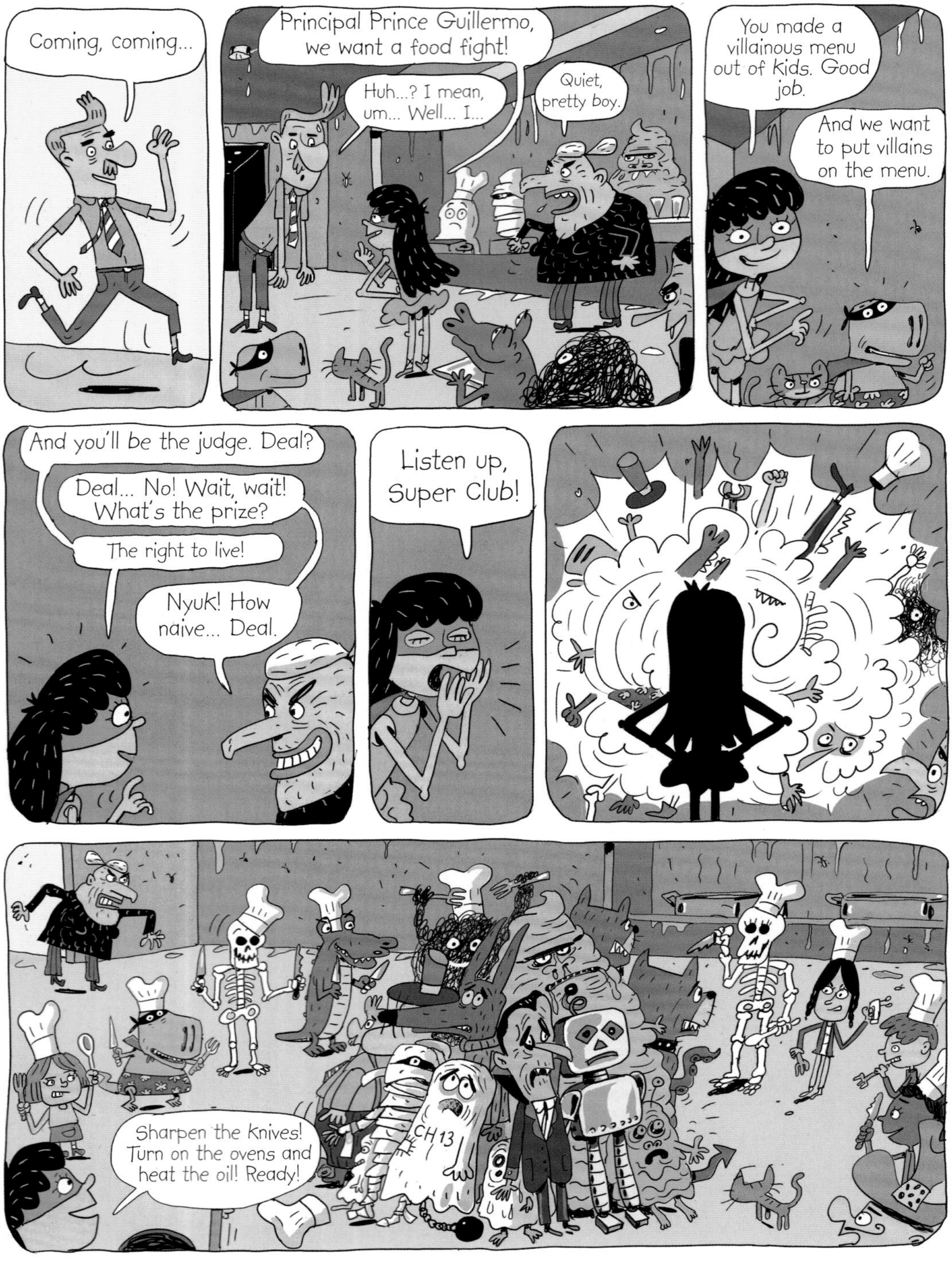
Coming, coming...
Principal Prince Guillermo, we want a food fight!
Huh...? I mean, um... Well... I...
Quiet, pretty boy.
You made a villainous menu out of Kids. Good job.
And we want to put villains on the menu.
And you'll be the judge. Deal?
Deal... No! Wait, wait! What's the prize?
The right to live!
Nyuk! How naive... Deal.
Listen up, Super Club!
CH 13
Sharpen the Knives! Turn on the ovens and heat the oil! Ready!

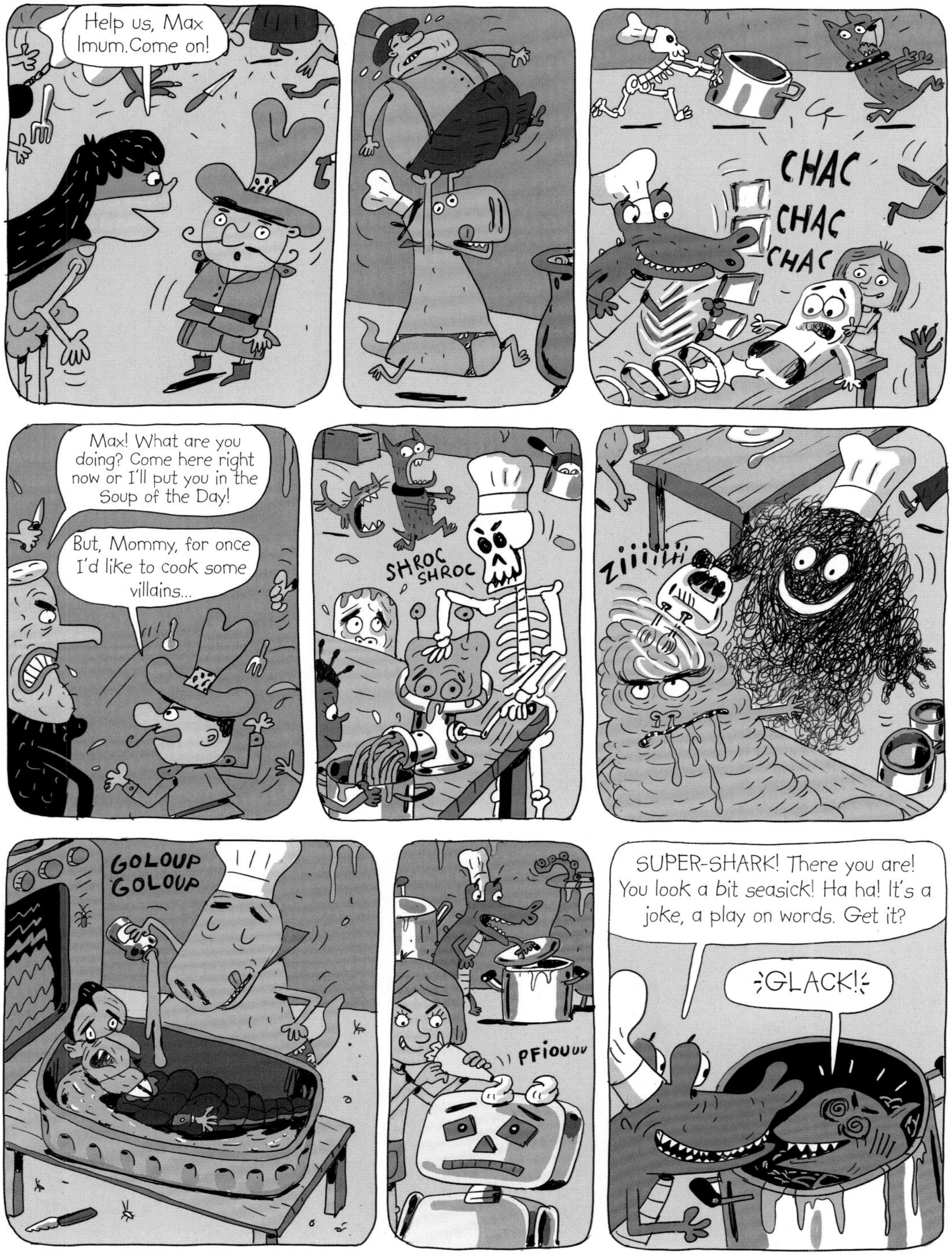

Help us, Max Imum. Come on!
CHAC
CHAC
CHAC
Max! What are you doing? Come here right now or I'll put you in the Soup of the Day!
But, Mommy, for once I'd like to cook some villains...
SHROC SHROC
ZIIIIIII
GOLOUP GOLOUP
PFIOUUU
SUPER-SHARK! There you are! You look a bit seasick! Ha ha! It's a joke, a play on words. Get it?
GLACK!

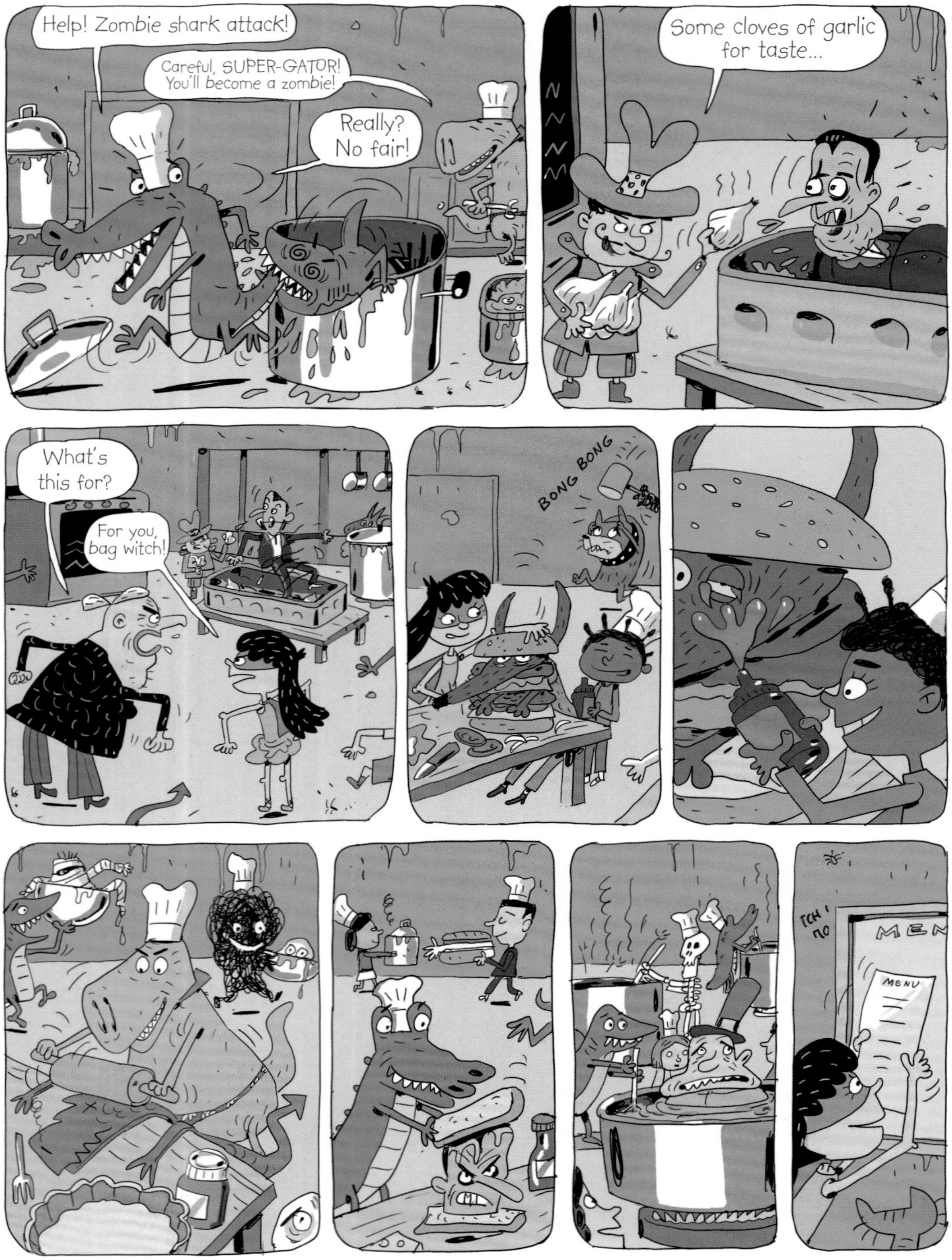
Help! Zombie shark attack!
Careful, SUPER-GATOR! You'll become a zombie!
Really? No fair!
Some cloves of garlic for taste...
What's this for?
For you, bag witch!
BONG BONG
TCH! TCH!
MENU
MENU

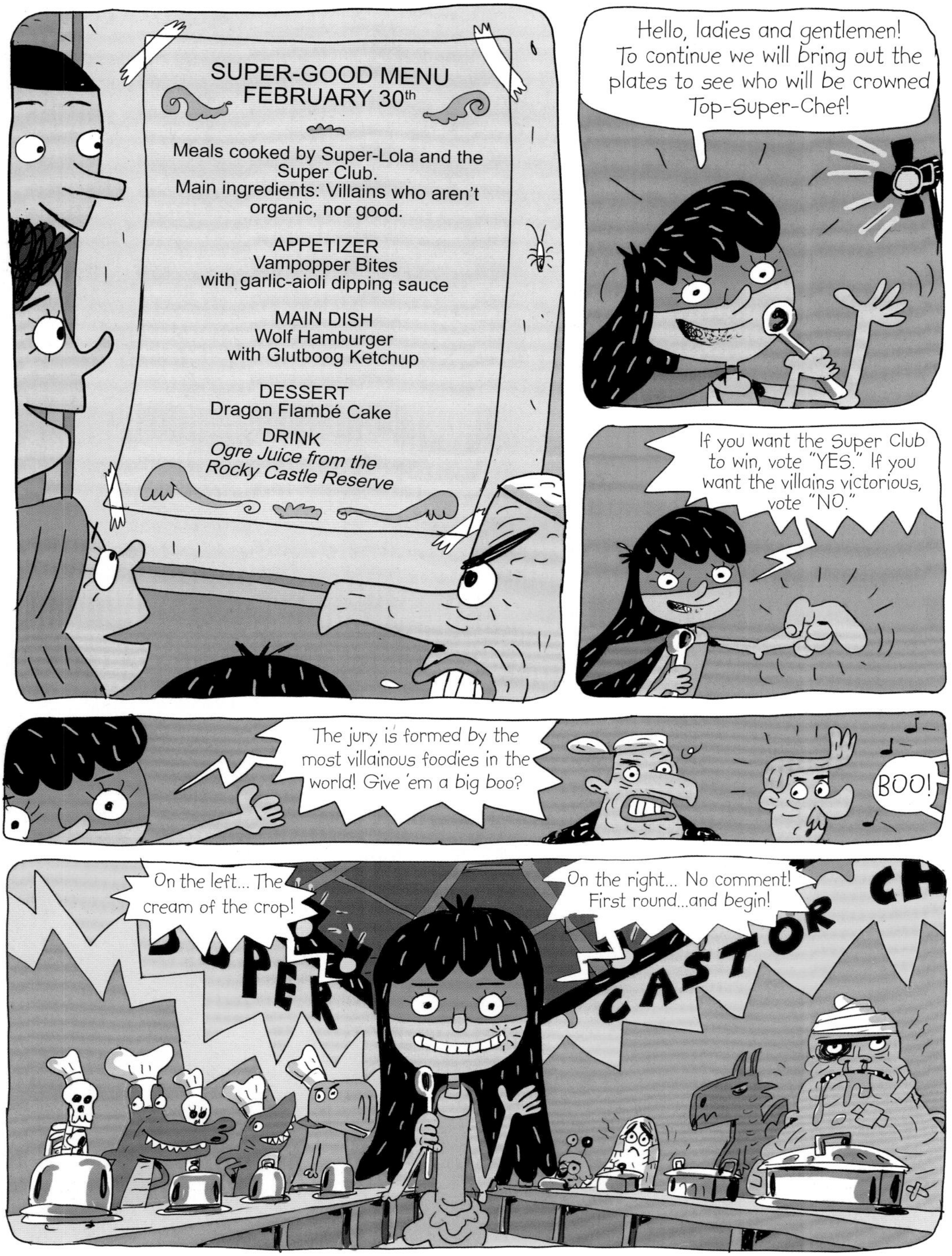
SUPER-GOOD MENU
FEBRUARY 30th
Meals cooked by Super-Lola and the Super Club.
Main ingredients: Villains who aren't organic, nor good.
APPETIZER
Vampopper Bites
with garlic-aioli dipping sauce
MAIN DISH
Wolf Hamburger
with Glutboog Ketchup
DESSERT
Dragon Flambé Cake
DRINK
Ogre Juice from the Rocky Castle Reserve
Hello, ladies and gentlemen! To continue we will bring out the plates to see who will be crowned Top-Super-Chef!
If you want the Super Club to win, vote "YES." If you want the villains victorious, vote "NO."
The jury is formed by the most villainous foodies in the world! Give 'em a big boo?
BOO!
On the left... The cream of the crop!
On the right... No comment! First round...and begin!
SUPER
CASTOR CH

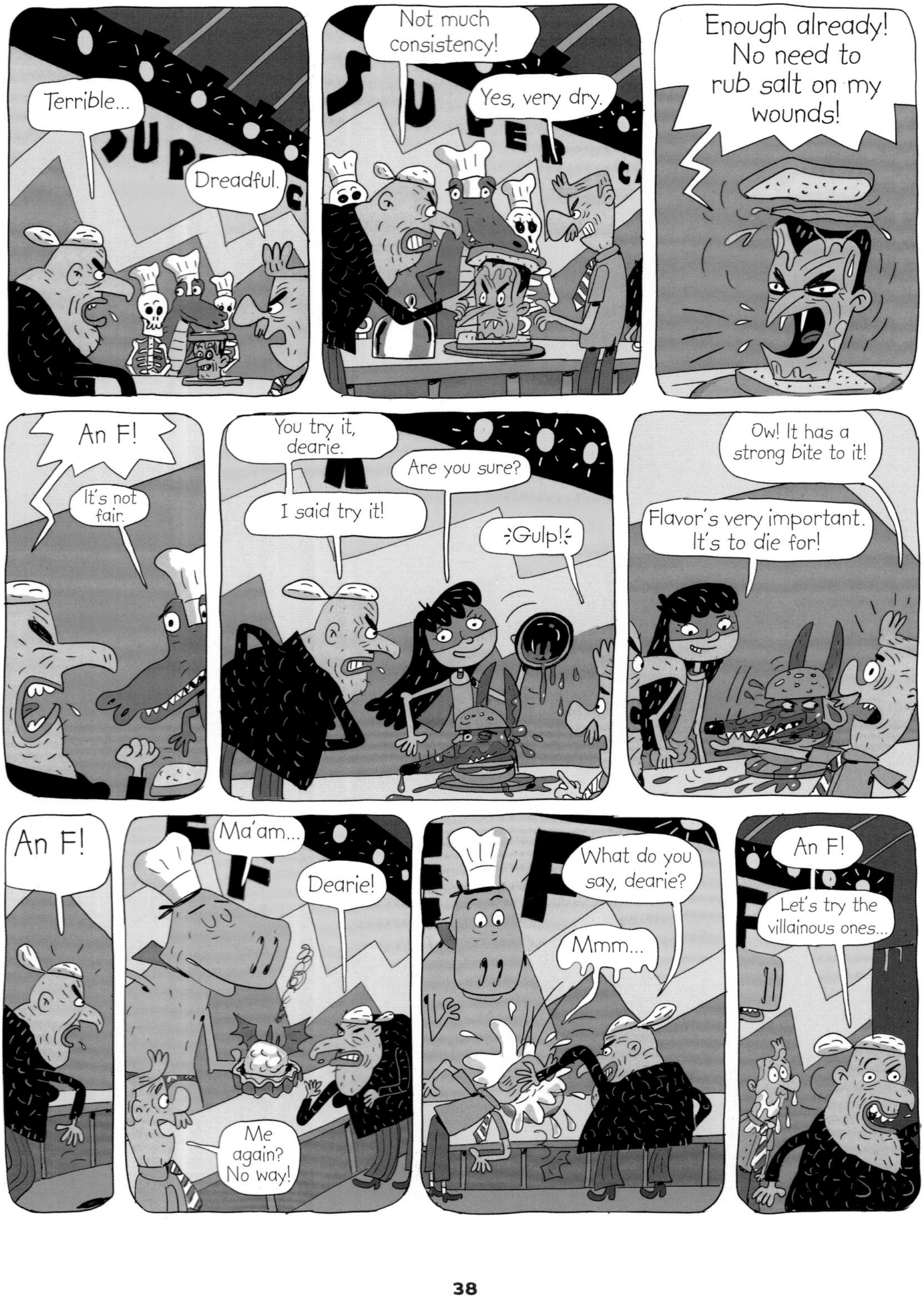

Terrible...
Dreadful.
SUPER
Not much consistency!
Yes, very dry.
Enough already! No need to rub salt on my wounds!
An F!
It's not fair.
You try it, dearie.
Are you sure?
I said try it!
Gulp!
Ow! It has a strong bite to it!
Flavor's very important. It's to die for!
An F!
Ma'am...
Dearie!
Me again? No way!
What do you say, dearie?
Mmm...
An F!
Let's try the villainous ones...

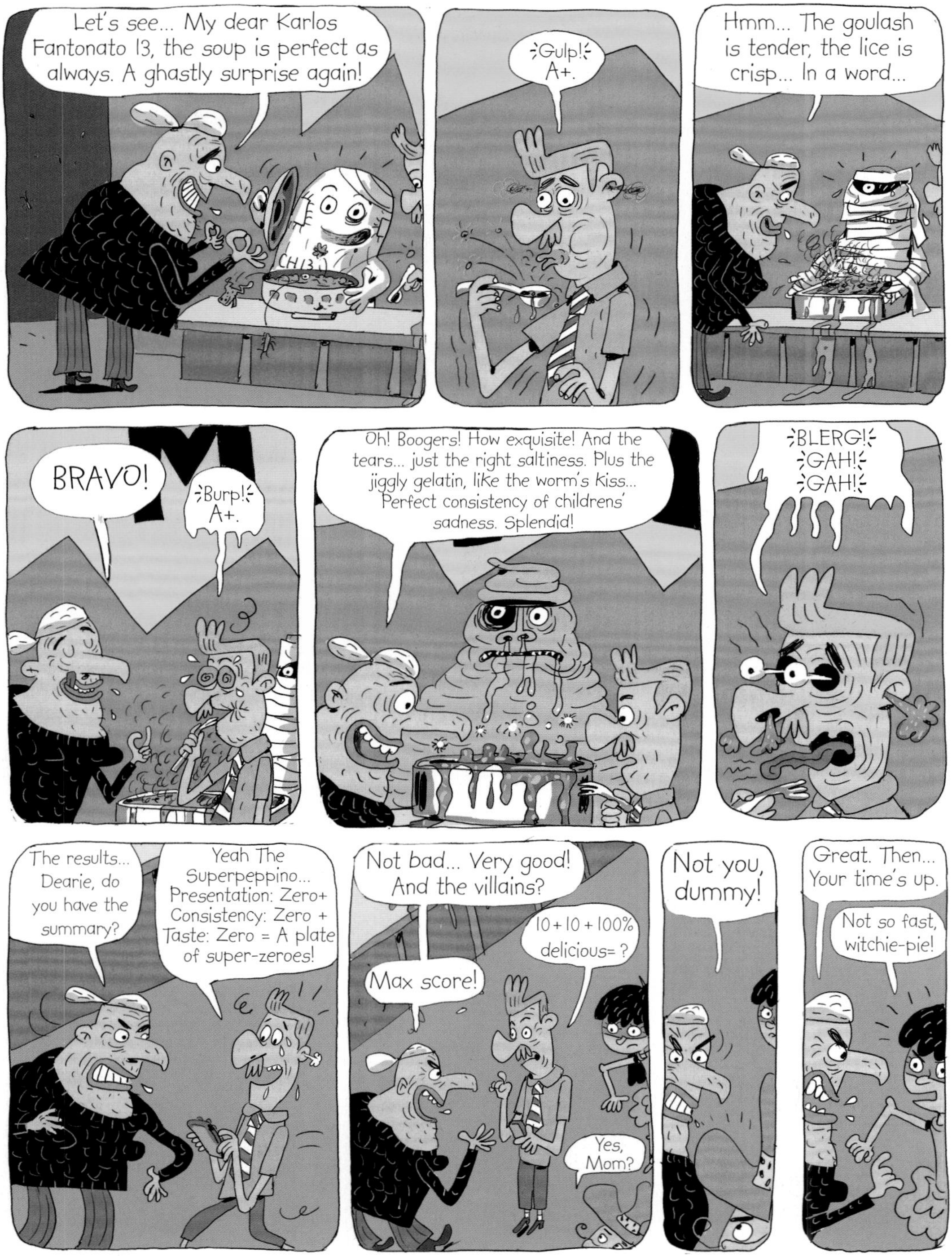

Let's see... My dear Karlos Fantonato 13, the soup is perfect as always. A ghastly surprise again!
CH13
Gulp! A+.
Hmm... The goulash is tender, the lice is crisp... In a word...
BRAVO!
Burp! A+.
Oh! Boogers! How exquisite! And the tears... just the right saltiness. Plus the jiggly gelatin, like the worm's Kiss... Perfect consistency of childrens' sadness. Splendid!
BLERG! GAH! GAH!
The results... Dearie, do you have the summary?
Yeah The Superpeppino... Presentation: Zero+ Consistency: Zero + Taste: Zero = A plate of super-zeroes!
Not bad... Very good! And the villains?
10 + 10 + 100% delicious= ?
Max score!
Yes, Mom?
Not you, dummy!
Great. Then... Your time's up.
Not so fast, witchie-pie!

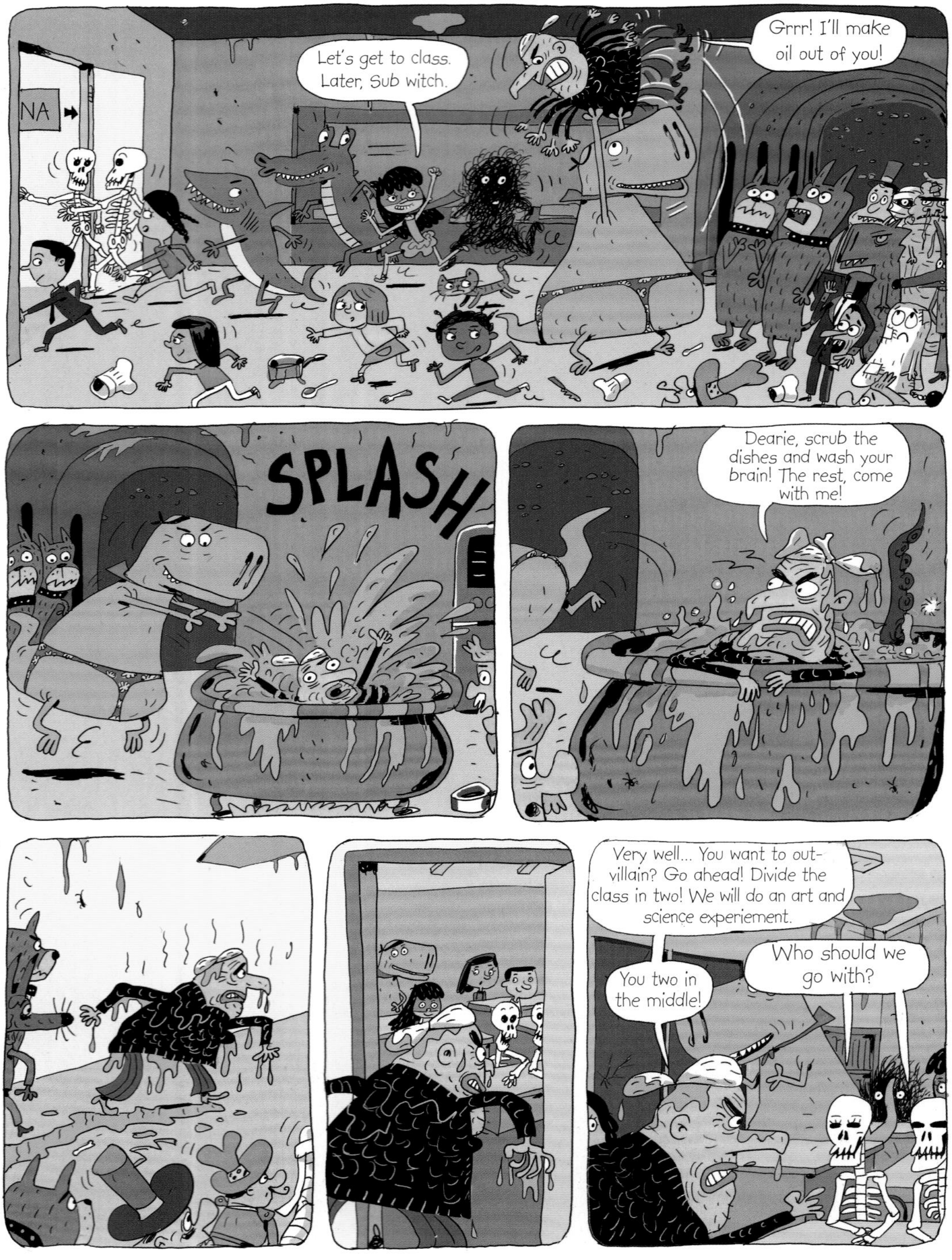

NA
Let's get to class. Later, Sub witch.
Grrr! I'll make oil out of you!
SPLASH
Dearie, scrub the dishes and wash your brain! The rest, come with me!
Very well... You want to out-villain? Go ahead! Divide the class in two! We will do an art and science experiement.
You two in the middle!
Who should we go with?

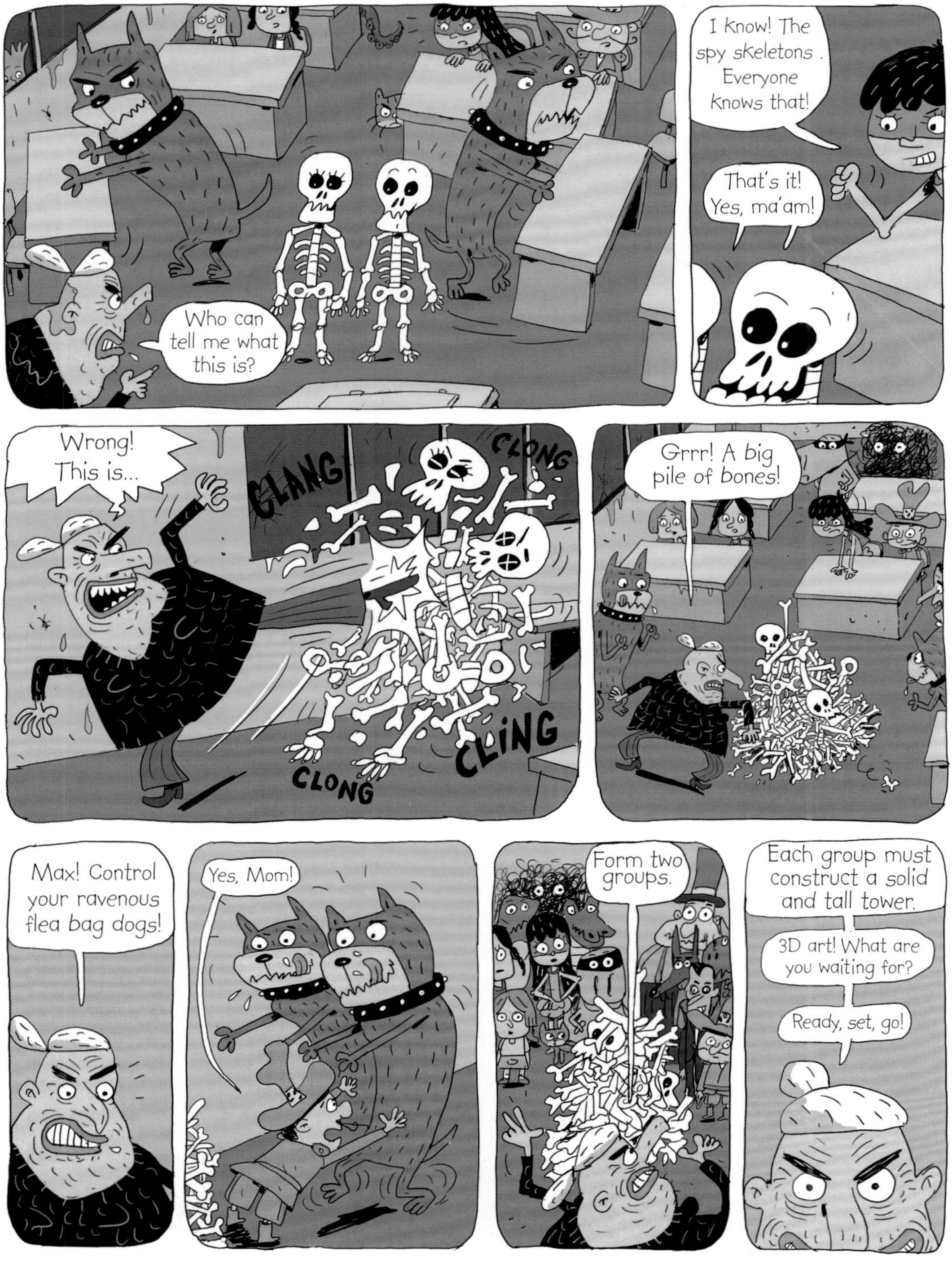
Who can tell me what this is?
I know! The spy skeletons . Everyone knows that!
That's it! Yes, ma'am!
Wrong! This is...
CLANG
CLONG
CLING
CLONG
Grrr! A big pile of bones!
Max! Control your ravenous flea bag dogs!
Yes, Mom!
Form two groups.
Each group must construct a solid and tall tower.
3D art! What are you waiting for?
Ready, set, go!

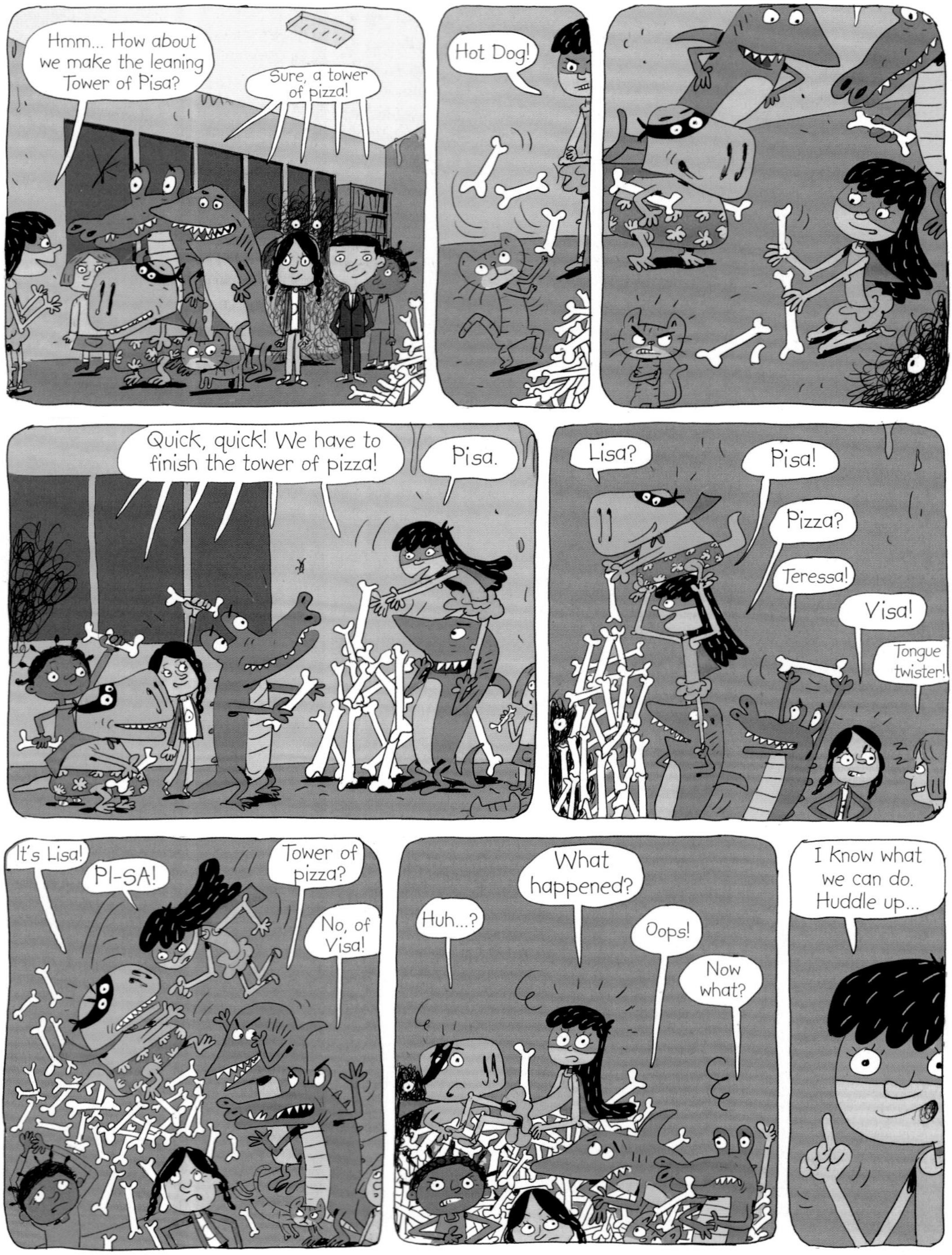

Hmm... How about we make the leaning Tower of Pisa?
Sure, a tower of pizza!
Hot Dog!
Quick, quick! We have to finish the tower of pizza!
Pisa.
Lisa?
Pisa!
Pizza?
Teressa!
Visa!
Tongue twister!
It's Lisa!
PI-SA!
Tower of pizza?
No, of Visa!
Huh...?
What happened?
Oops!
Now what?
I know what we can do. Huddle up...

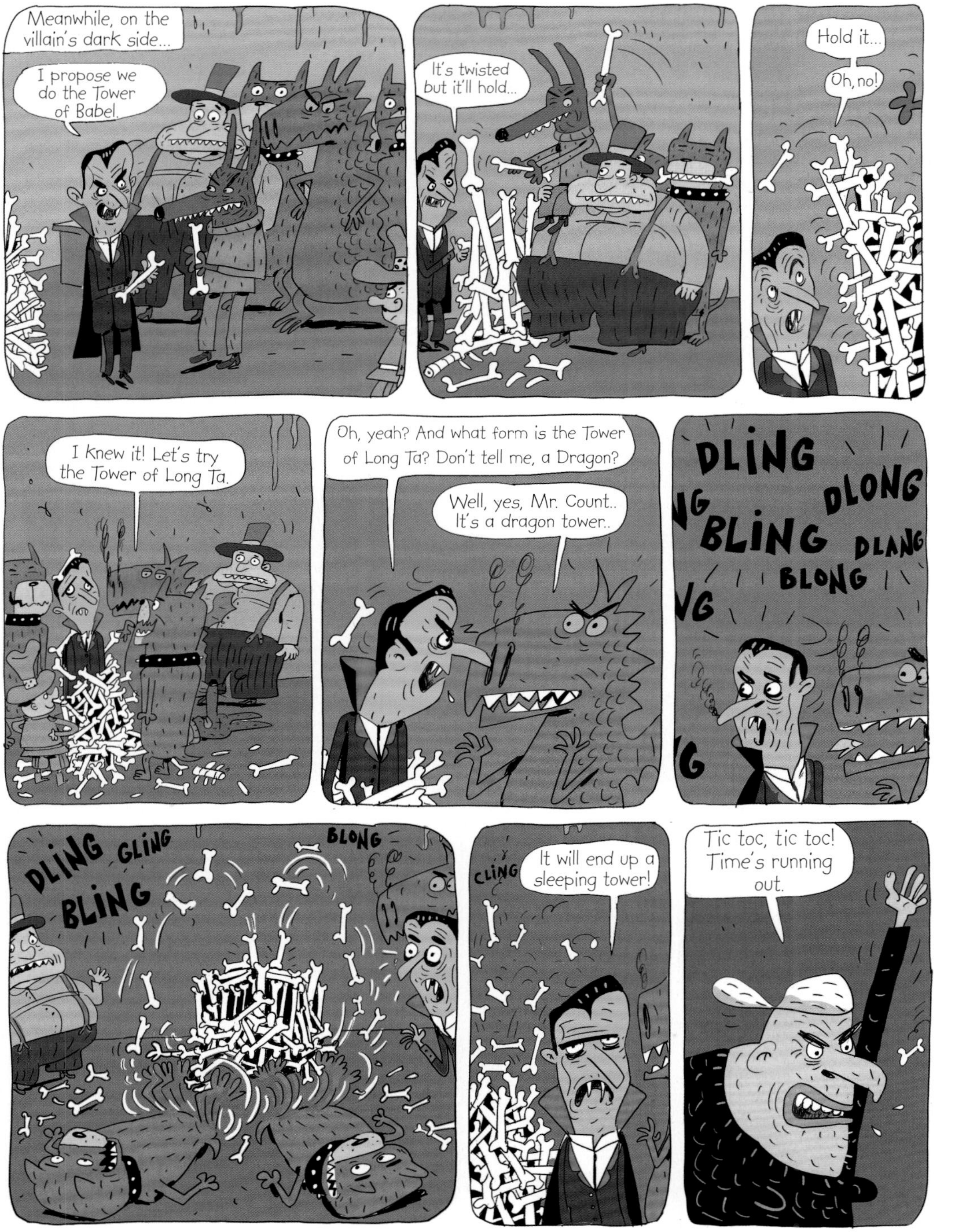
Meanwhile, on the villain's dark side...
I propose we do the Tower of Babel.
It's twisted but it'll hold...
Hold it...
Oh, no!
I knew it! Let's try the Tower of Long Ta.
Oh, yeah? And what form is the Tower of Long Ta? Don't tell me, a Dragon?
Well, yes, Mr. Count.. It's a dragon tower..
DLING
DLONG
BLING
DLANG
BLONG
DLING
GLING
BLONG
BLING
CLING
It will end up a sleeping tower!
Tic toc, tic toc! Time's running out.

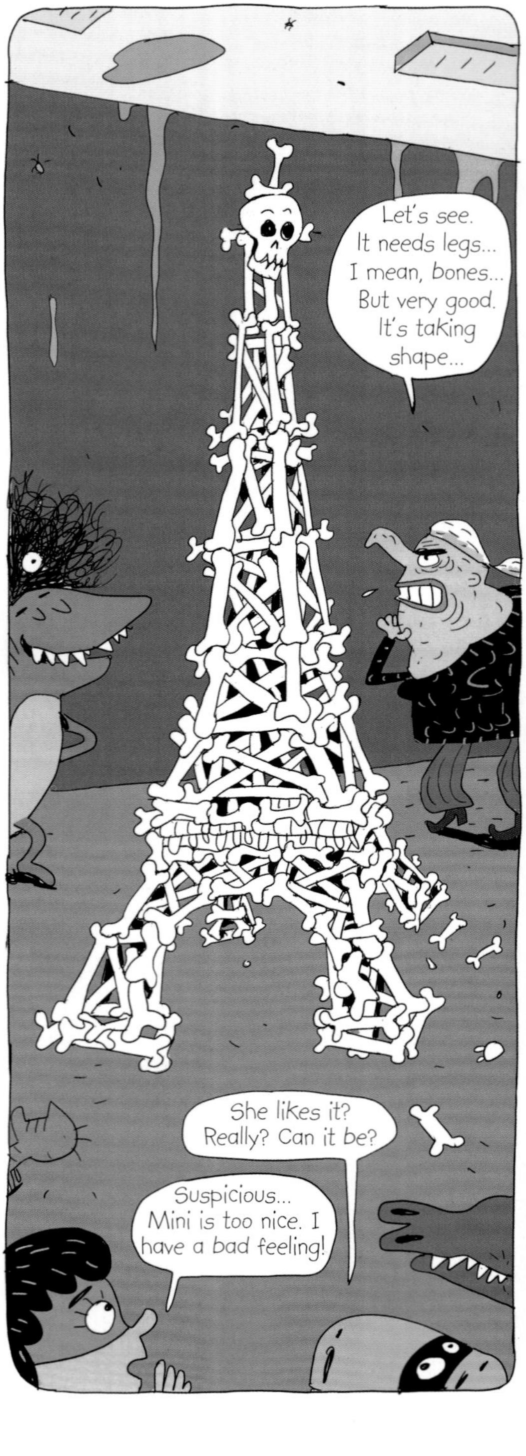
Let's see. It needs legs... I mean, bones... But very good. It's taking shape...
She likes it? Really? Can it be?
Suspicious... Mini is too nice. I have a bad feeling!

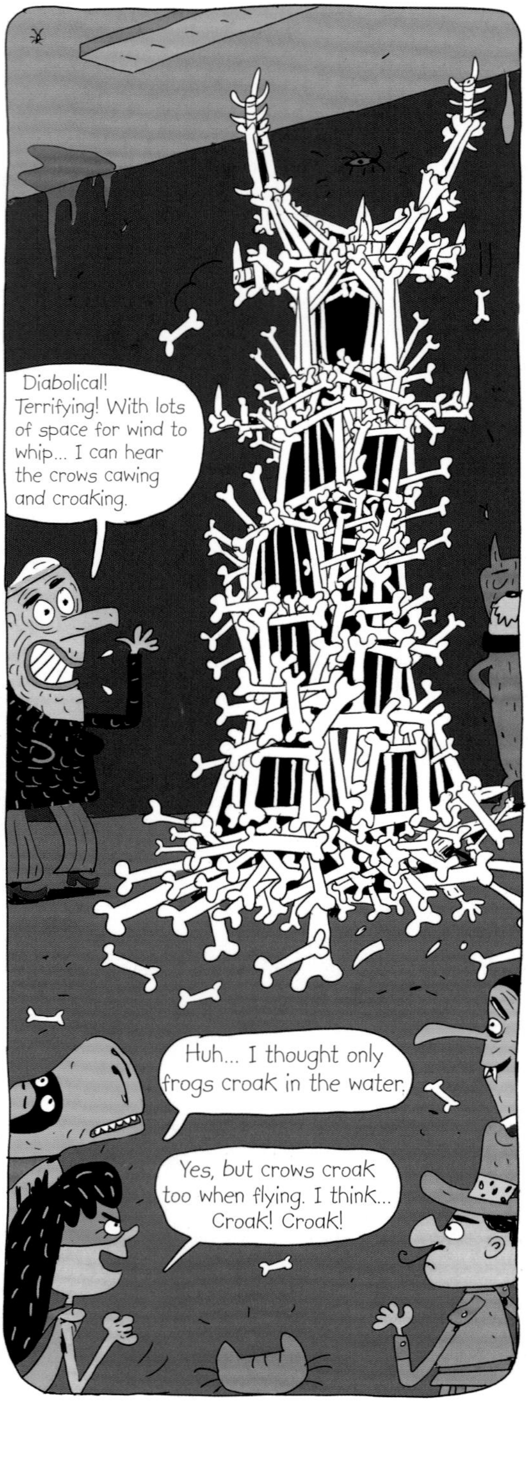
Diabolical! Terrifying! With lots of space for wind to whip... I can hear the crows cawing and croaking.
Huh... I thought only frogs croak in the water.
Yes, but crows croak too when flying. I think... Croak! Croak!

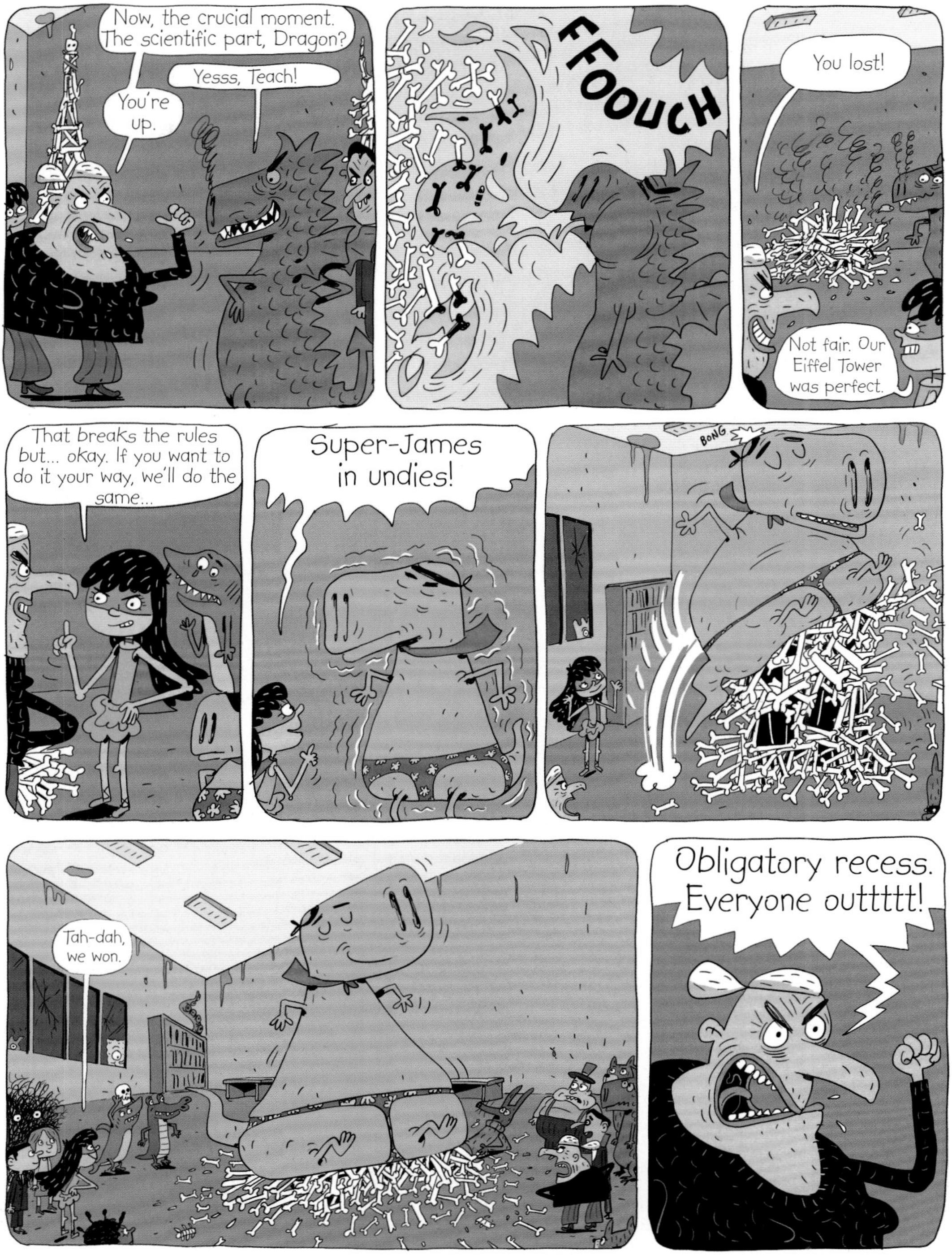
Now, the crucial moment. The scientific part, Dragon?
You're up.
Yesss, Teach!
FFOOUCH
You lost!
Not fair. Our Eiffel Tower was perfect.
That breaks the rules but... okay. If you want to do it your way, we'll do the same...
Super-James in undies!
BONG
Tah-dah, we won.
Obligatory recess. Everyone outttttt!

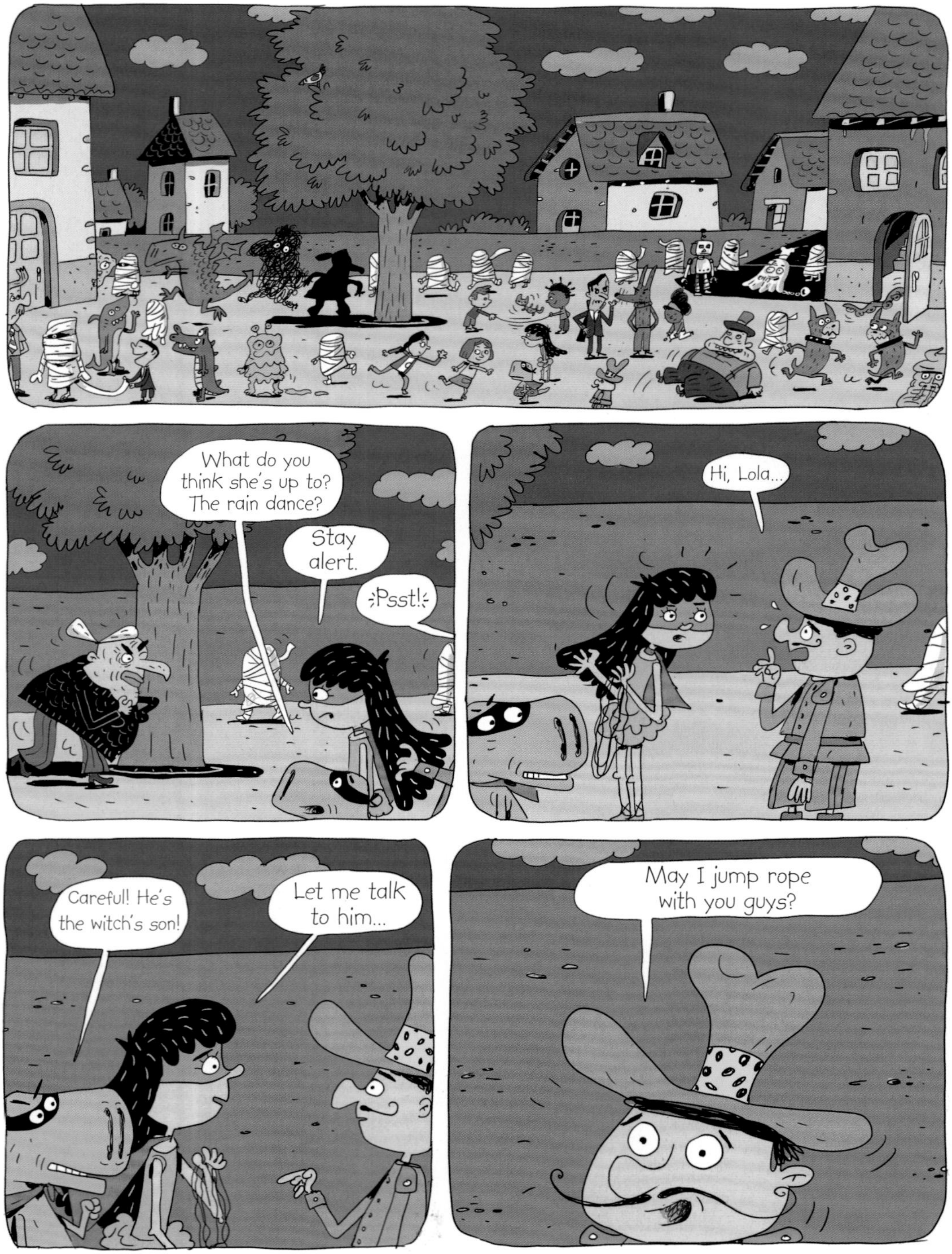
What do you think she's up to? The rain dance?
Stay alert.
Psst!
Hi, Lola...
Careful! He's the witch's son!
Let me talk to him...
May I jump rope with you guys?

...29...

YAHOOO! YAHOO!

...99...

Might I know what you're doing?

Hundred!

Max! You want to jump? Very well!

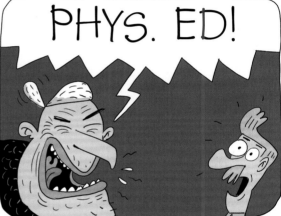

PHYS. ED!

Now we are going to have a physical education class. Very good! This is a bomb. You must throw it to attack. If the ball hits you... you're a prisoner. Or even worse: zombies, vampires, and ogres! Nyuk!

Bag witch! You'll see who's the champs at dodge ball.

TWEE

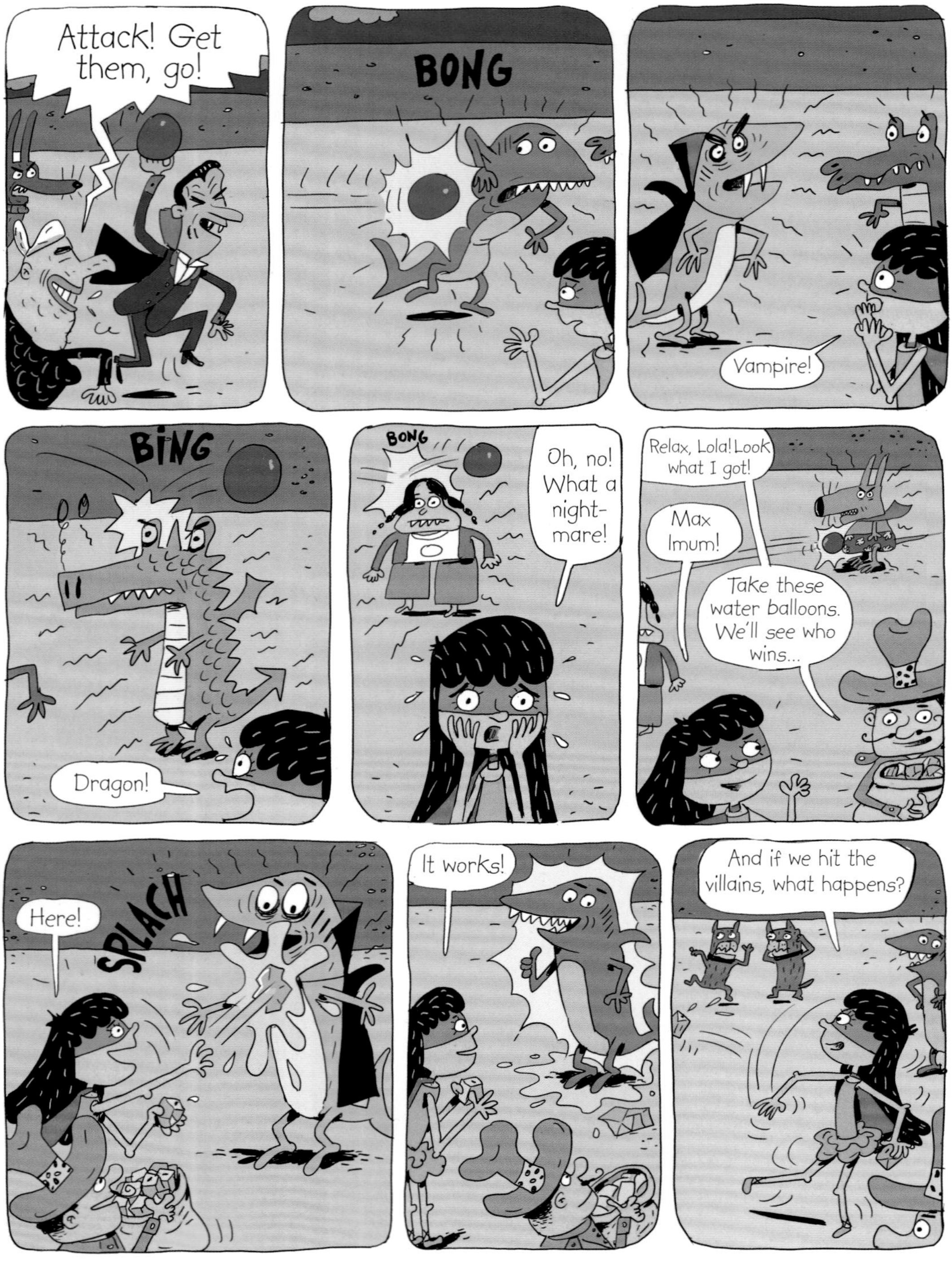
Attack! Get them, go!
BONG
Vampire!
BING
Dragon!
BONG
Oh, no! What a night-mare!
Relax, Lola! Look what I got!
Max Imum!
Take these water balloons. We'll see who wins...
Here!
SPLACH
It works!
And if we hit the villains, what happens?

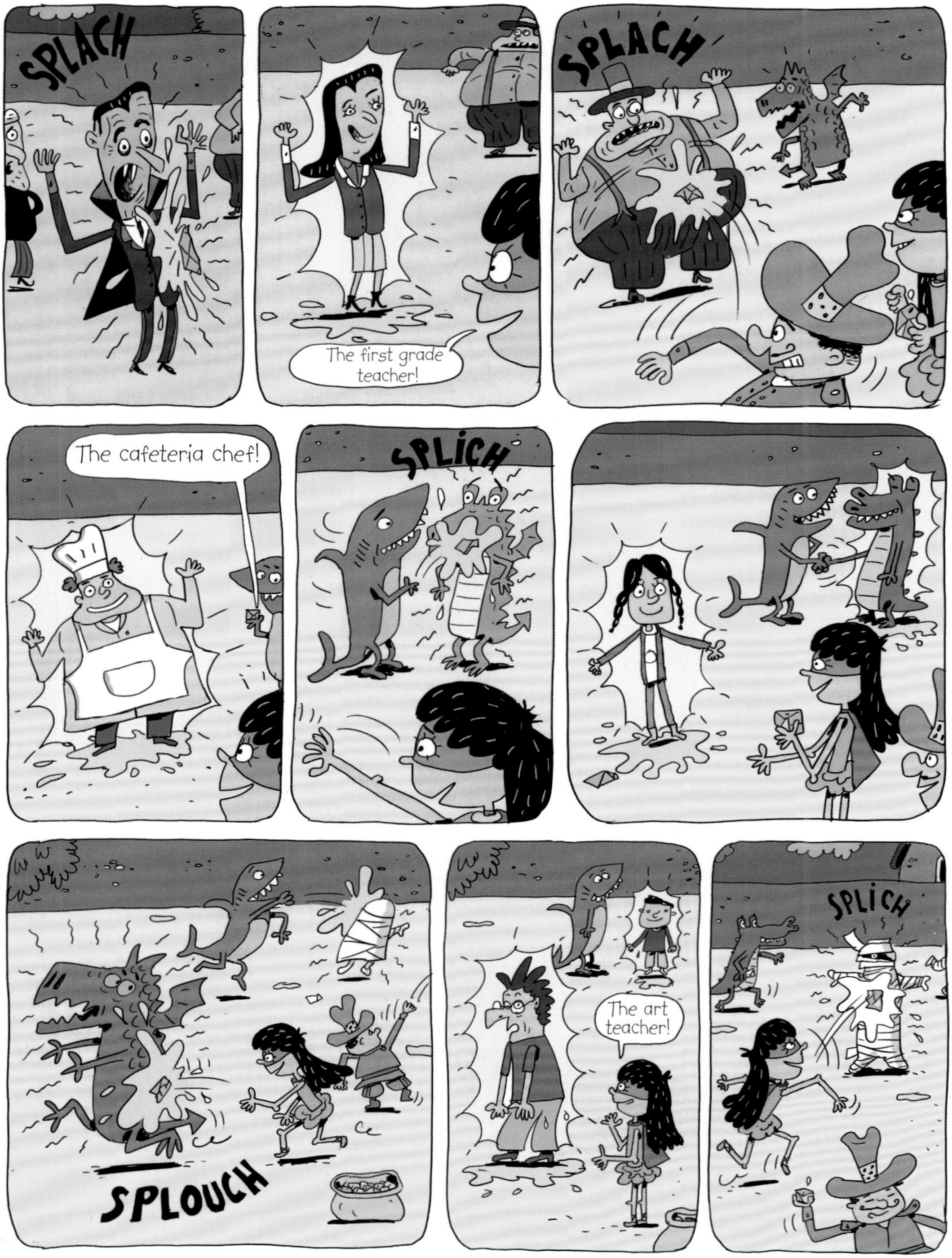
SPLACH
The first grade teacher!
SPLACH
The cafeteria chef!
SPLICH
SPLOUCH
The art teacher!
SPLICH

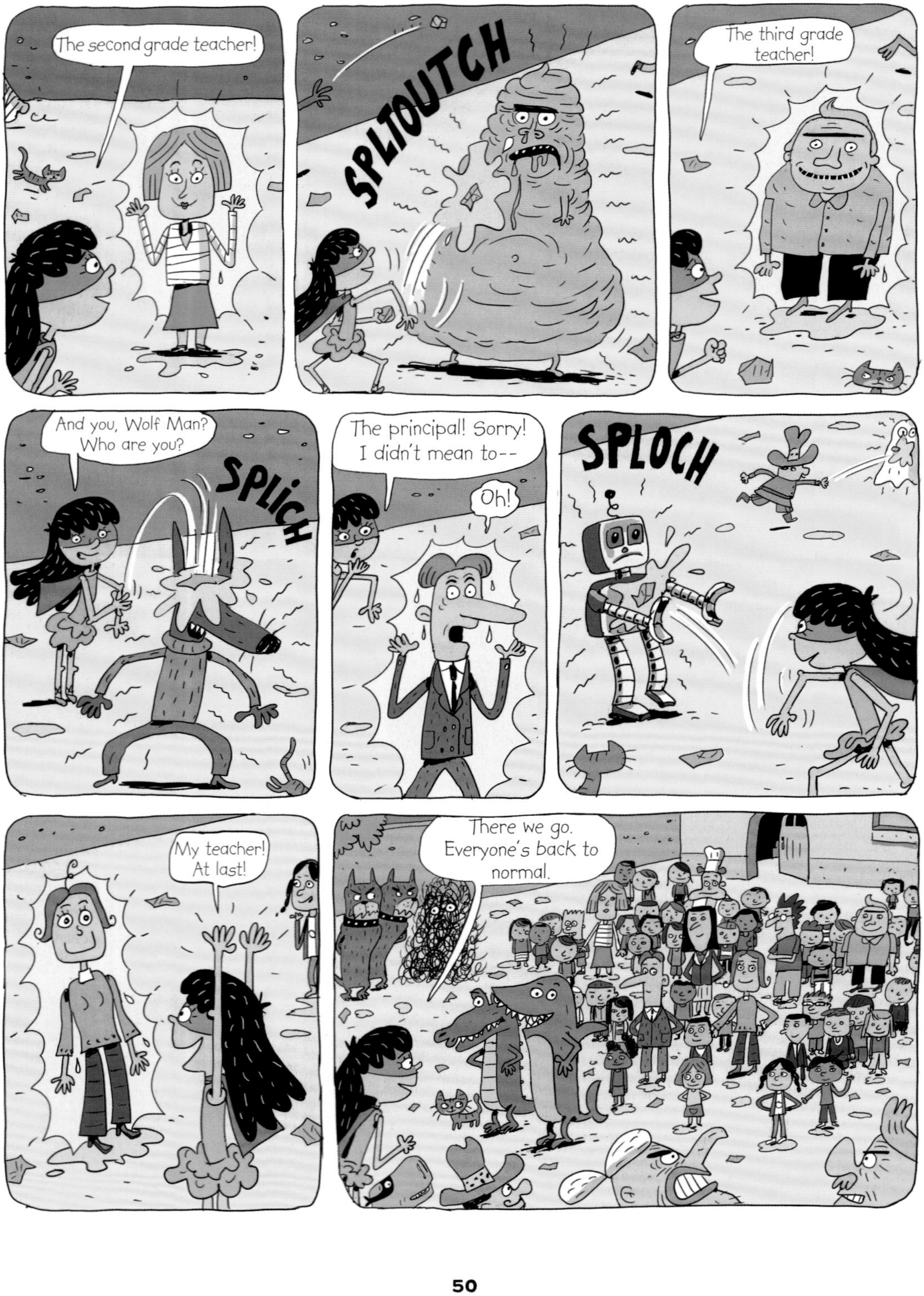
The second grade teacher!
SPLTOUTCH
The third grade teacher!
And you, Wolf Man? Who are you?
SPLICH
The principal! Sorry! I didn't mean to--
Oh!
SPLOCH
My teacher! At last!
There we go. Everyone's back to normal.

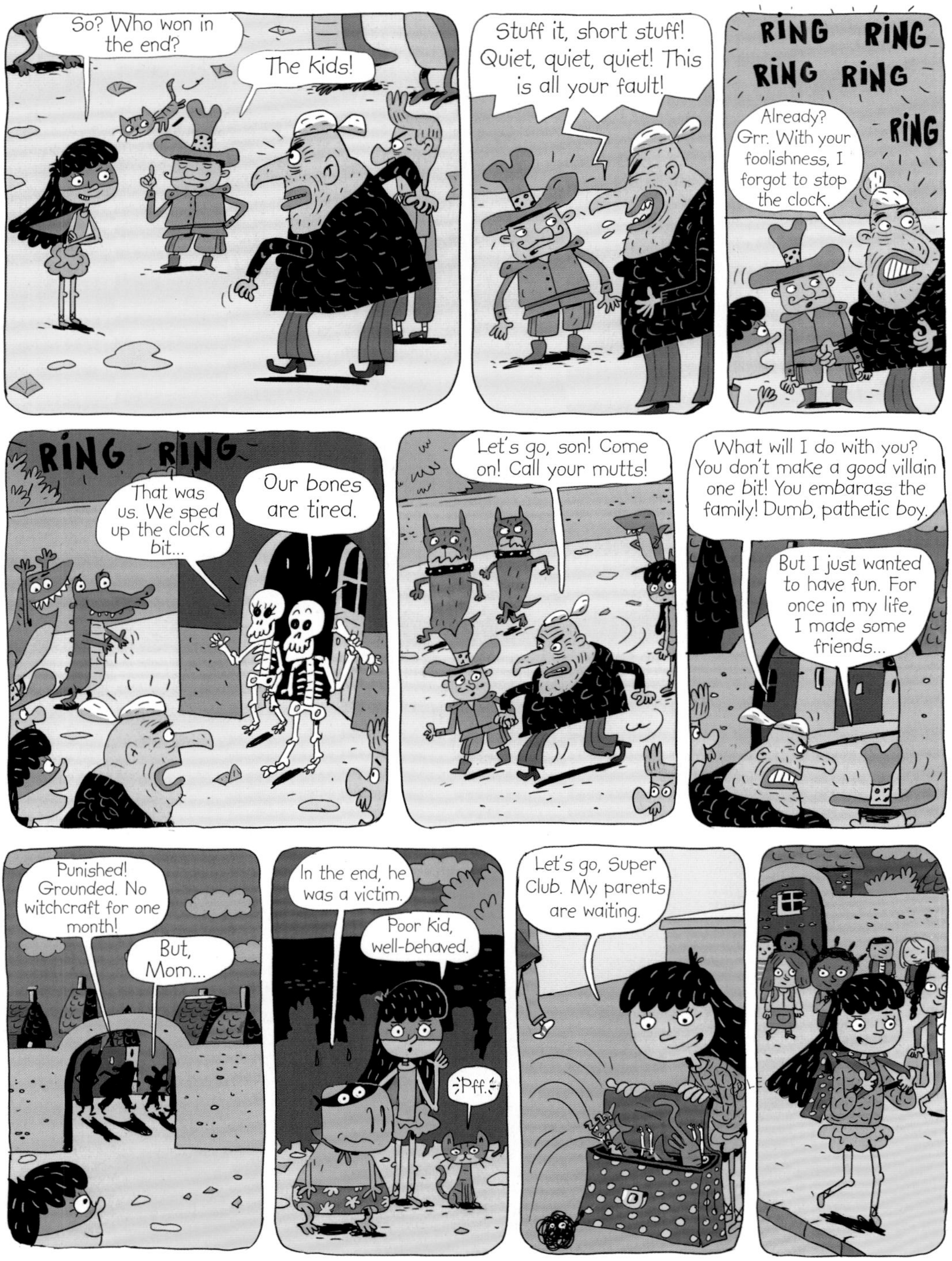

So? Who won in the end?
The kids!
Stuff it, short stuff! Quiet, quiet, quiet! This is all your fault!
RING RING RING RING RING
Already? Grr. With your foolishness, I forgot to stop the clock.
RING RING
That was us. We sped up the clock a bit...
Our bones are tired.
Let's go, son! Come on! Call your mutts!
What will I do with you? You don't make a good villain one bit! You embarass the family! Dumb, pathetic boy.
But I just wanted to have fun. For once in my life, I made some friends...
Punished! Grounded. No witchcraft for one month!
But, Mom...
In the end, he was a victim.
Poor kid, well-behaved.
Pff.
Let's go, Super Club. My parents are waiting.

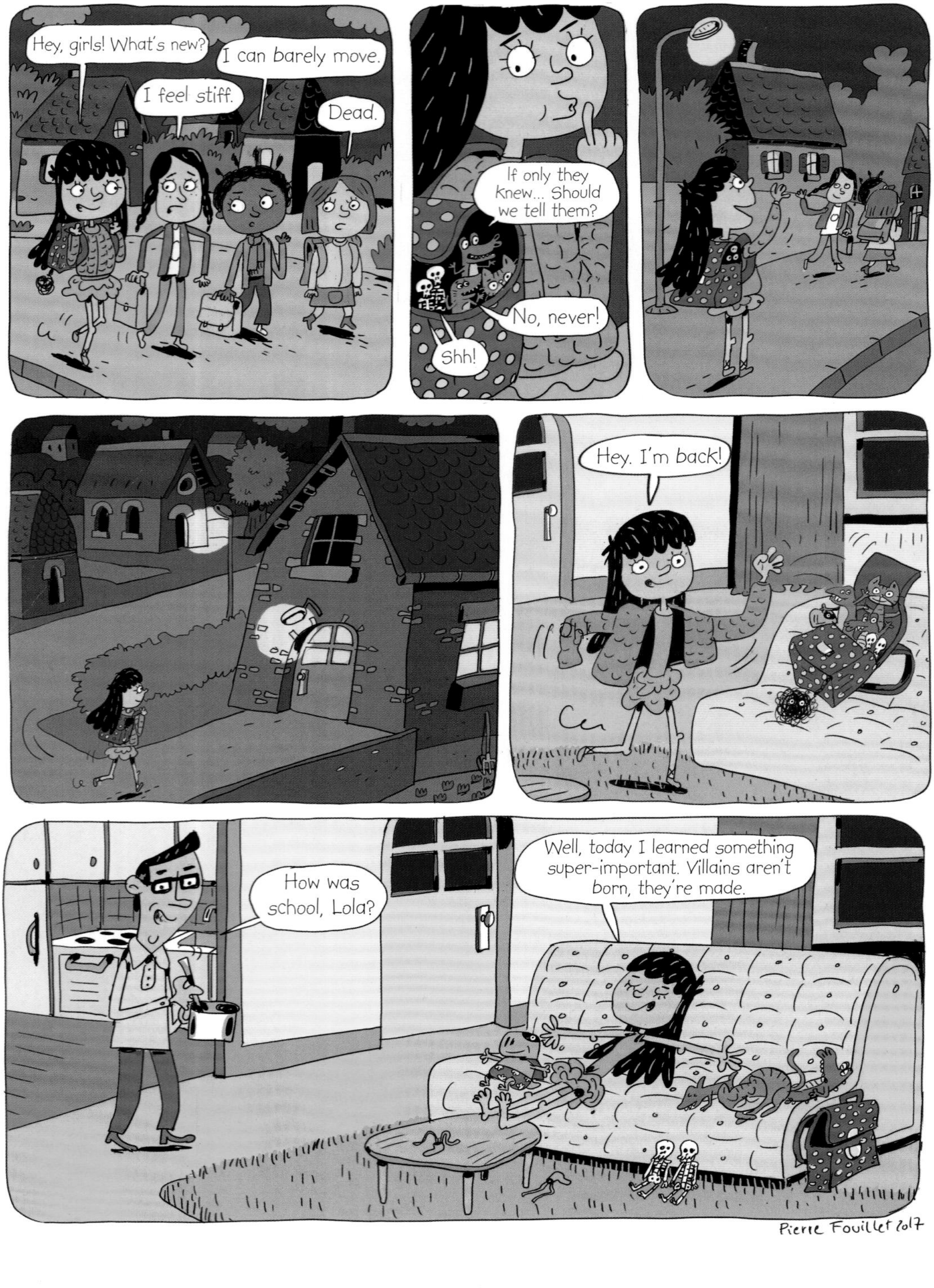
Hey, girls! What's new?
I feel stiff.
I can barely move.
Dead.
If only they knew... Should we tell them?
No, never!
Shh!
Hey. I'm back!
How was school, Lola?
Well, today I learned something super-important. Villains aren't born, they're made.
Pierre Fouillet 2017

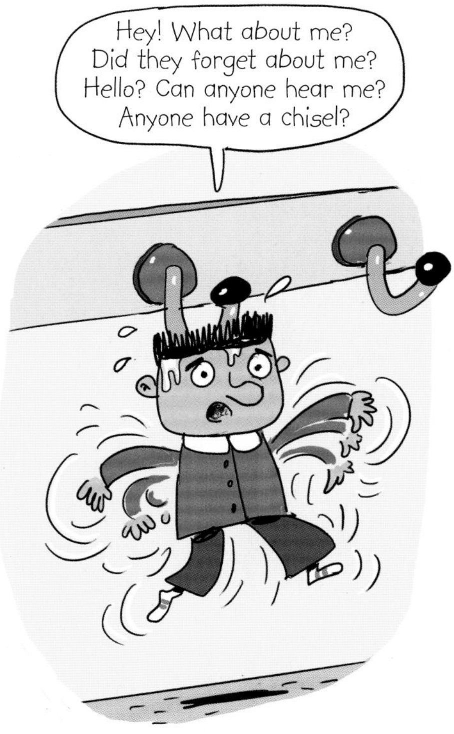
Hey! What about me? Did they forget about me? Hello? Can anyone hear me? Anyone have a chisel?

Lola's SUPER CLUB

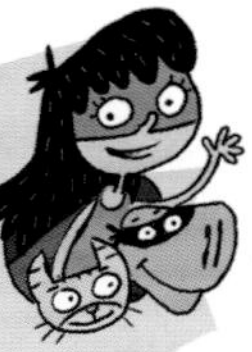

"MY GRAMPY IS THE KING OF SPORTS"

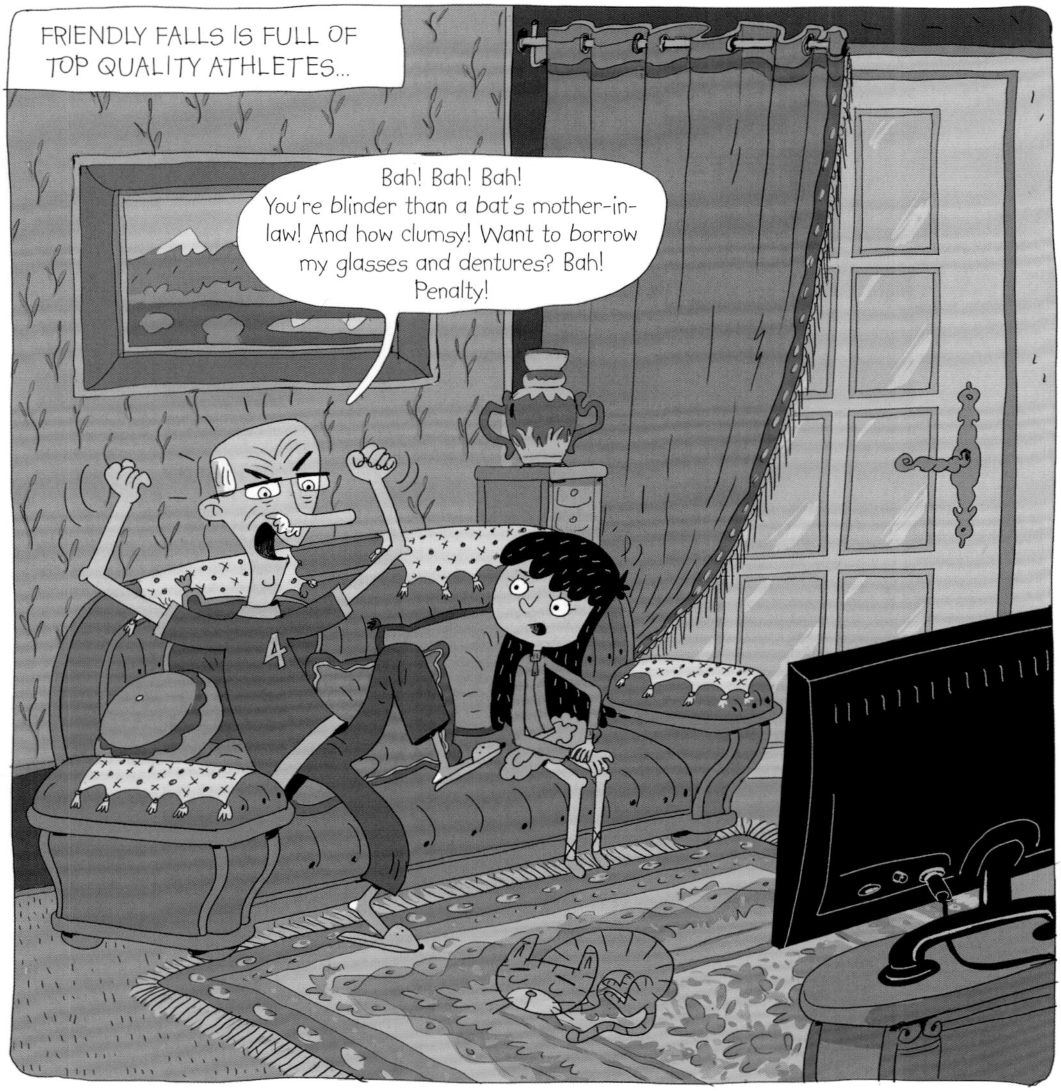

FRIENDLY FALLS IS FULL OF TOP QUALITY ATHLETES...
Bah! Bah! Bah! You're blinder than a bat's mother-in-law! And how clumsy! Want to borrow my glasses and dentures? Bah! Penalty!
4

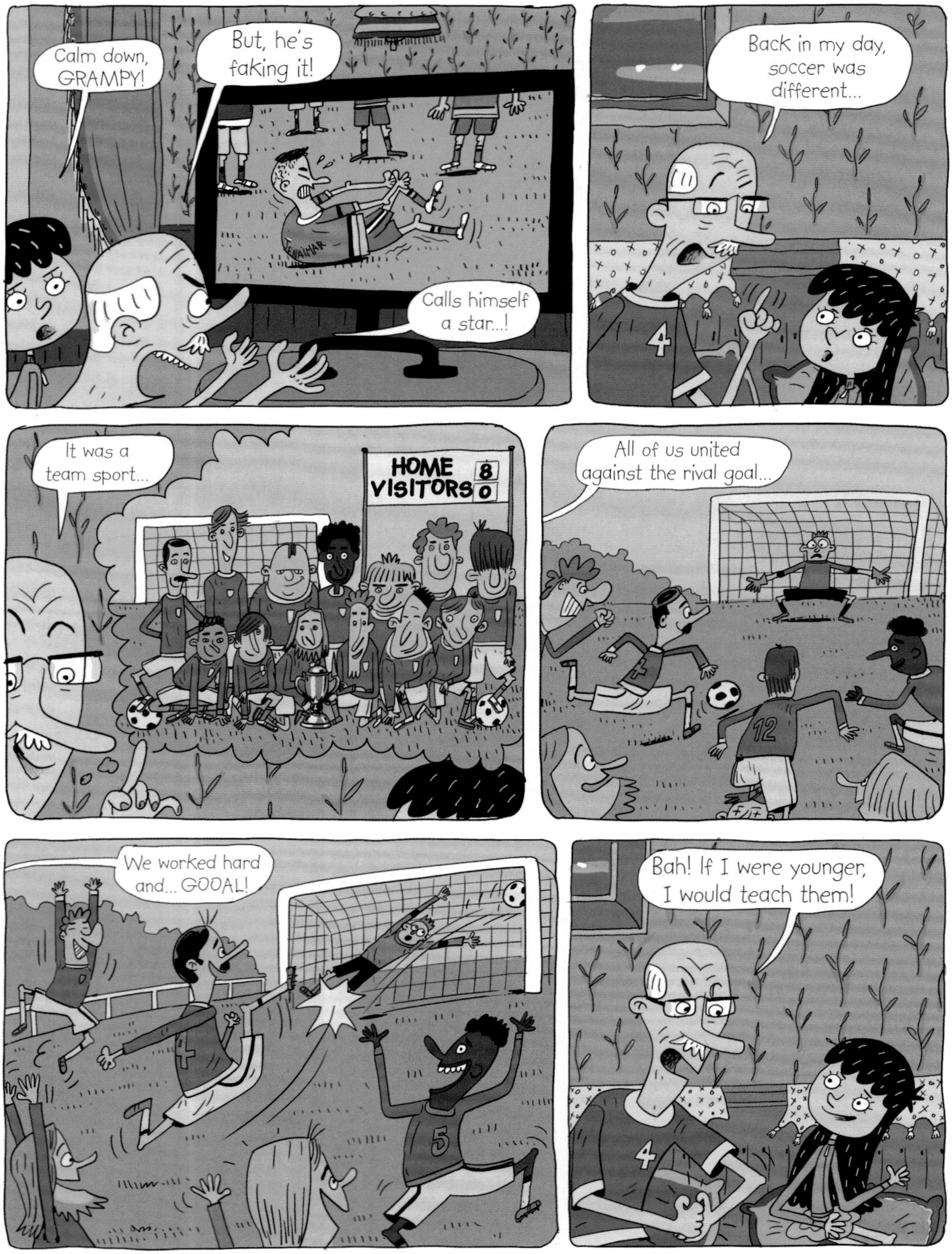
Calm down, GRAMPY!
But, he's faking it!
Calls himself a star...!
Back in my day, soccer was different...
It was a team sport...
HOME 8
VISITORS 0
All of us united against the rival goal...
We worked hard and... GOOAL!
Bah! If I were younger, I would teach them!

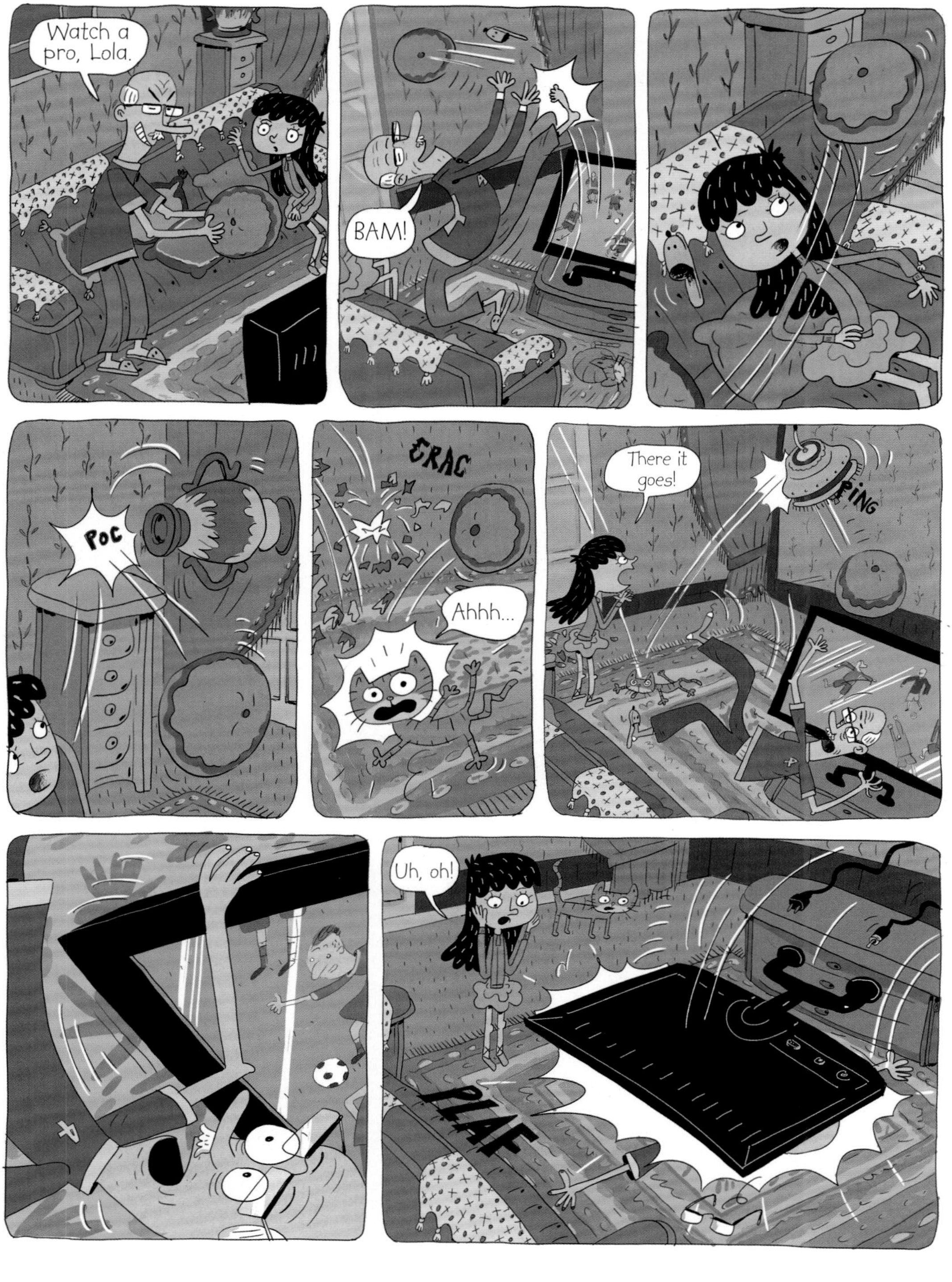
Watch a pro, Lola.
BAM!
POC
CRAC
Ahhh...
There it goes!
PING
Uh, oh!
PLAF

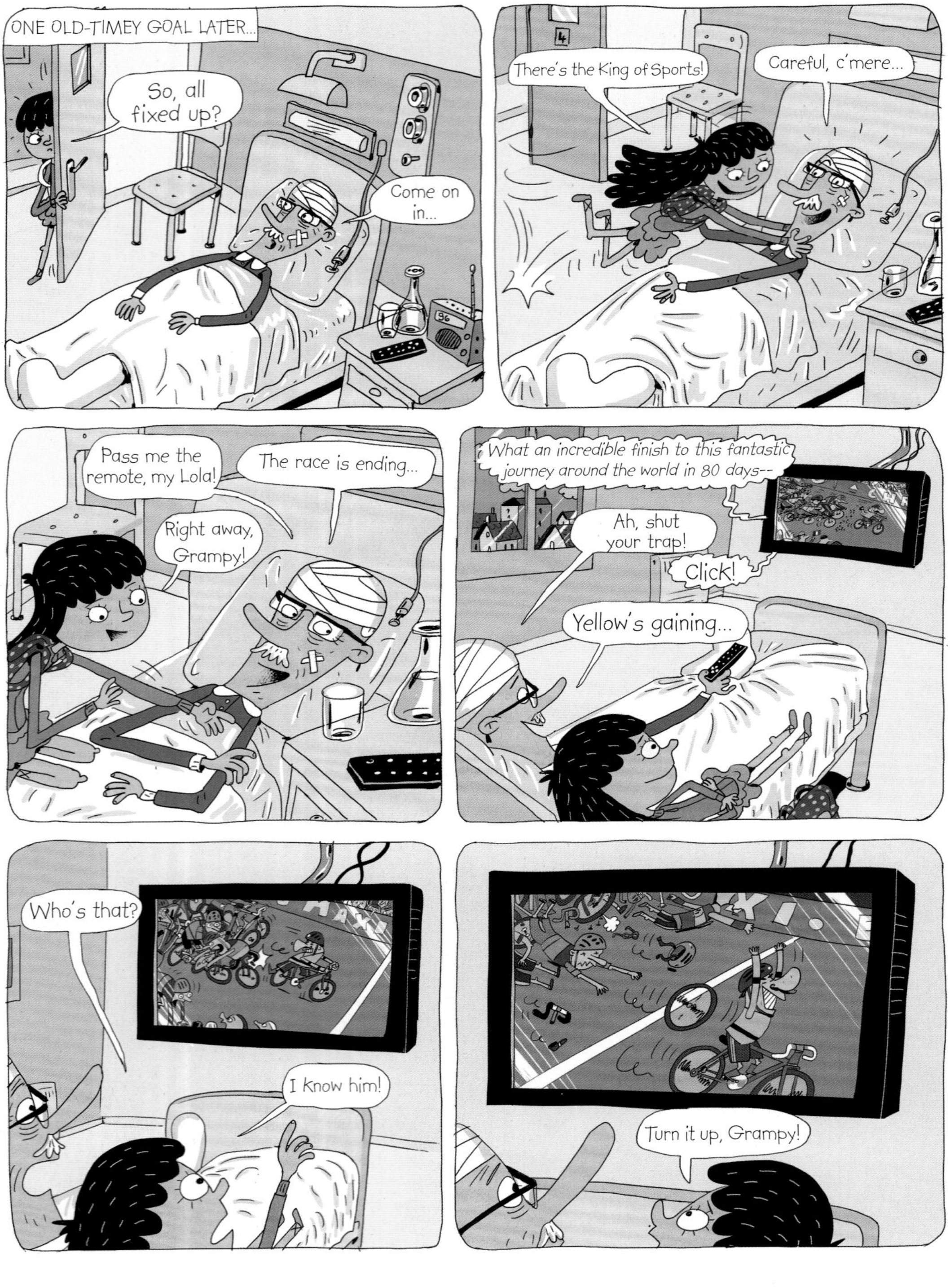
ONE OLD-TIMEY GOAL LATER...
So, all fixed up?
Come on in...
There's the King of Sports!
Careful, c'mere...
Pass me the remote, my Lola!
The race is ending...
Right away, Grampy!
What an incredible finish to this fantastic journey around the world in 80 days--
Ah, shut your trap!
Click!
Yellow's gaining...
Who's that?
I know him!
Turn it up, Grampy!

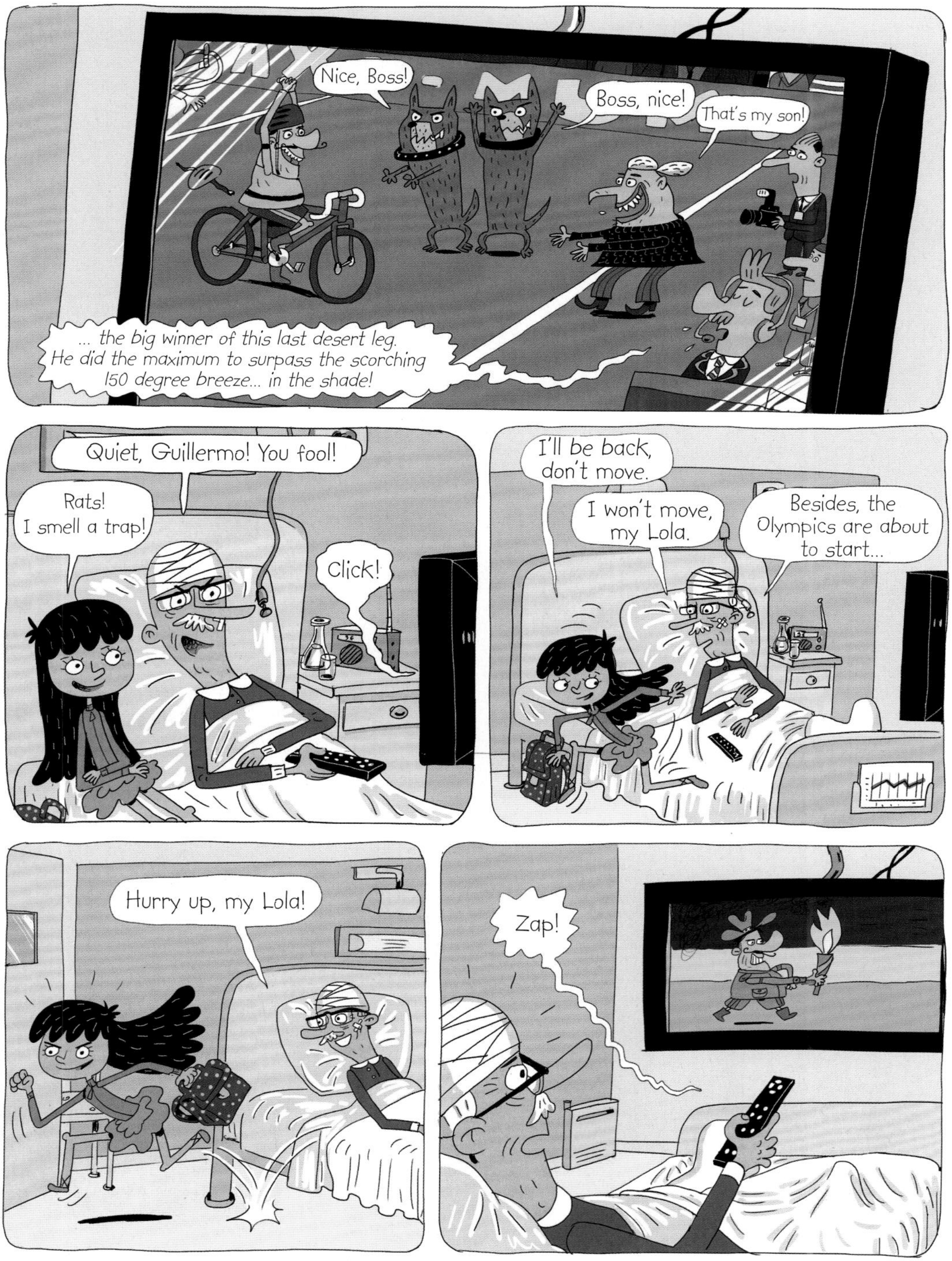
Nice, Boss!
Boss, nice!
That's my son!
... the big winner of this last desert leg. He did the maximum to surpass the scorching 150 degree breeze... in the shade!
Quiet, Guillermo! You fool!
Rats! I smell a trap!
Click!
I'll be back, don't move.
I won't move, my Lola.
Besides, the Olympics are about to start...
Hurry up, my Lola!
Zap!

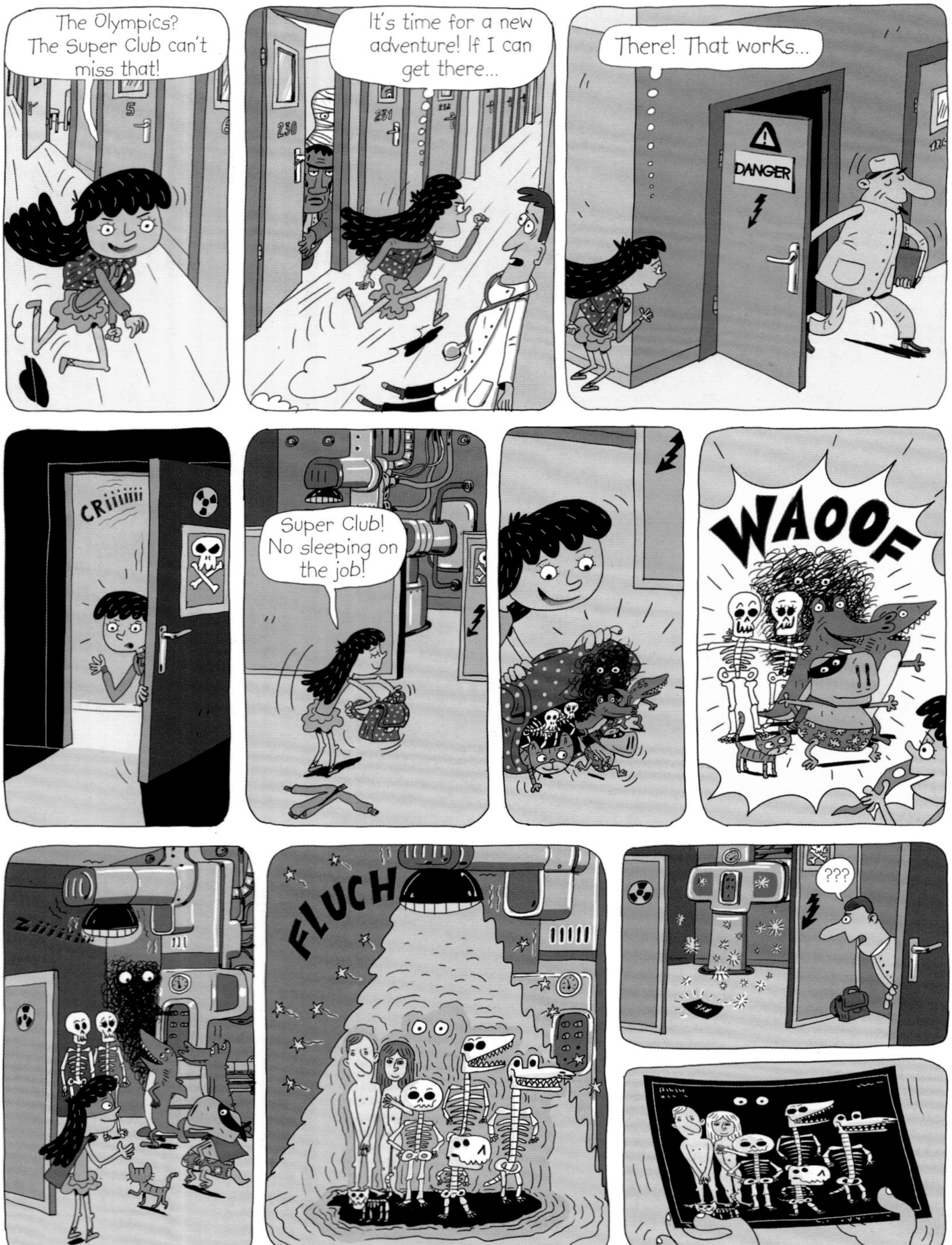
The Olympics? The Super Club can't miss that!
It's time for a new adventure! If I can get there...
There! That works...
DANGER
CRiiiiiii
Super Club! No sleeping on the job!
WAOOF
Ziiiiiii
FLUCH
???

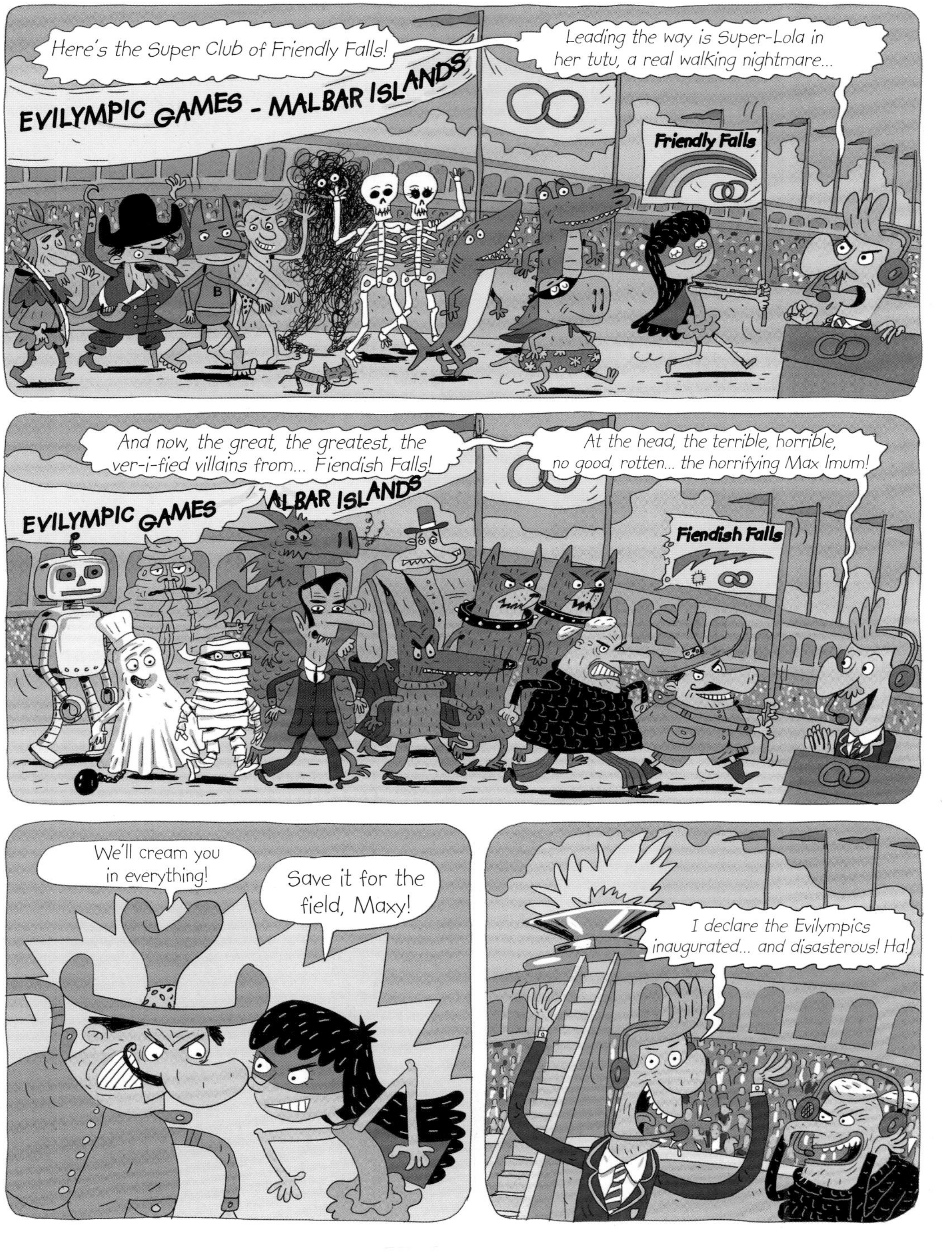

Here's the Super Club of Friendly Falls!
Leading the way is Super-Lola in her tutu, a real walking nightmare...
EVILYMPIC GAMES - MALBAR ISLANDS
Friendly Falls
And now, the great, the greatest, the ver-i-fied villains from... Fiendish Falls!
At the head, the terrible, horrible, no good, rotten... the horrifying Max Imum!
EVILYMPIC GAMES
ALBAR ISLANDS
Fiendish Falls
We'll cream you in everything!
Save it for the field, Maxy!
I declare the Evilympics inaugurated... and disasterous! Ha!

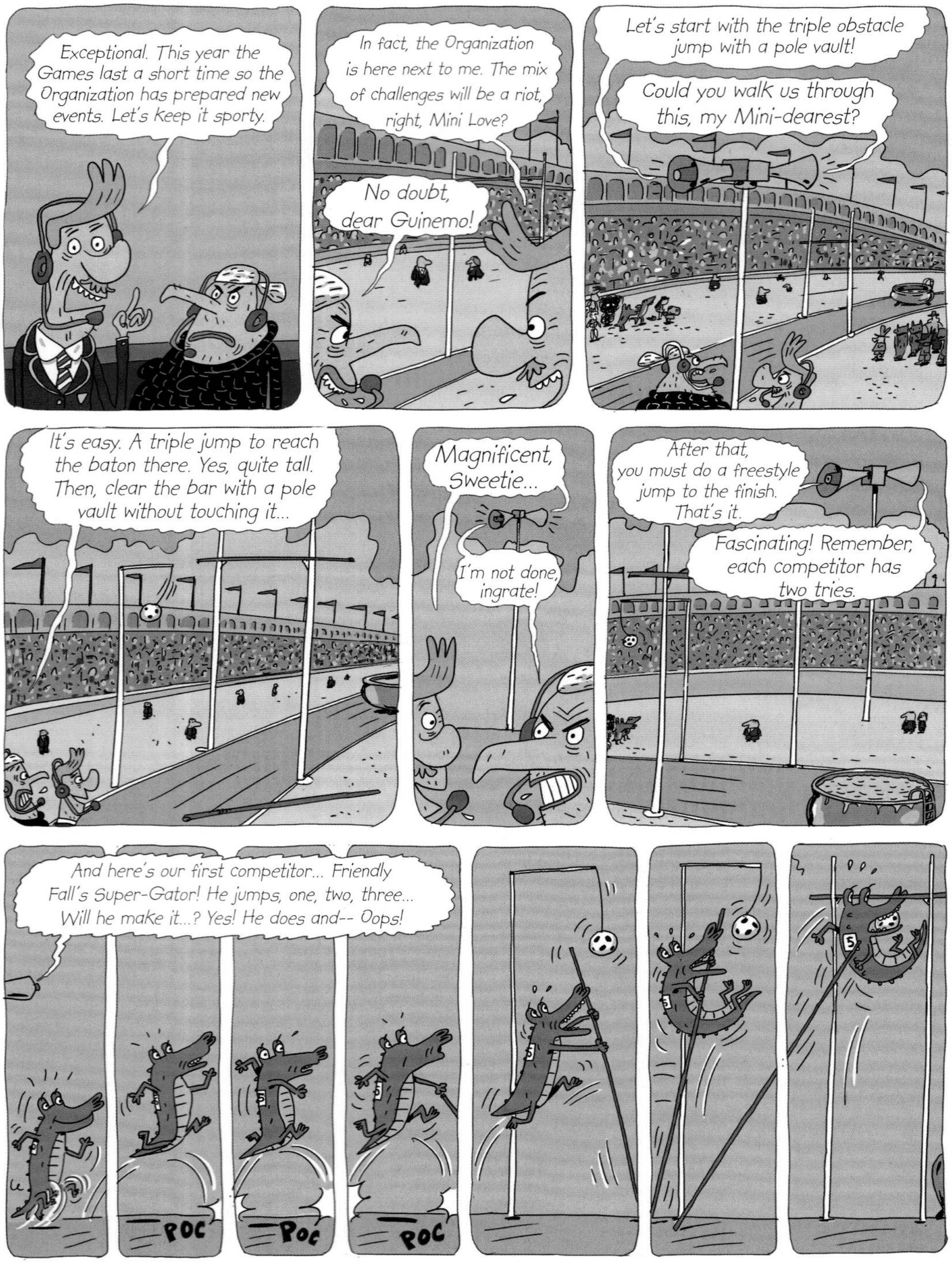
Exceptional. This year the Games last a short time so the Organization has prepared new events. Let's keep it sporty.
In fact, the Organization is here next to me. The mix of challenges will be a riot, right, Mini Love?
No doubt, dear Guinemo!
Let's start with the triple obstacle jump with a pole vault!
Could you walk us through this, my Mini-dearest?
It's easy. A triple jump to reach the baton there. Yes, quite tall. Then, clear the bar with a pole vault without touching it...
Magnificent, Sweetie...
I'm not done, ingrate!
After that, you must do a freestyle jump to the finish. That's it.
Fascinating! Remember, each competitor has two tries.
And here's our first competitor... Friendly Fall's Super-Gator! He jumps, one, two, three... Will he make it...? Yes! He does and-- Oops!
POC
POC
POC

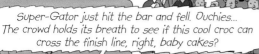
Super-Gator just hit the bar and fell. Ouchies... The crowd holds its breath to see if this cool croc can cross the finish line, right, baby cakes?

BONG

SPLOSH

Right as rain. Nyuk!

POC

No fair.

It seems Super-Gator isn't fit to continue... He's being carried out in a stretcher.

No fair!

Well..., that's one down! Nyuk nyuk!

But why did I agree to participating in this?

POC

POC

POC

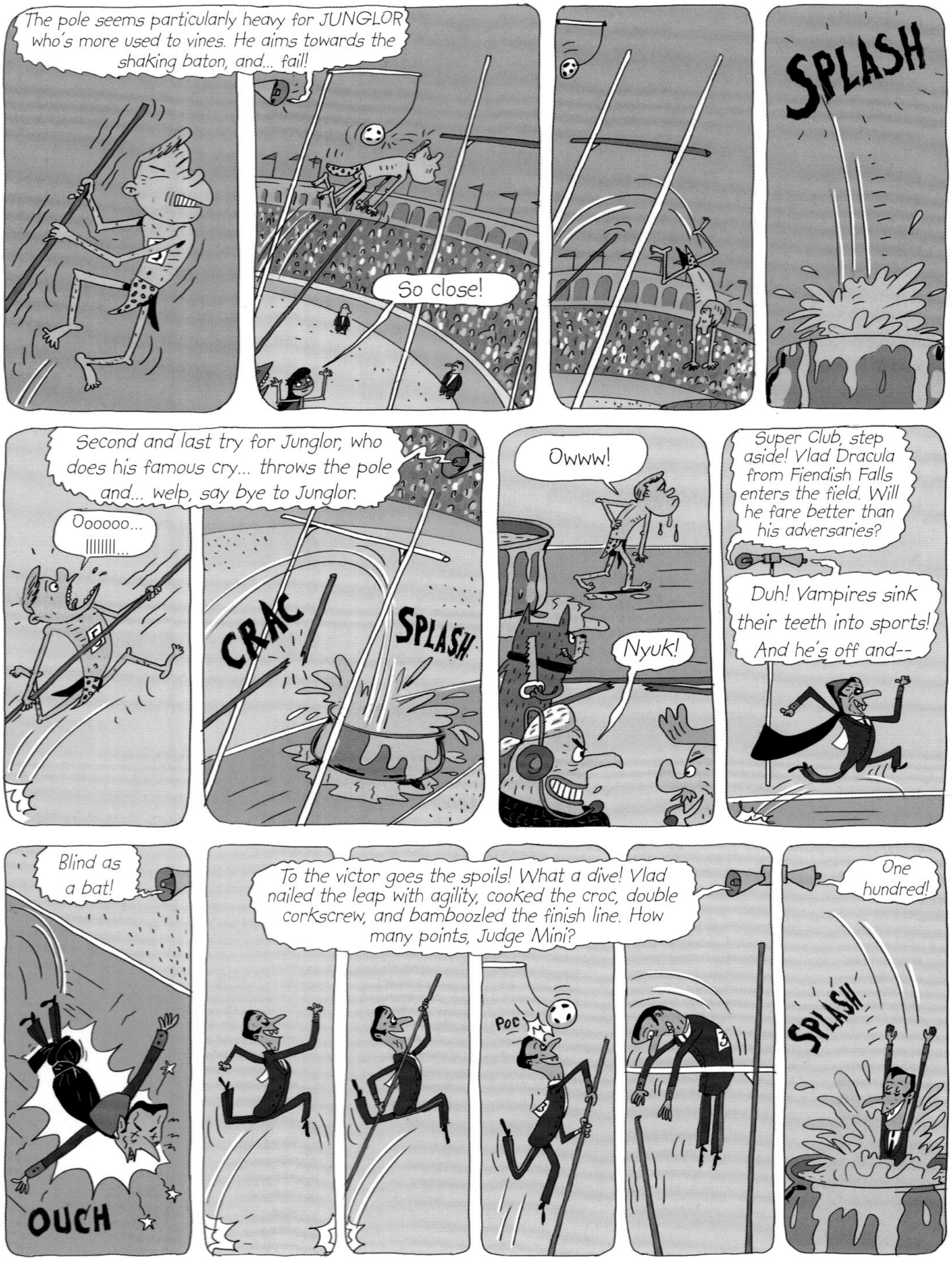
The pole seems particularly heavy for JUNGLOR who's more used to vines. He aims towards the shaking baton, and... fail!
So close!
SPLASH
Second and last try for Junglor, who does his famous cry... throws the pole and... welp, say bye to Junglor.
Oooooo... lllllll...
CRAC
SPLASH
Owww!
Nyuk!
Super Club, step aside! Vlad Dracula from Fiendish Falls enters the field. Will he fare better than his adversaries?
Duh! Vampires sink their teeth into sports! And he's off and--
Blind as a bat!
OUCH
To the victor goes the spoils! What a dive! Vlad nailed the leap with agility, cooked the croc, double corkscrew, and bamboozled the finish line. How many points, Judge Mini?
POC
One hundred!
SPLASH

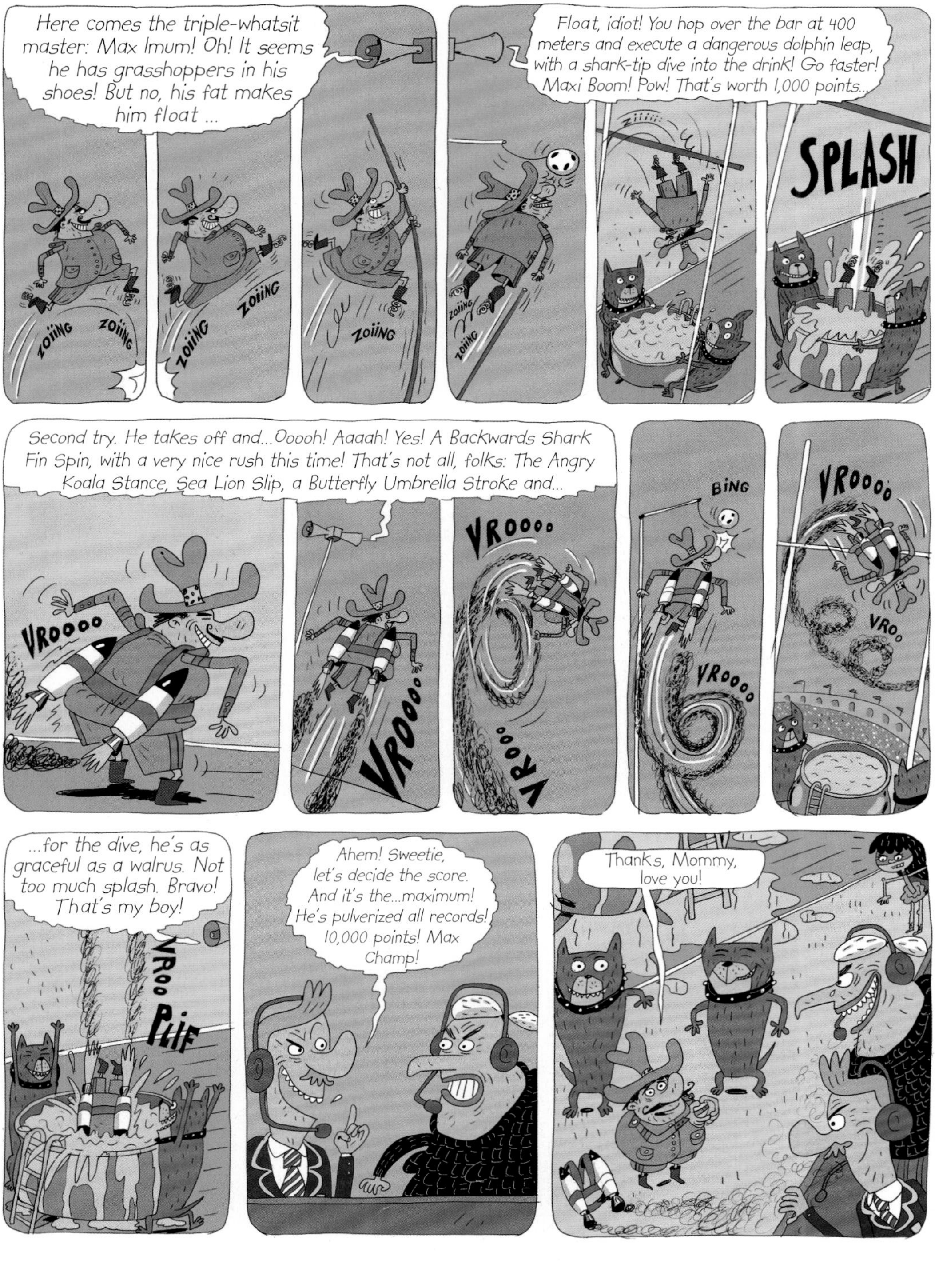
Here comes the triple-whatsit master: Max Imum! Oh! It seems he has grasshoppers in his shoes! But no, his fat makes him float ...
ZOIING ZOIING
ZOIING ZOIING
ZOIING
Float, idiot! You hop over the bar at 400 meters and execute a dangerous dolphin leap, with a shark-tip dive into the drink! Go faster! Maxi Boom! Pow! That's worth 1,000 points...
ZOIING ZOIING
SPLASH
Second try. He takes off and...Ooooh! Aaaah! Yes! A Backwards Shark Fin Spin, with a very nice rush this time! That's not all, folks: The Angry Koala Stance, Sea Lion Slip, a Butterfly Umbrella Stroke and...
VROOOO
VROOOO
VROOOO
VROOOO
BING
VROOOO
VROOOO
VROO
...for the dive, he's as graceful as a walrus. Not too much splash. Bravo! That's my boy!
VROO
PLIF
Ahem! Sweetie, let's decide the score. And it's the...maximum! He's pulverized all records! 10,000 points! Max Champ!
Thanks, Mommy, love you!

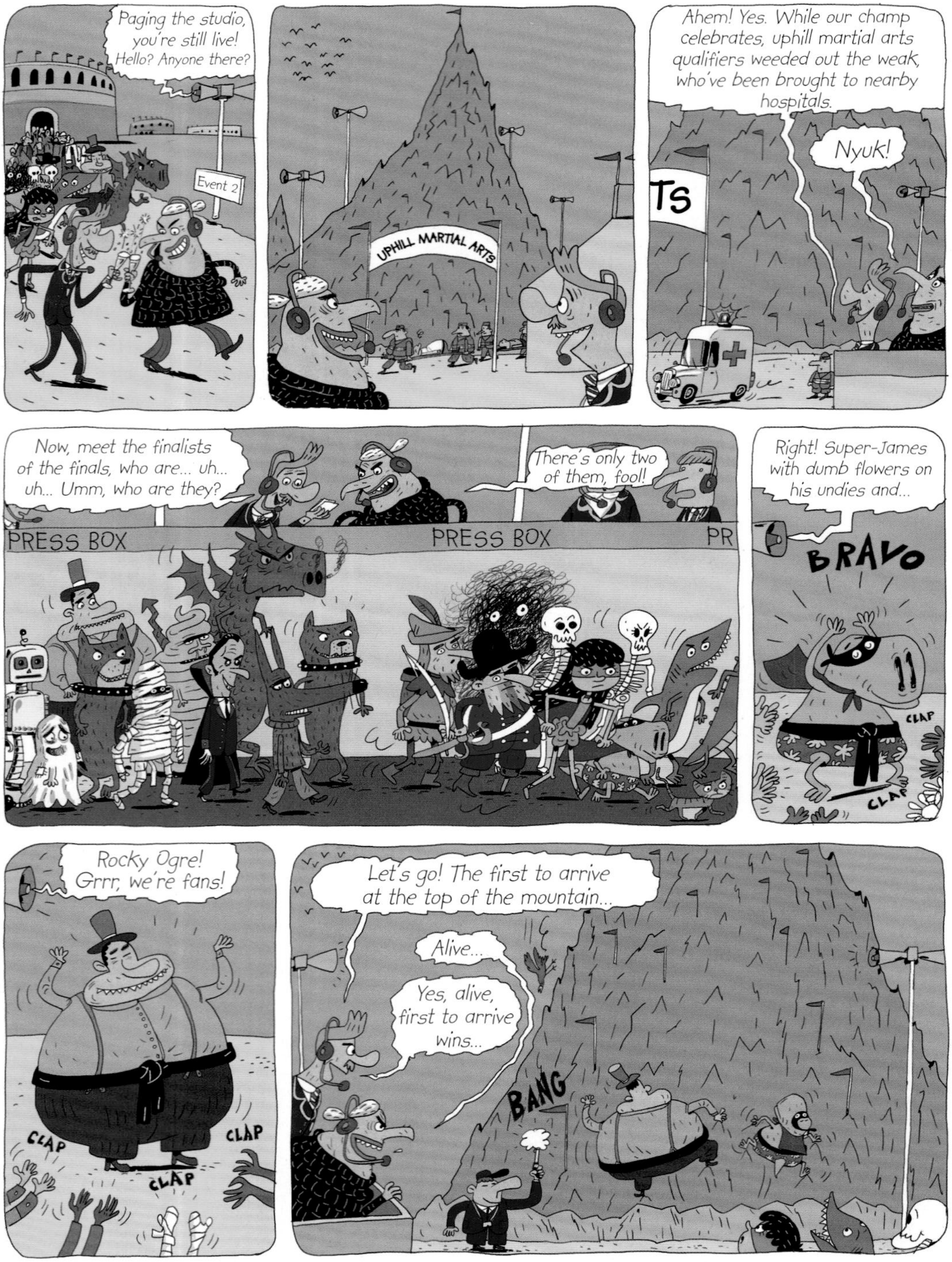
Paging the studio, you're still live! Hello? Anyone there?
Event 2
UPHILL MARTIAL ARTS
Ahem! Yes. While our champ celebrates, uphill martial arts qualifiers weeded out the weak, who've been brought to nearby hospitals.
Nyuk!
TS
Now, meet the finalists of the finals, who are... uh... uh... Umm, who are they?
There's only two of them, fool!
PRESS BOX
PRESS BOX
PR
Right! Super-James with dumb flowers on his undies and...
BRAVO
CLAP
CLAP
Rocky Ogre! Grrr, we're fans!
CLAP
CLAP
CLAP
Let's go! The first to arrive at the top of the mountain...
Alive...
Yes, alive, first to arrive wins...
BANG

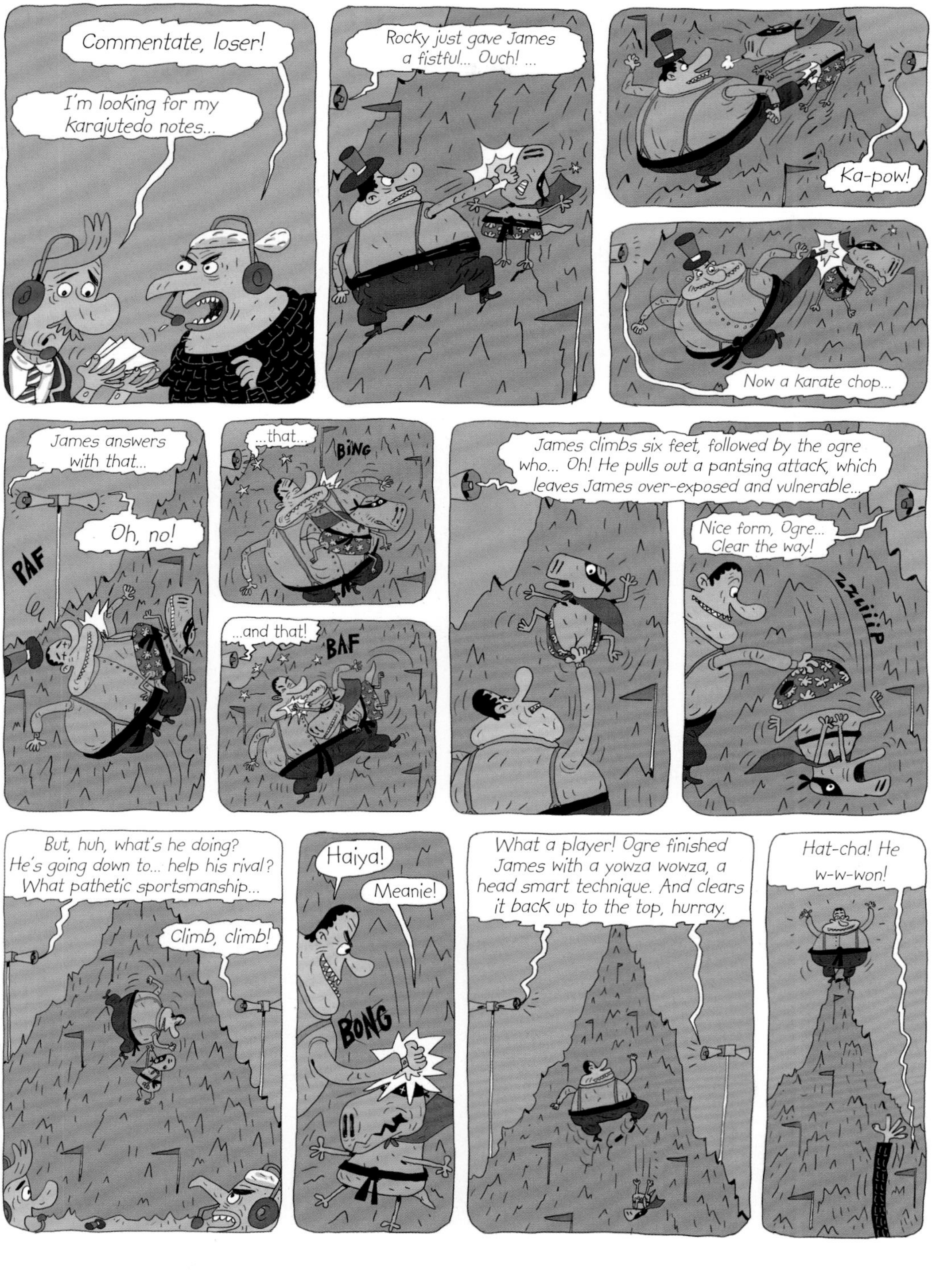
Commentate, loser!
I'm looking for my karajutedo notes...
Rocky just gave James a fistful... Ouch! ...
Ka-pow!
Now a karate chop...
James answers with that...
Oh, no!
PAF
...that...
BING
...and that!
BAF
James climbs six feet, followed by the ogre who... Oh! He pulls out a pantsing attack, which leaves James over-exposed and vulnerable...
Nice form, Ogre... Clear the way!
ZZLIIIIP
But, huh, what's he doing? He's going down to... help his rival? What pathetic sportsmanship...
Climb, climb!
Haiya!
Meanie!
BONG
What a player! Ogre finished James with a yowza wowza, a head smart technique. And clears it back up to the top, hurray.
Hat-cha! He w-w-won!

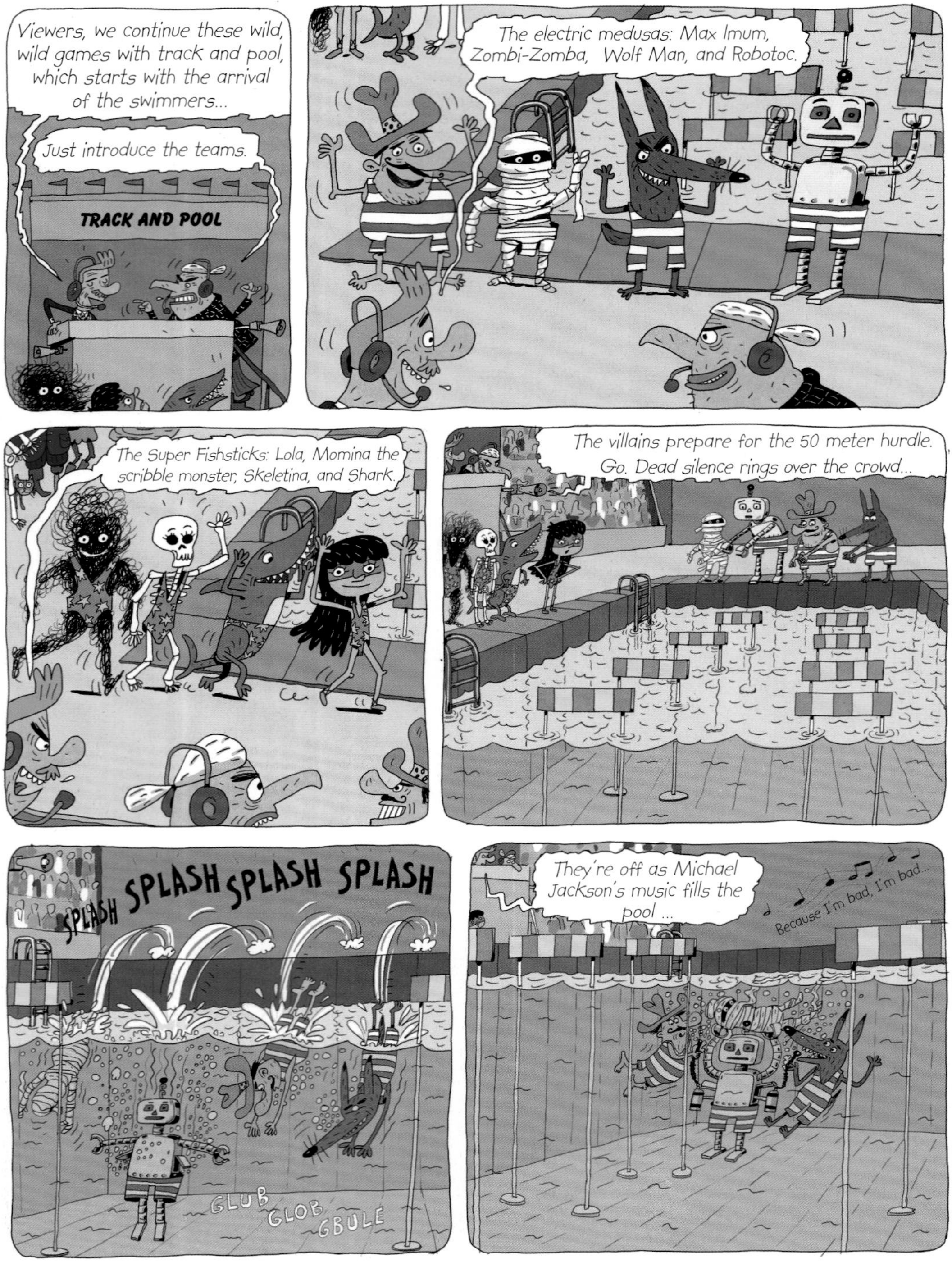
Viewers, we continue these wild, wild games with track and pool, which starts with the arrival of the swimmers...
Just introduce the teams.
TRACK AND POOL
The electric medusas: Max Imum, Zombi-Zomba, Wolf Man, and Robotoc.
The Super Fishsticks: Lola, Momina the scribble monster, Skeletina, and Shark.
The villains prepare for the 50 meter hurdle. Go. Dead silence rings over the crowd...
SPLASH SPLASH SPLASH SPLASH
GLUB GLOB GBULE
They're off as Michael Jackson's music fills the pool ...
Because I'm bad, I'm bad...

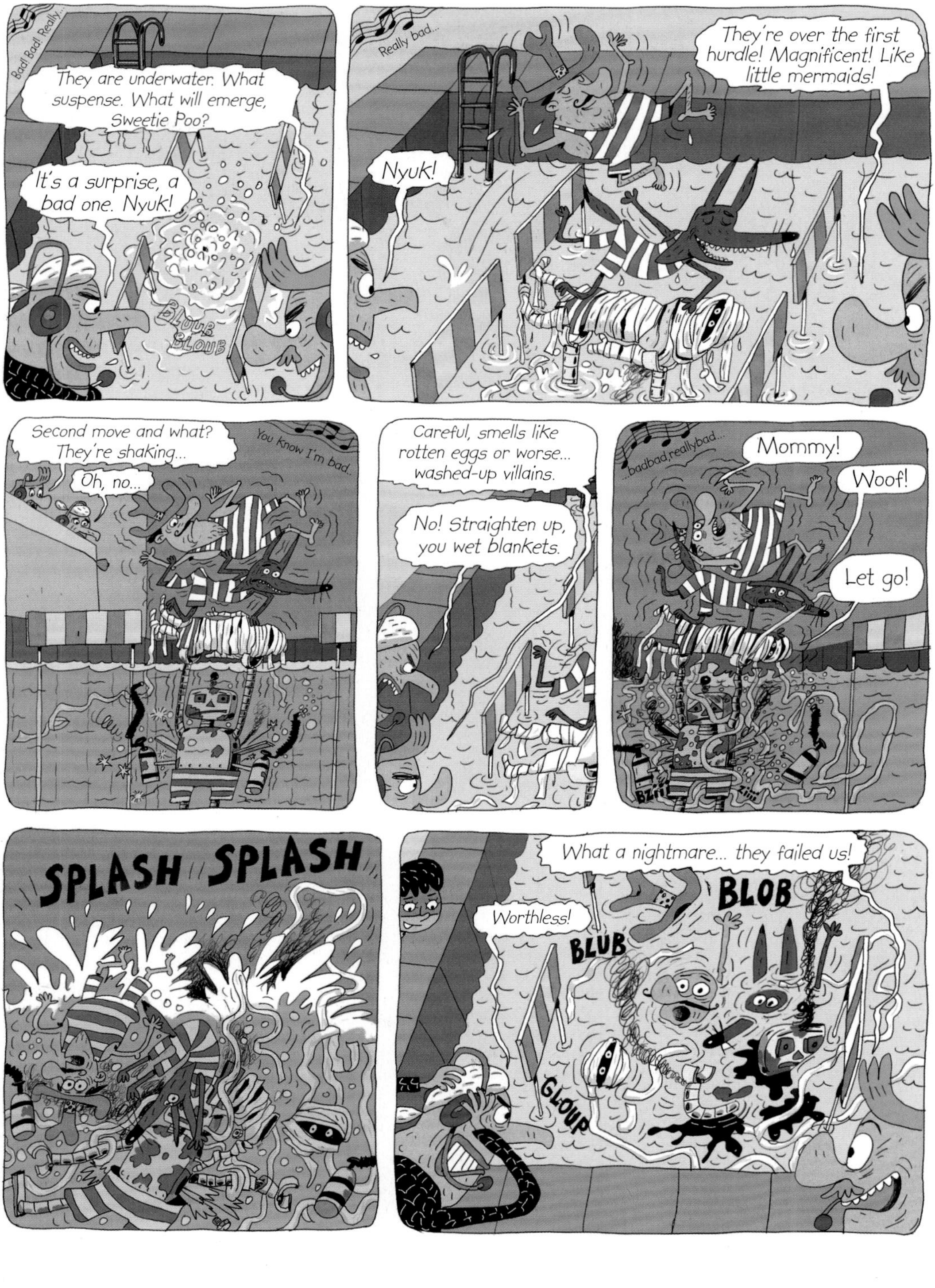
Bad! Bad! Really...
They are underwater. What suspense. What will emerge, Sweetie Poo?
It's a surprise, a bad one. Nyuk!
BLOUB BLOUB
Really bad...
They're over the first hurdle! Magnificent! Like little mermaids!
Nyuk!
Second move and what? They're shaking...
You know I'm bad..
Oh, no...
Careful, smells like rotten eggs or worse... washed-up villains.
No! Straighten up, you wet blankets.
...badbad,reallybad...
Mommy!
Woof!
Let go!
SPLASH SPLASH
What a nightmare... they failed us!
Worthless!
BLOB
BLUB
GLOUP

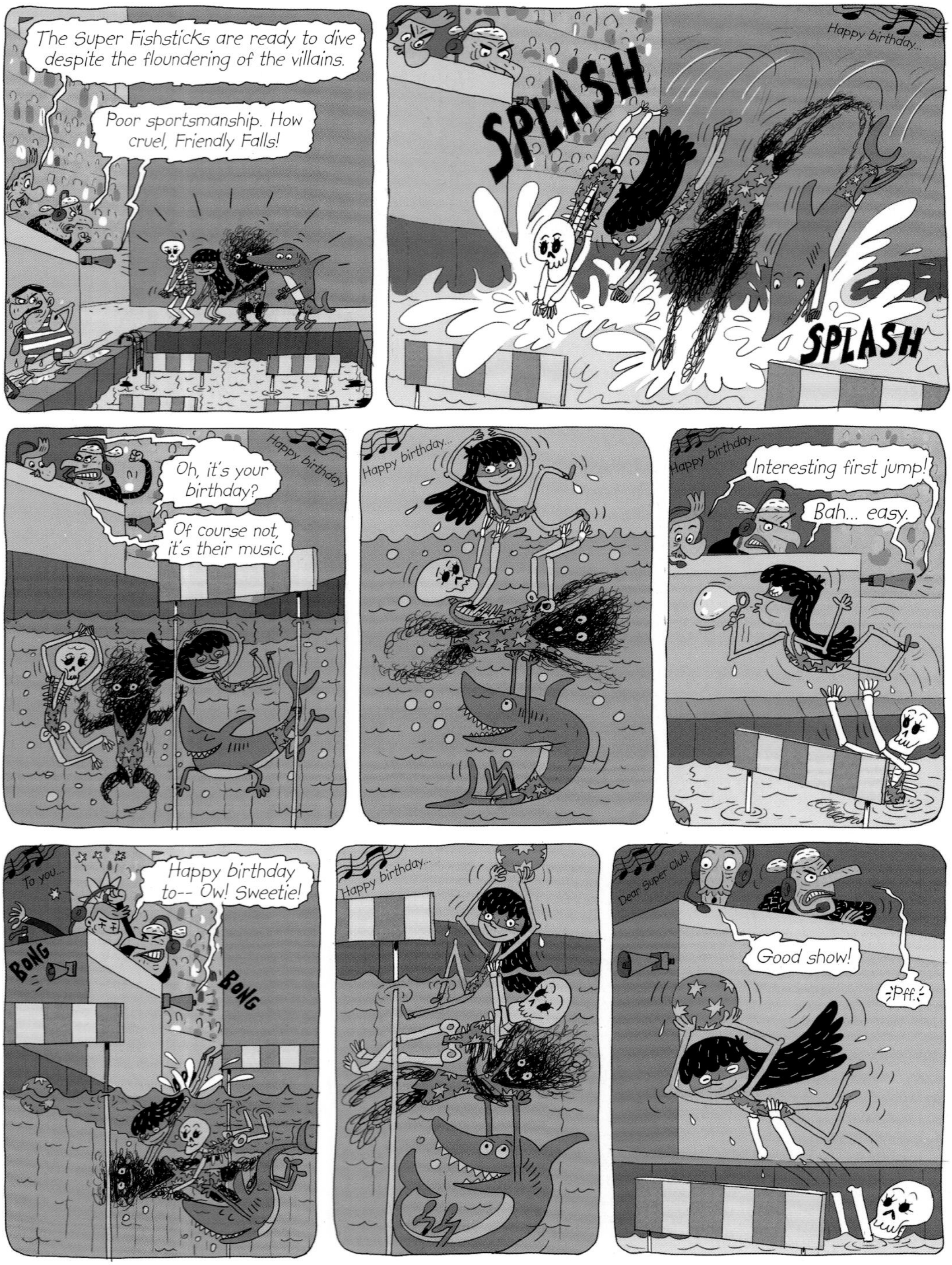
The Super Fishsticks are ready to dive despite the floundering of the villains.
Poor sportsmanship. How cruel, Friendly Falls!
SPLASH
Happy birthday...
SPLASH
Happy birthday
Oh, it's your birthday?
Of course not, it's their music.
Happy birthday...
Happy birthday...
Interesting first jump!
Bah... easy.
To you...
Happy birthday to-- Ow! Sweetie!
BONG
BONG
Happy birthday...
Dear Super Club!
Good show!
Pff.

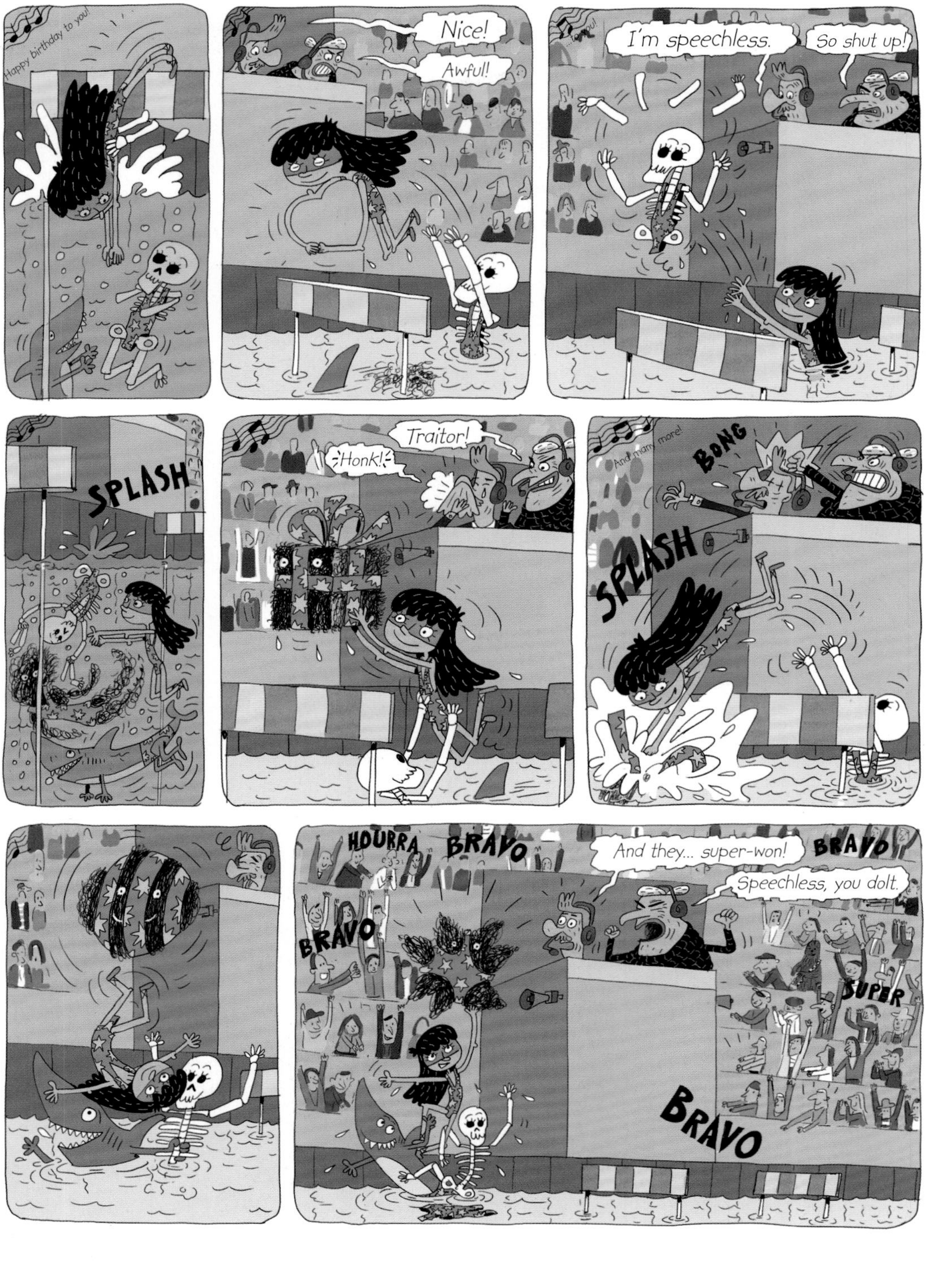

Happy birthday to you!
Nice!
Awful!
I'm speechless.
So shut up!
SPLASH
Traitor!
Honk!
And many more!
BONG
SPLASH
HOURRA
BRAVO
And they... super-won!
BRAVO
Speechless, you dolt.
BRAVO
SUPER
BRAVO

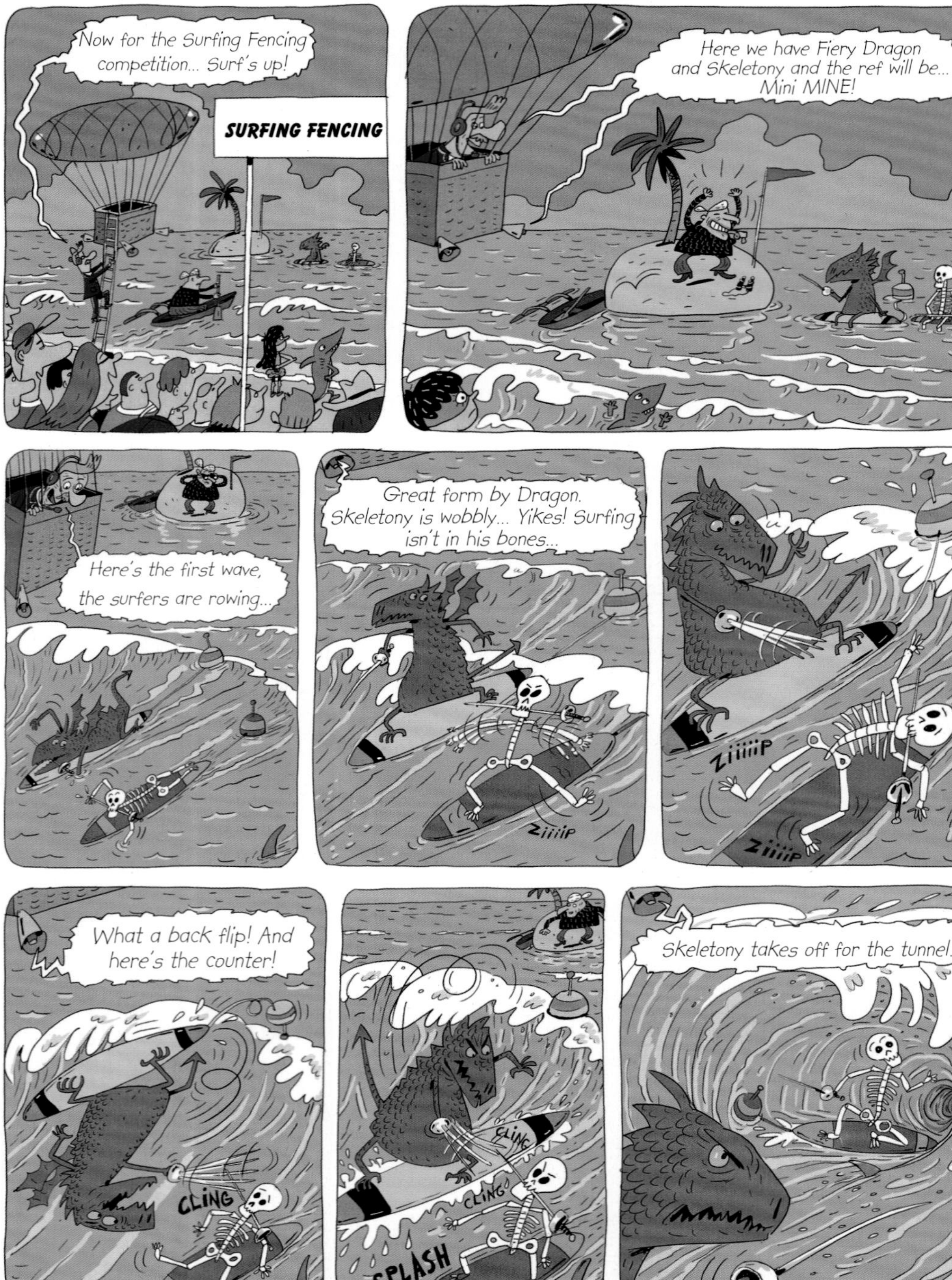

Now for the Surfing Fencing competition... Surf's up!
SURFING FENCING
Here we have Fiery Dragon and Skeletony and the ref will be... Mini MINE!
Here's the first wave, the surfers are rowing...
Great form by Dragon. Skeletony is wobbly... Yikes! Surfing isn't in his bones...
ZIIIIP
ZIIIIP
ZIIIIP
What a back flip! And here's the counter!
CLING
CLING
CLING
SPLASH
Skeletony takes off for the tunnel...

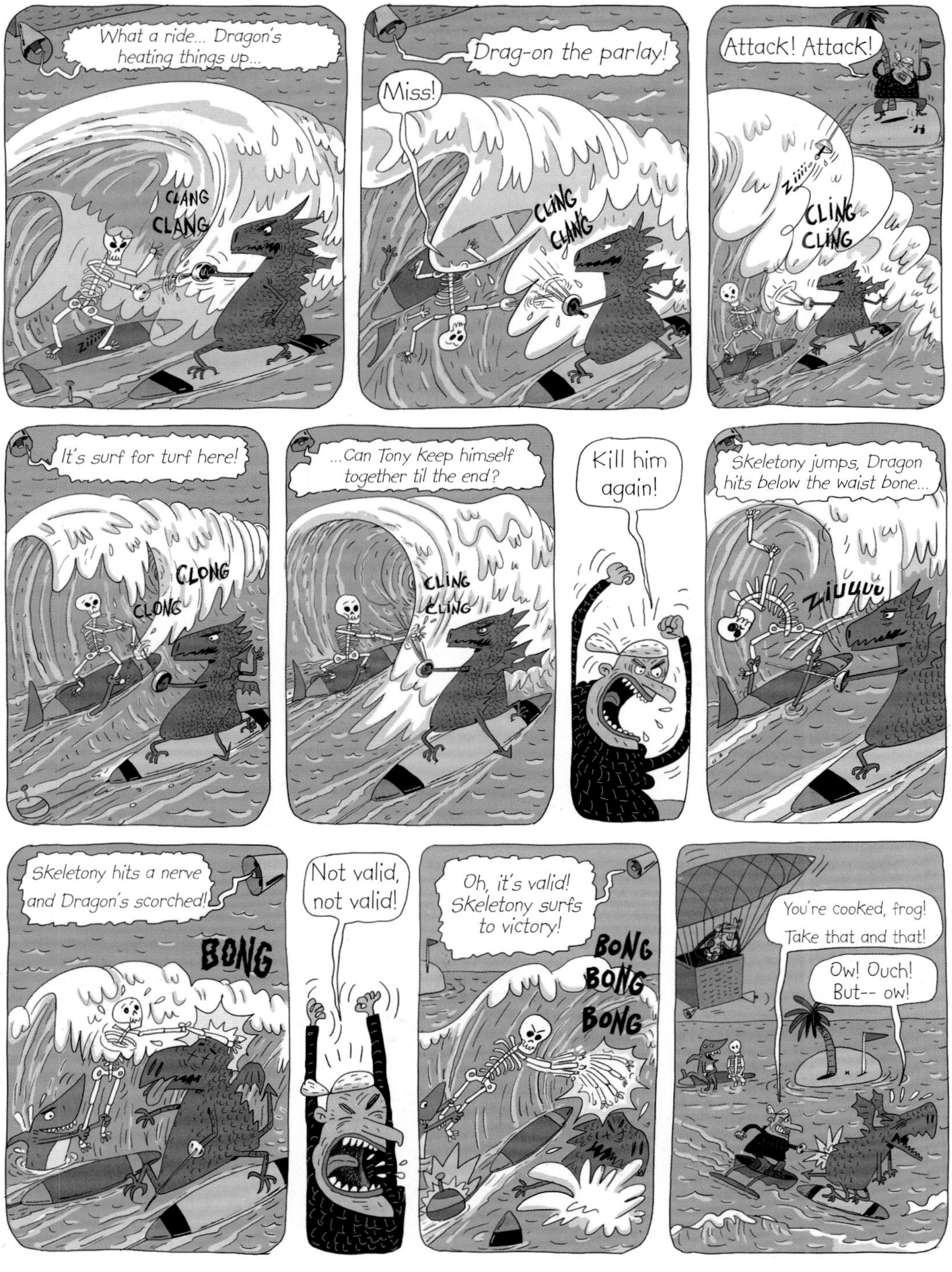
What a ride... Dragon's heating things up...
CLANG
CLANG
ziiii
Drag-on the parlay!
Miss!
CLING
CLANG
Attack! Attack!
Ziiiii
CLING
CLING
It's surf for turf here!
CLONG
CLONG
...Can Tony keep himself together til the end?
CLING
CLING
Kill him again!
Skeletony jumps, Dragon hits below the waist bone...
ZIUUUU
Skeletony hits a nerve and Dragon's scorched!
BONG
Not valid, not valid!
Oh, it's valid! Skeletony surfs to victory!
BONG
BONG
BONG
You're cooked, frog! Take that and that!
Ow! Ouch! But-- ow!

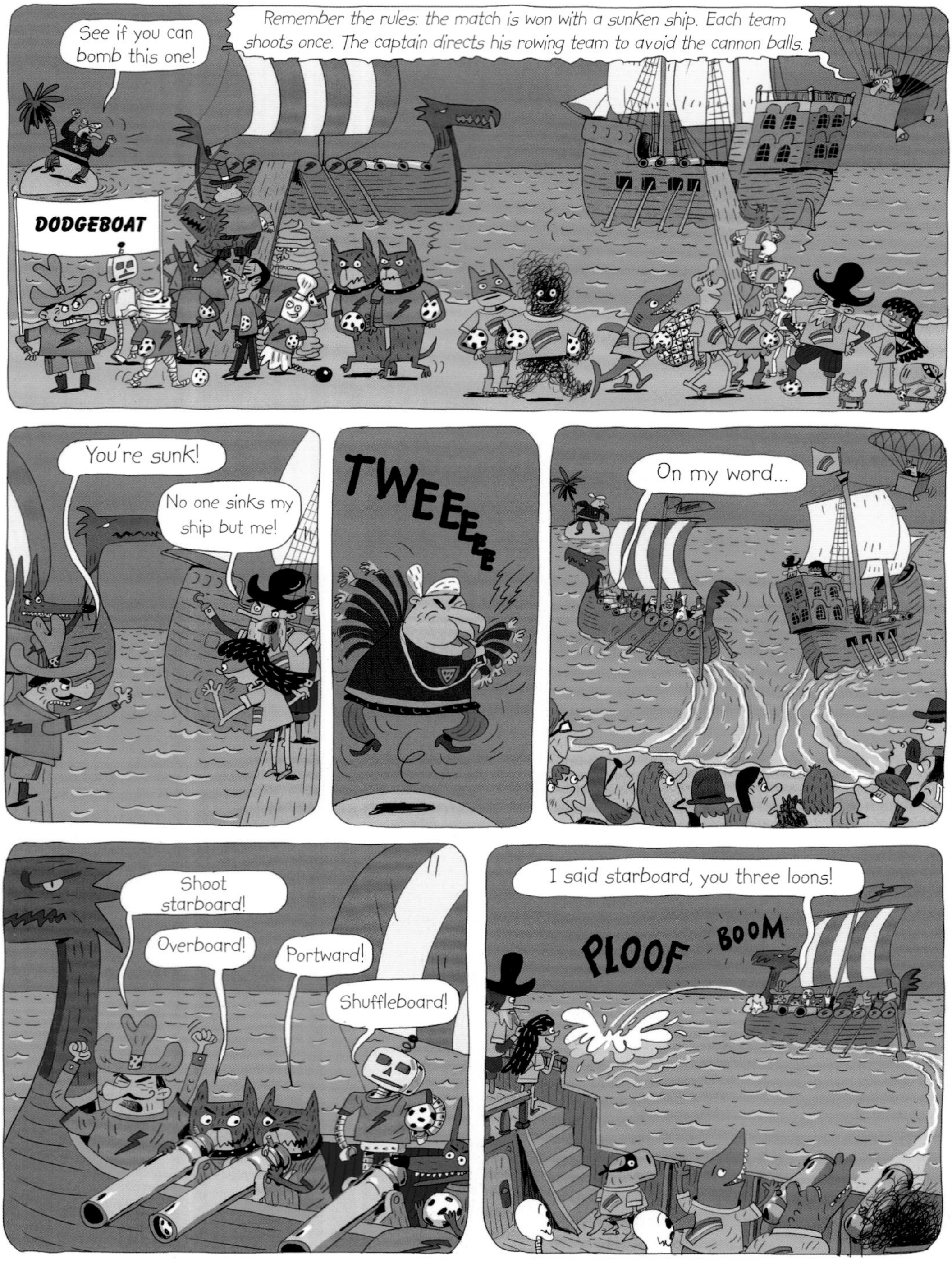
See if you can bomb this one!
Remember the rules: the match is won with a sunken ship. Each team shoots once. The captain directs his rowing team to avoid the cannon balls.
DODGEBOAT
You're sunk!
No one sinks my ship but me!
TWEEEEEE
On my word...
Shoot starboard!
Overboard!
Portward!
Shuffleboard!
I said starboard, you three loons!
PLOOF
BOOM

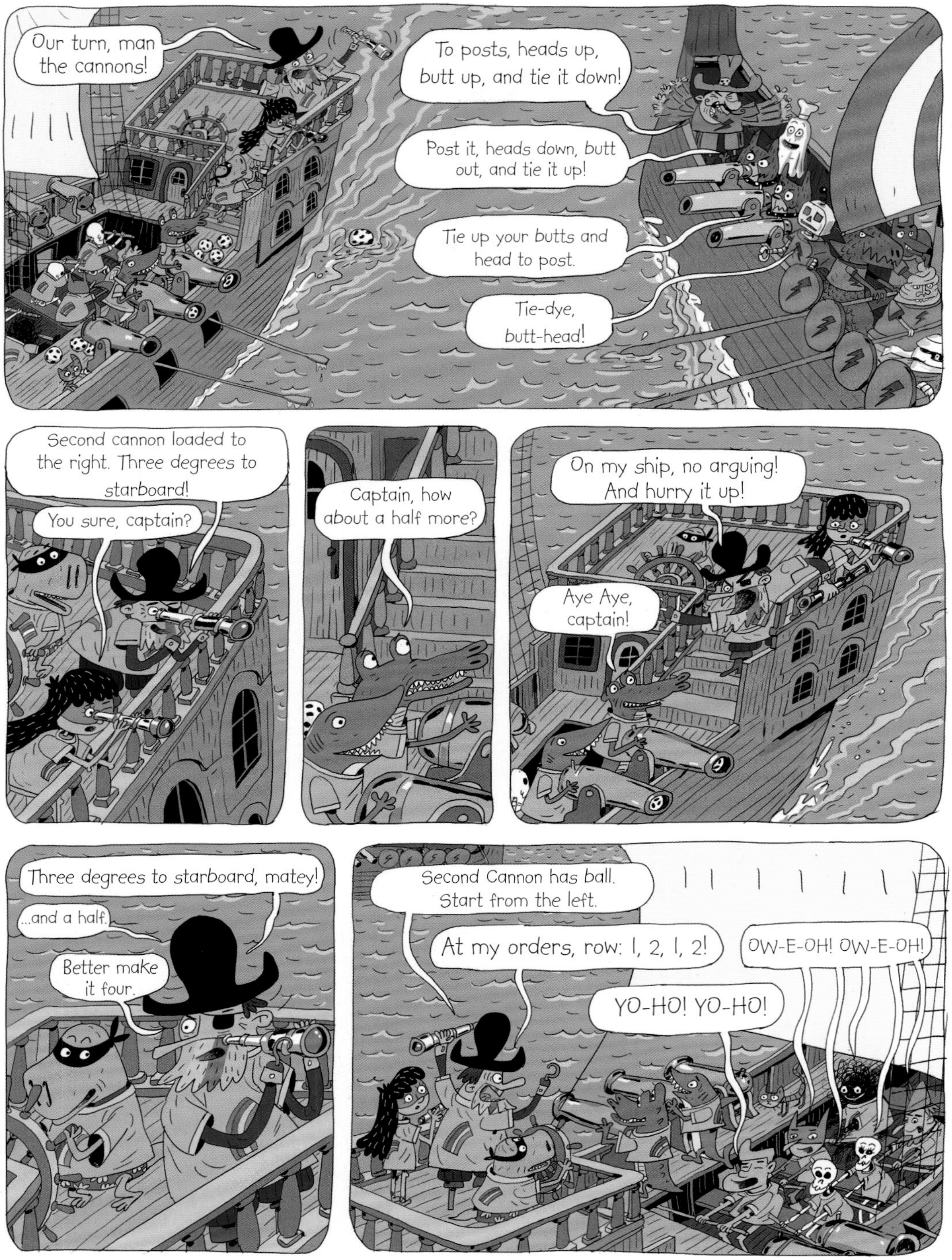
Our turn, man the cannons!
To posts, heads up, butt up, and tie it down!
Post it, heads down, butt out, and tie it up!
Tie up your butts and head to post.
Tie-dye, butt-head!
Second cannon loaded to the right. Three degrees to starboard!
You sure, captain?
Captain, how about a half more?
On my ship, no arguing! And hurry it up!
Aye Aye, captain!
Three degrees to starboard, matey!
...and a half.
Better make it four.
Second Cannon has ball. Start from the left.
At my orders, row: 1, 2, 1, 2!
OW-E-OH! OW-E-OH!
YO-HO! YO-HO!

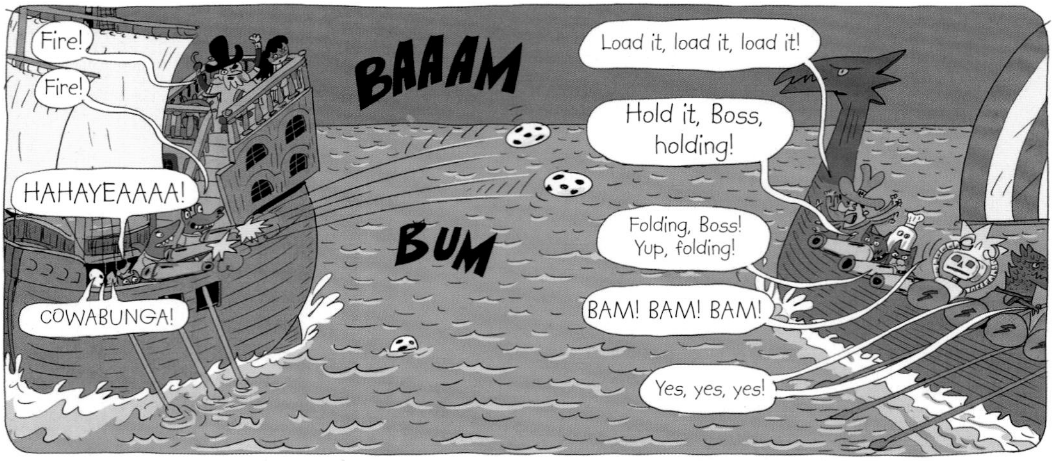
Fire!
Fire!
HAHAYEAAAA!
COWABUNGA!
BAAAM
BUM
Load it, load it, load it!
Hold it, Boss, holding!
Folding, Boss! Yup, folding!
BAM! BAM! BAM!
Yes, yes, yes!

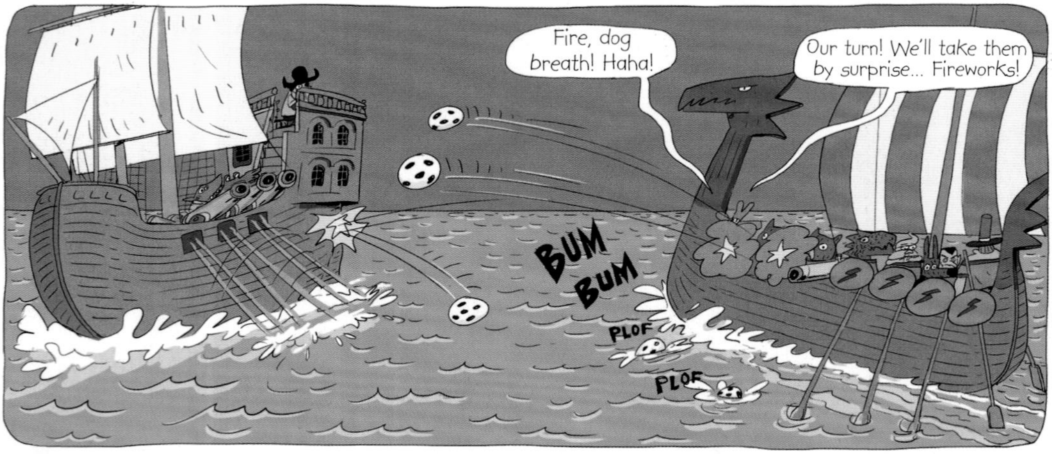
Fire, dog breath! Haha!
Our turn! We'll take them by surprise... Fireworks!
BUM
BUM
PLOF
PLOF

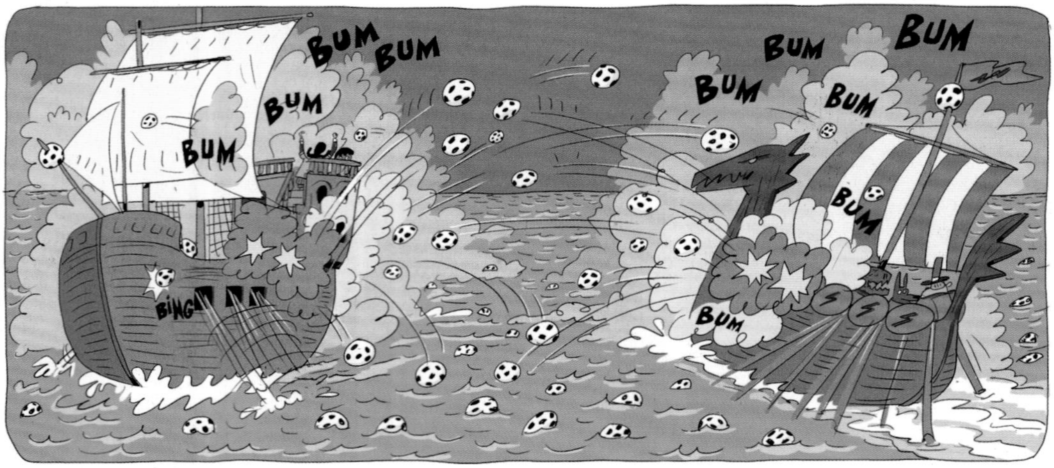
BUM
BUM
BUM
BUM
BING
BUM
BUM
BUM
BUM
BUM
BUM

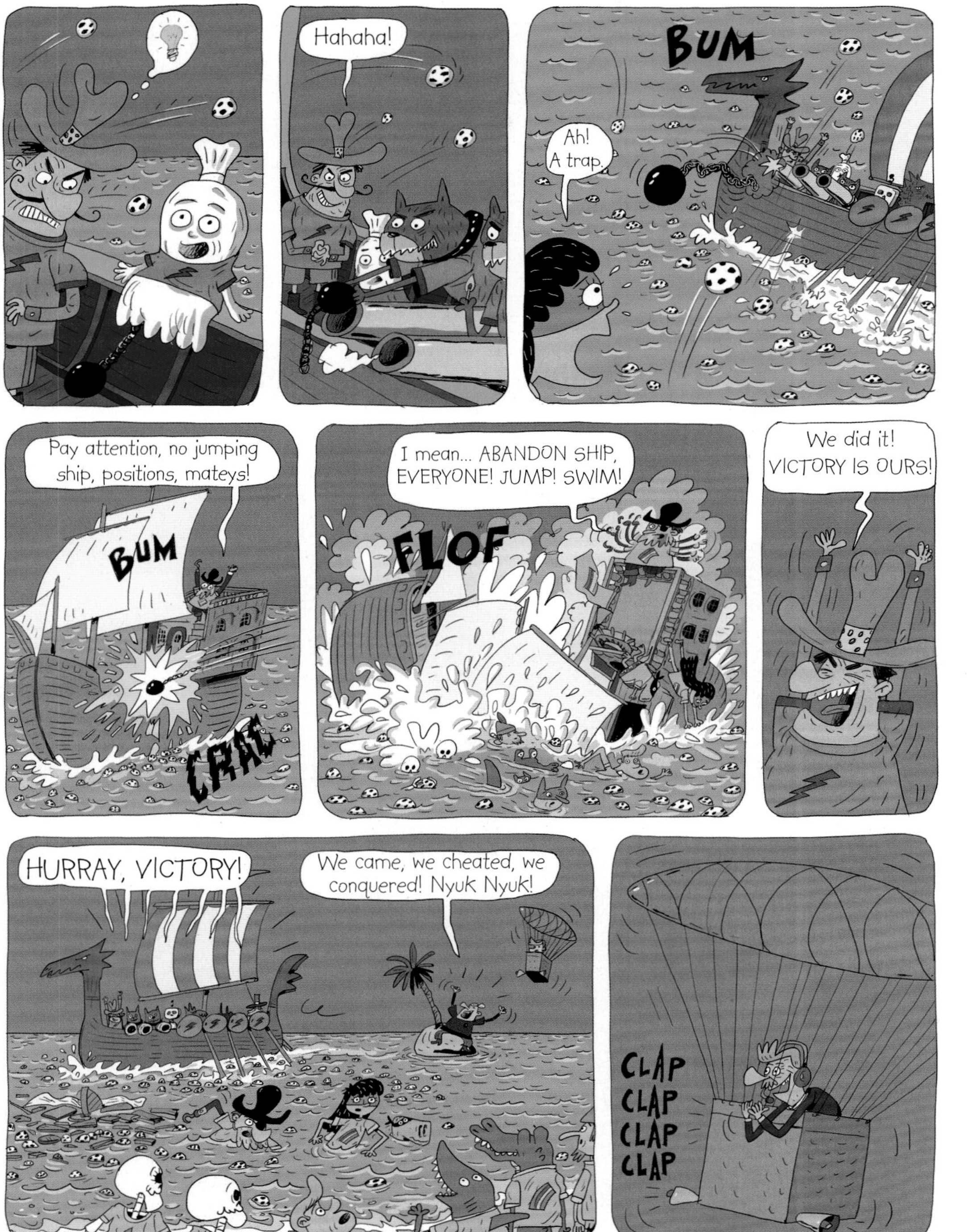
Hahaha!
BUM
Ah!
A trap.
Pay attention, no jumping ship, positions, mateys!
BUM
CRAC
I mean... ABANDON SHIP, EVERYONE! JUMP! SWIM!
FLOF
We did it! VICTORY IS OURS!
HURRAY, VICTORY!
We came, we cheated, we conquered! Nyuk Nyuk!
CLAP
CLAP
CLAP
CLAP

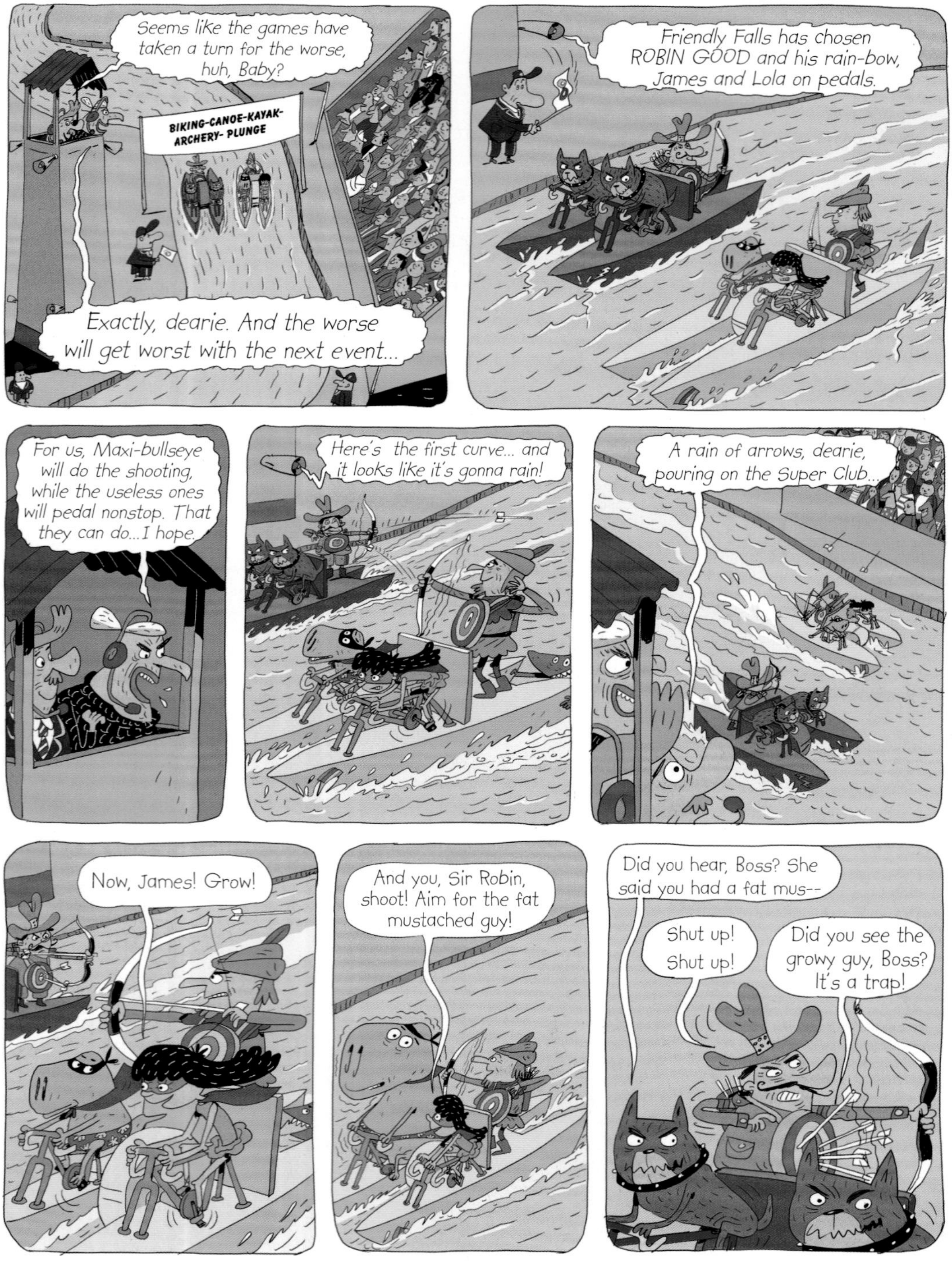
Seems like the games have taken a turn for the worse, huh, Baby?
BIKING-CANOE-KAYAK-ARCHERY- PLUNGE
Exactly, dearie. And the worse will get worst with the next event...
Friendly Falls has chosen ROBIN GOOD and his rain-bow, James and Lola on pedals.
For us, Maxi-bullseye will do the shooting, while the useless ones will pedal nonstop. That they can do...I hope.
Here's the first curve... and it looks like it's gonna rain!
A rain of arrows, dearie, pouring on the Super Club...
Now, James! Grow!
And you, Sir Robin, shoot! Aim for the fat mustached guy!
Did you hear, Boss? She said you had a fat mus--
Shut up! Shut up!
Did you see the growy guy, Boss? It's a trap!

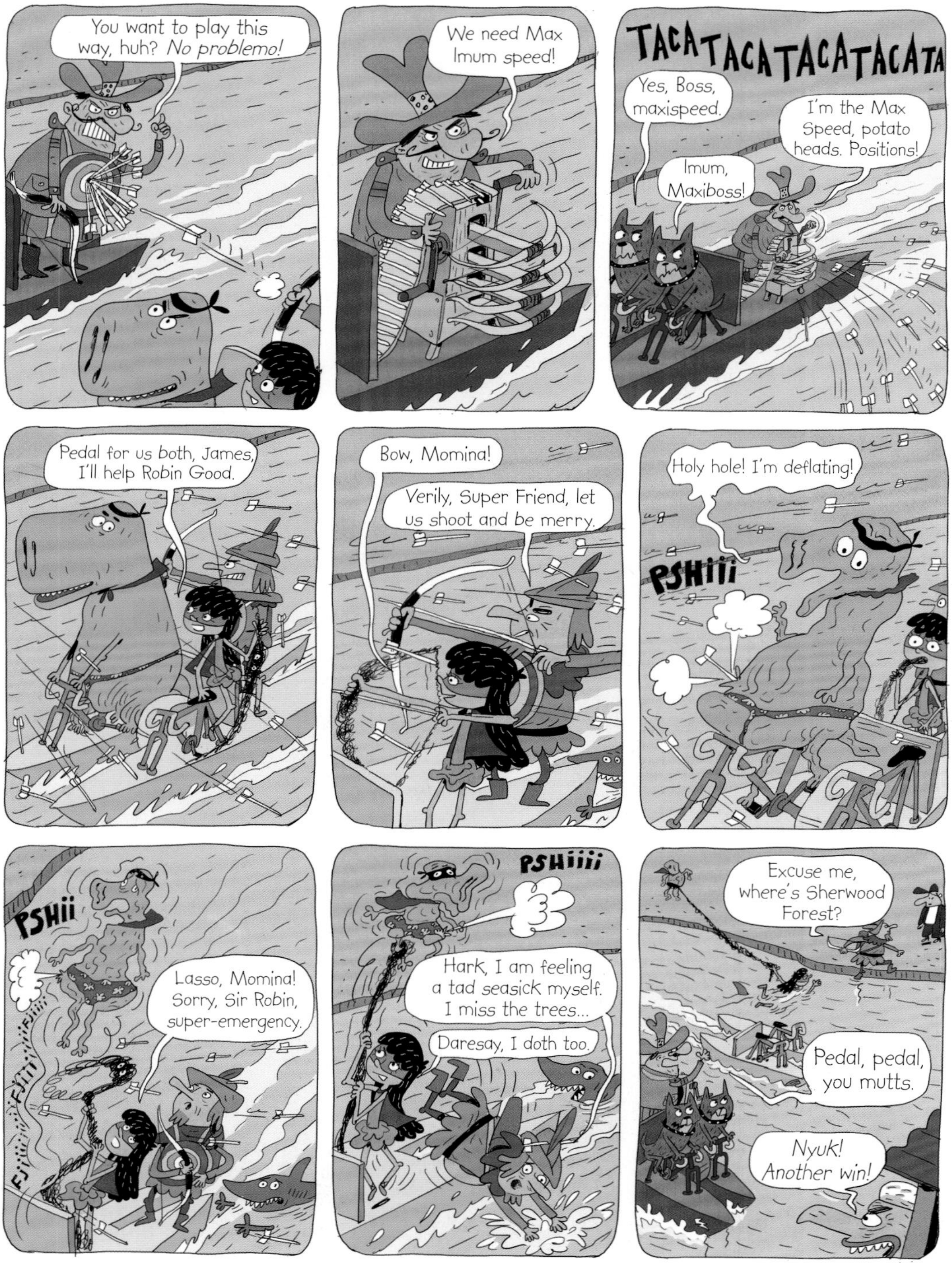
You want to play this way, huh? No problemo!
We need Max Imum speed!
TACATACATACATACATACATA
Yes, Boss, maxispeed.
I'm the Max Speed, potato heads. Positions!
Imum, Maxiboss!
Pedal for us both, James, I'll help Robin Good.
Bow, Momina!
Verily, Super Friend, let us shoot and be merry.
Holy hole! I'm deflating!
PSHiii
PSHii
Lasso, Momina! Sorry, Sir Robin, super-emergency.
PSHiiii
Hark, I am feeling a tad seasick myself. I miss the trees...
Daresay, I doth too.
Excuse me, where's Sherwood Forest?
Pedal, pedal, you mutts.
Nyuk! Another win!

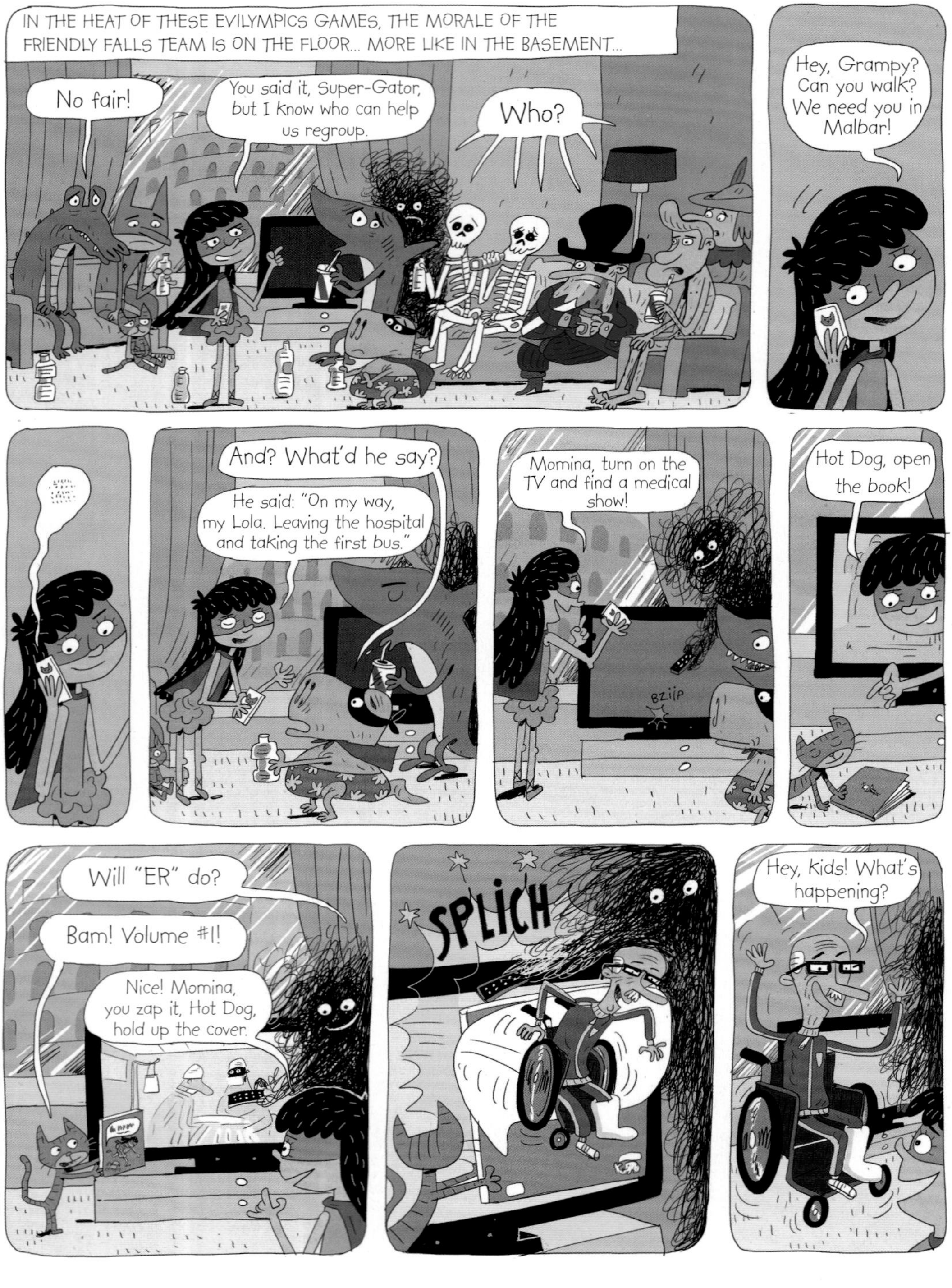
IN THE HEAT OF THESE EVILYMPICS GAMES, THE MORALE OF THE FRIENDLY FALLS TEAM IS ON THE FLOOR... MORE LIKE IN THE BASEMENT...
No fair!
You said it, Super-Gator, but I know who can help us regroup.
Who?
Hey, Grampy? Can you walk? We need you in Malbar!
And? What'd he say?
He said: "On my way, my Lola. Leaving the hospital and taking the first bus."
Momina, turn on the TV and find a medical show!
BZIIP
Hot Dog, open the book!
Will "ER" do?
Bam! Volume #1!
Nice! Momina, you zap it, Hot Dog, hold up the cover.
SPLICH
Hey, Kids! What's happening?

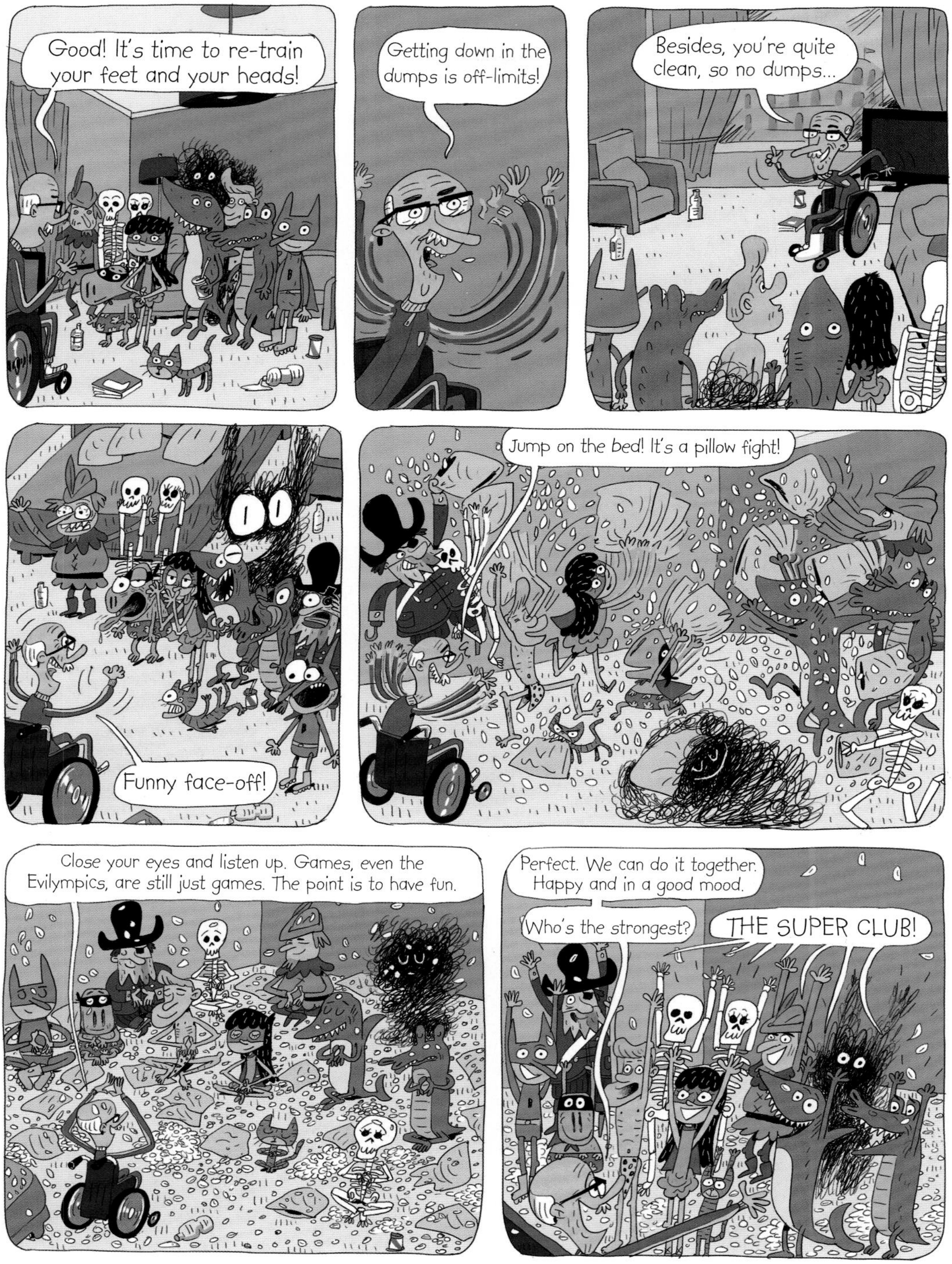

Good! It's time to re-train your feet and your heads!
Getting down in the dumps is off-limits!
Besides, you're quite clean, so no dumps...
Funny face-off!
Jump on the bed! It's a pillow fight!
Close your eyes and listen up. Games, even the Evilympics, are still just games. The point is to have fun.
Perfect. We can do it together. Happy and in a good mood.
Who's the strongest?
THE SUPER CLUB!

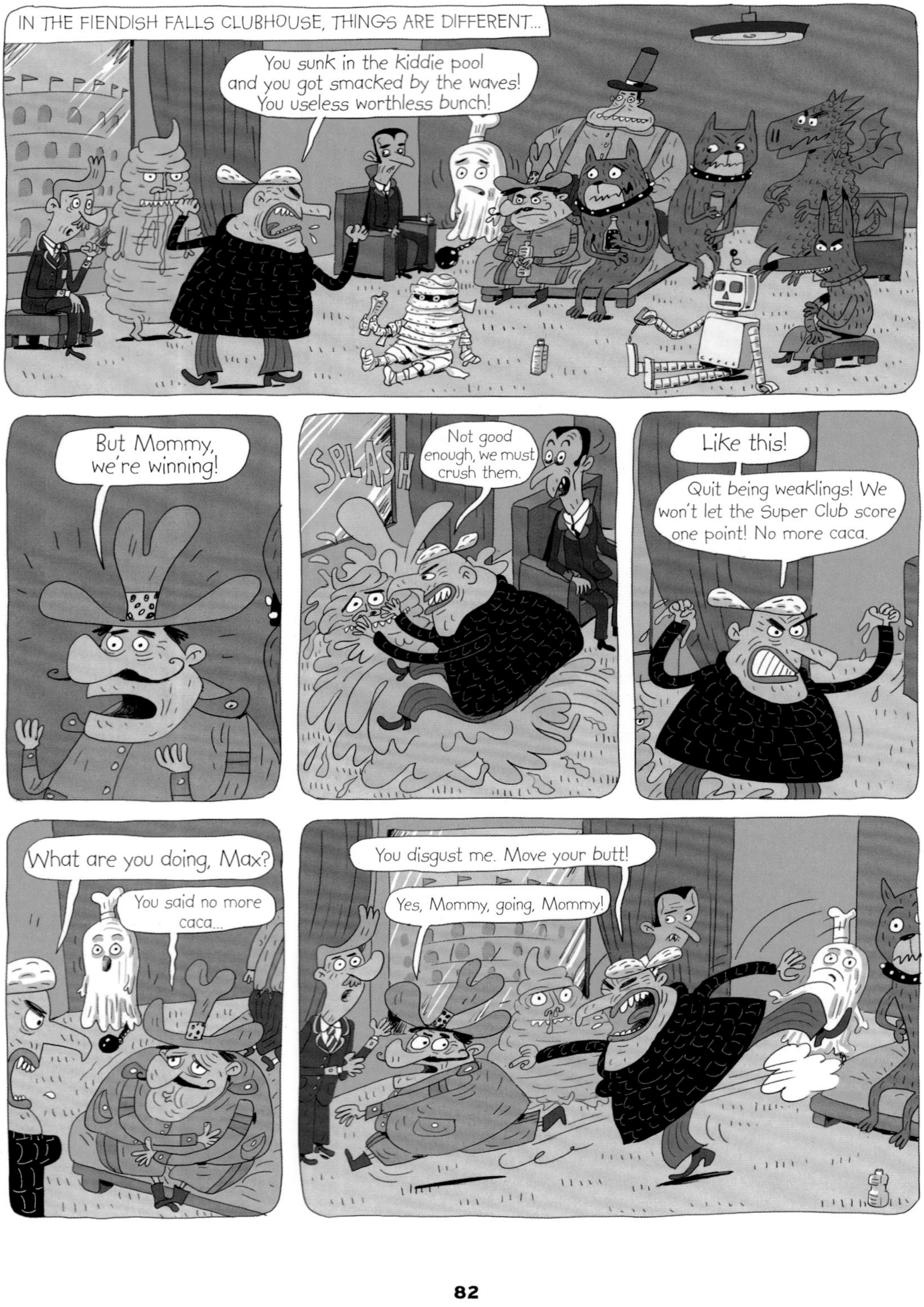
IN THE FIENDISH FALLS CLUBHOUSE, THINGS ARE DIFFERENT...
You sunk in the kiddie pool and you got smacked by the waves! You useless worthless bunch!
But Mommy, we're winning!
SPLASH
Not good enough, we must crush them.
Like this!
Quit being weaklings! We won't let the Super Club score one point! No more caca.
What are you doing, Max?
You said no more caca...
You disgust me. Move your butt!
Yes, Mommy, going, Mommy!

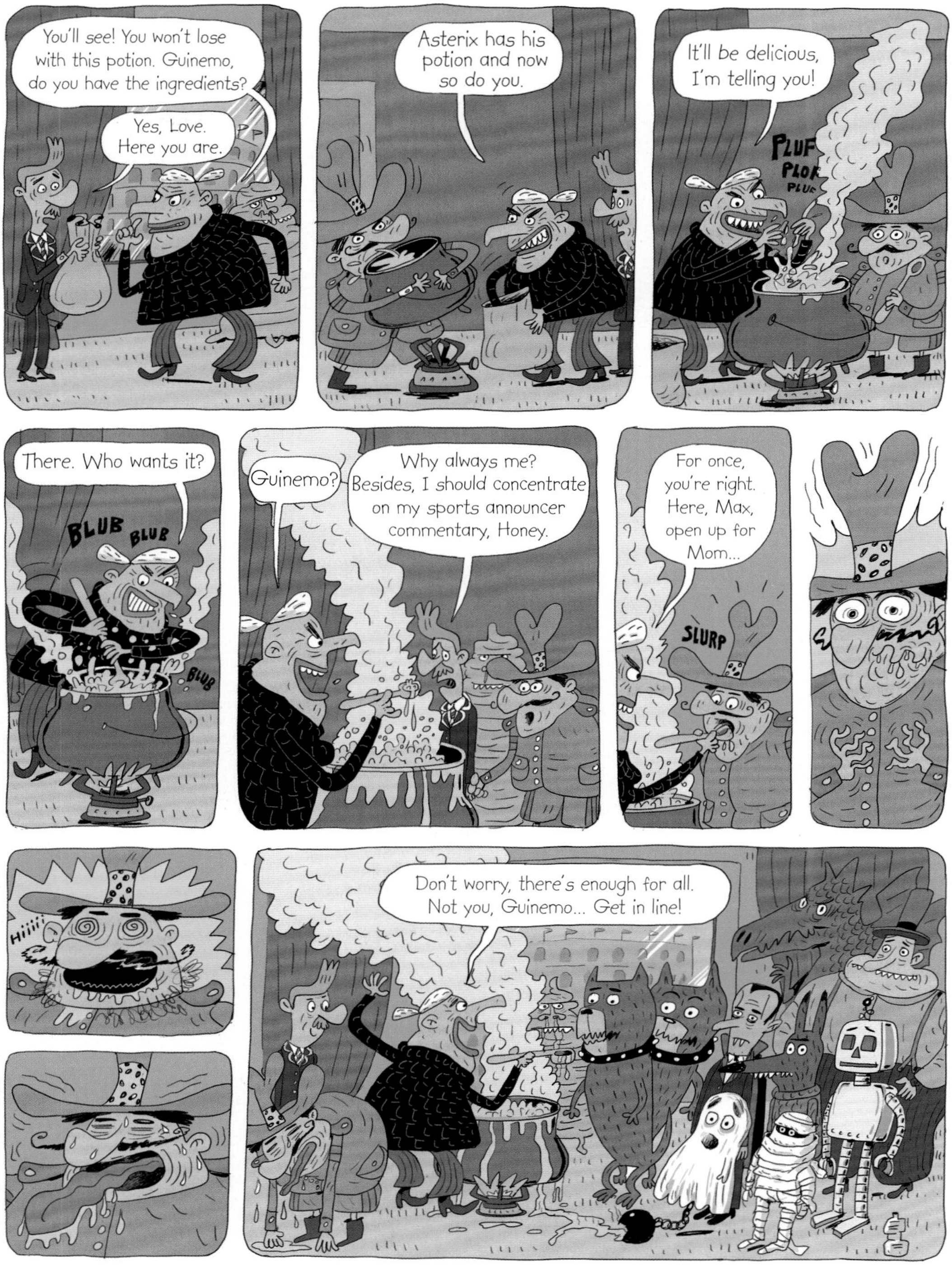
You'll see! You won't lose with this potion. Guinemo, do you have the ingredients?
Yes, Love. Here you are.
Asterix has his potion and now so do you.
It'll be delicious, I'm telling you!
PLUF
PLOF
PLUF
There. Who wants it?
BLUB
BLUB
BLUB
Guinemo?
Why always me? Besides, I should concentrate on my sports announcer commentary, Honey.
For once, you're right. Here, Max, open up for Mom...
SLURP
Hiiiii
Don't worry, there's enough for all. Not you, Guinemo... Get in line!

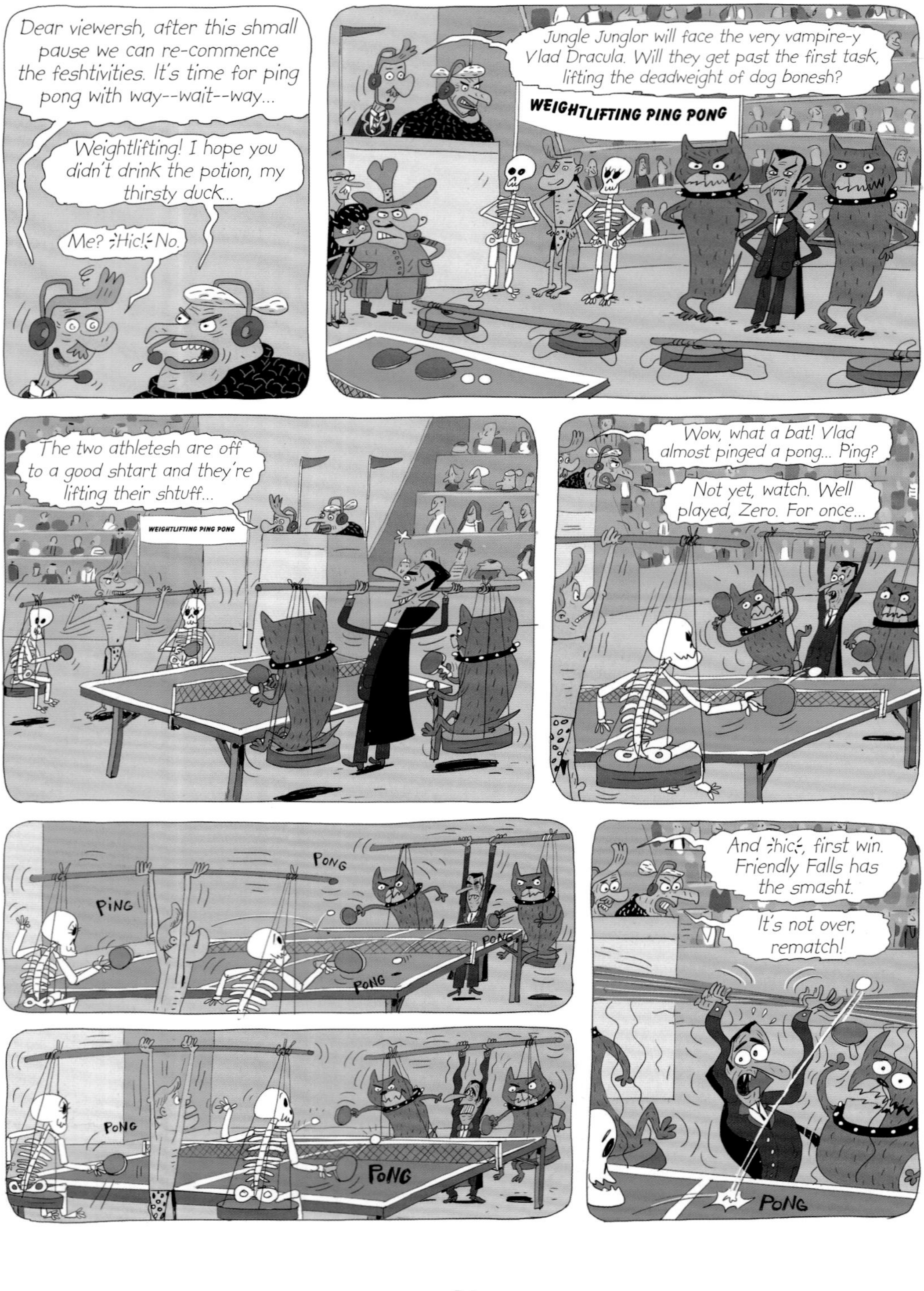
Dear viewersh, after this shmall pause we can re-commence the feshtivities. It's time for ping pong with way--wait--way...
Weightlifting! I hope you didn't drink the potion, my thirsty duck...
Me? ~Hic!~ No.
Jungle Junglor will face the very vampire-y Vlad Dracula. Will they get past the first task, lifting the deadweight of dog bonesh?
WEIGHTLIFTING PING PONG
The two athletesh are off to a good shtart and they're lifting their shtuff...
WEIGHTLIFTING PING PONG
Wow, what a bat! Vlad almost pinged a pong... Ping?
Not yet, watch. Well played, Zero. For once...
PING
PONG
PONG
PONG
And ~hic~, first win. Friendly Falls has the smasht.
It's not over, rematch!
PONG
PONG
PONG

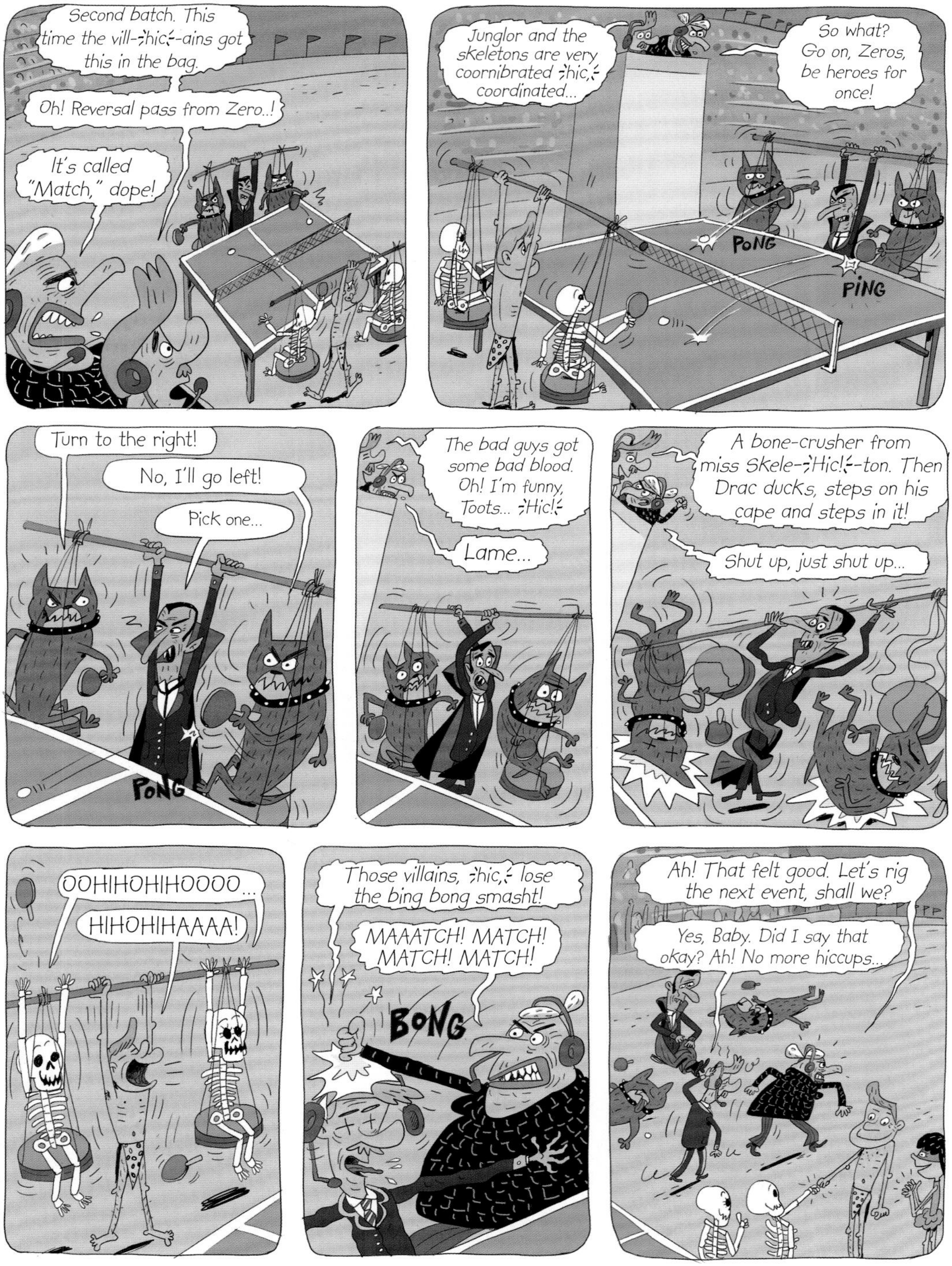
Second batch. This time the vill-;hic;-ains got this in the bag.
Oh! Reversal pass from Zero..!
It's called "Match," dope!
Junglor and the skeletons are very coornibrated ;hic; coordinated...
So what? Go on, Zeros, be heroes for once!
PONG
PING
Turn to the right!
No, I'll go left!
Pick one...
PONG
The bad guys got some bad blood. Oh! I'm funny, Toots... ;Hic!;
Lame...
A bone-crusher from miss Skele-;Hic!;-ton. Then Drac ducks, steps on his cape and steps in it!
Shut up, just shut up...
OOHIHOHIHOOOO...
HIHOHIHAAAA!
Those villains, ;hic; lose the bing bong smasht!
MAAATCH! MATCH! MATCH! MATCH!
BONG
Ah! That felt good. Let's rig the next event, shall we?
Yes, Baby. Did I say that okay? Ah! No more hiccups...

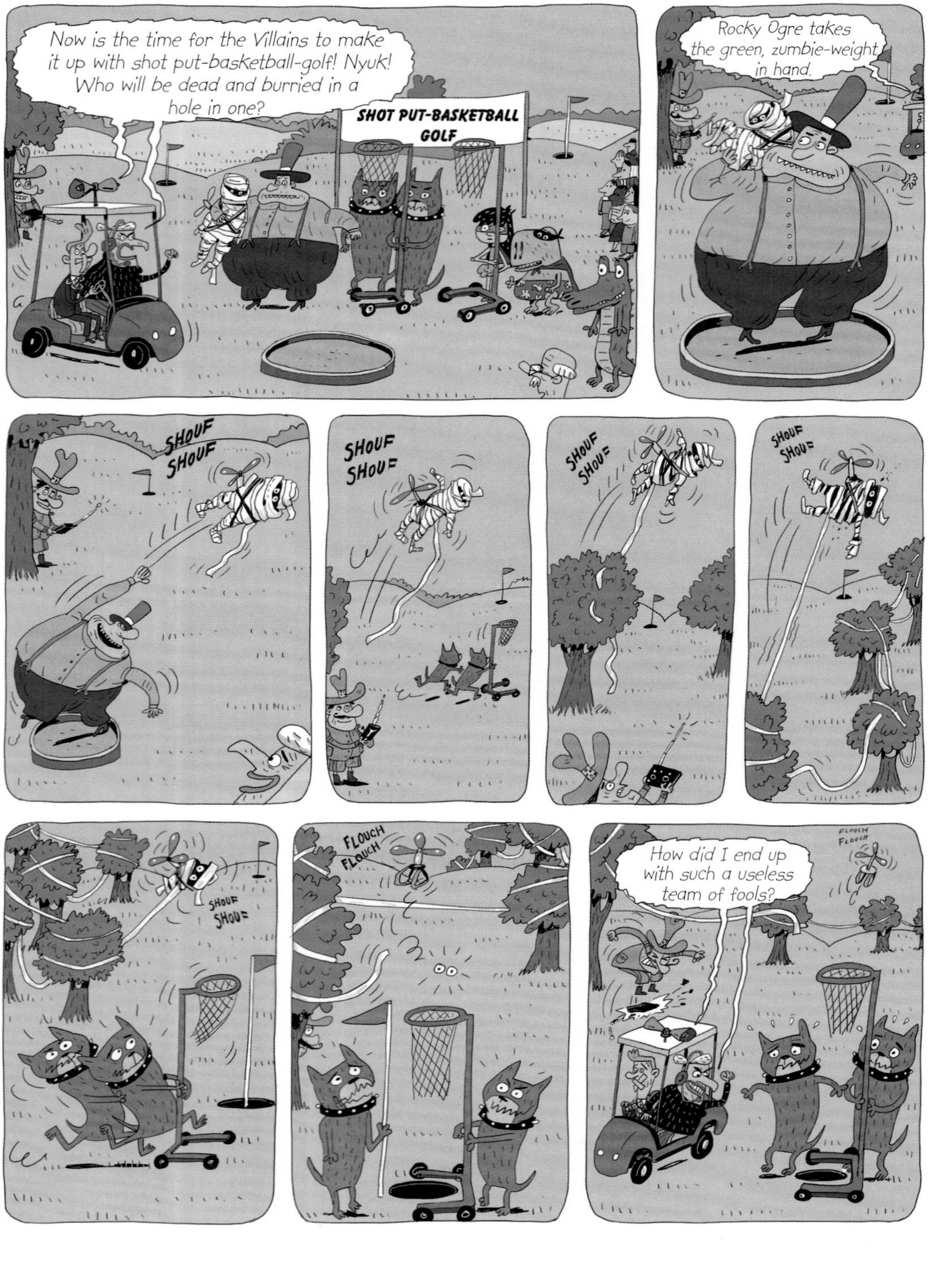

Now is the time for the Villains to make it up with shot put-basketball-golf! Nyuk! Who will be dead and burried in a hole in one?
SHOT PUT-BASKETBALL GOLF
Rocky Ogre takes the green, zumbie-weight in hand.
SHOUF SHOUF
SHOUF SHOUF
SHOUF SHOUF
SHOUF SHOUF
SHOUF SHOUF
FLOUCH FLOUCH
How did I end up with such a useless team of fools?
FLOUCH FLOUCH

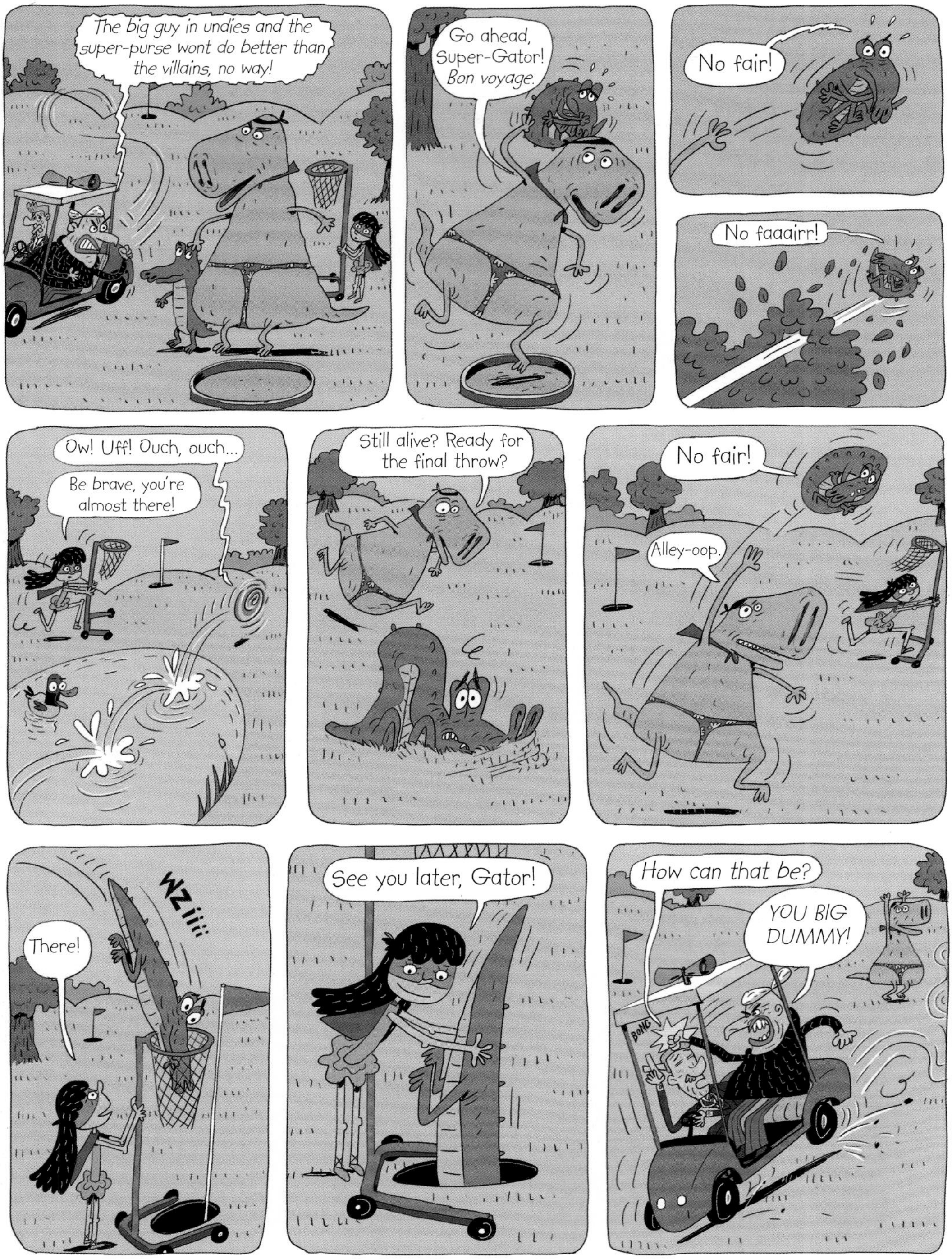
The big guy in undies and the super-purse wont do better than the villains, no way!
Go ahead, Super-Gator! Bon voyage.
No fair!
No faaairr!
Ow! Uff! Ouch, ouch...
Be brave, you're almost there!
Still alive? Ready for the final throw?
No fair!
Alley-oop.
There!
WZiiii
See you later, Gator!
How can that be?
YOU BIG DUMMY!
BONG

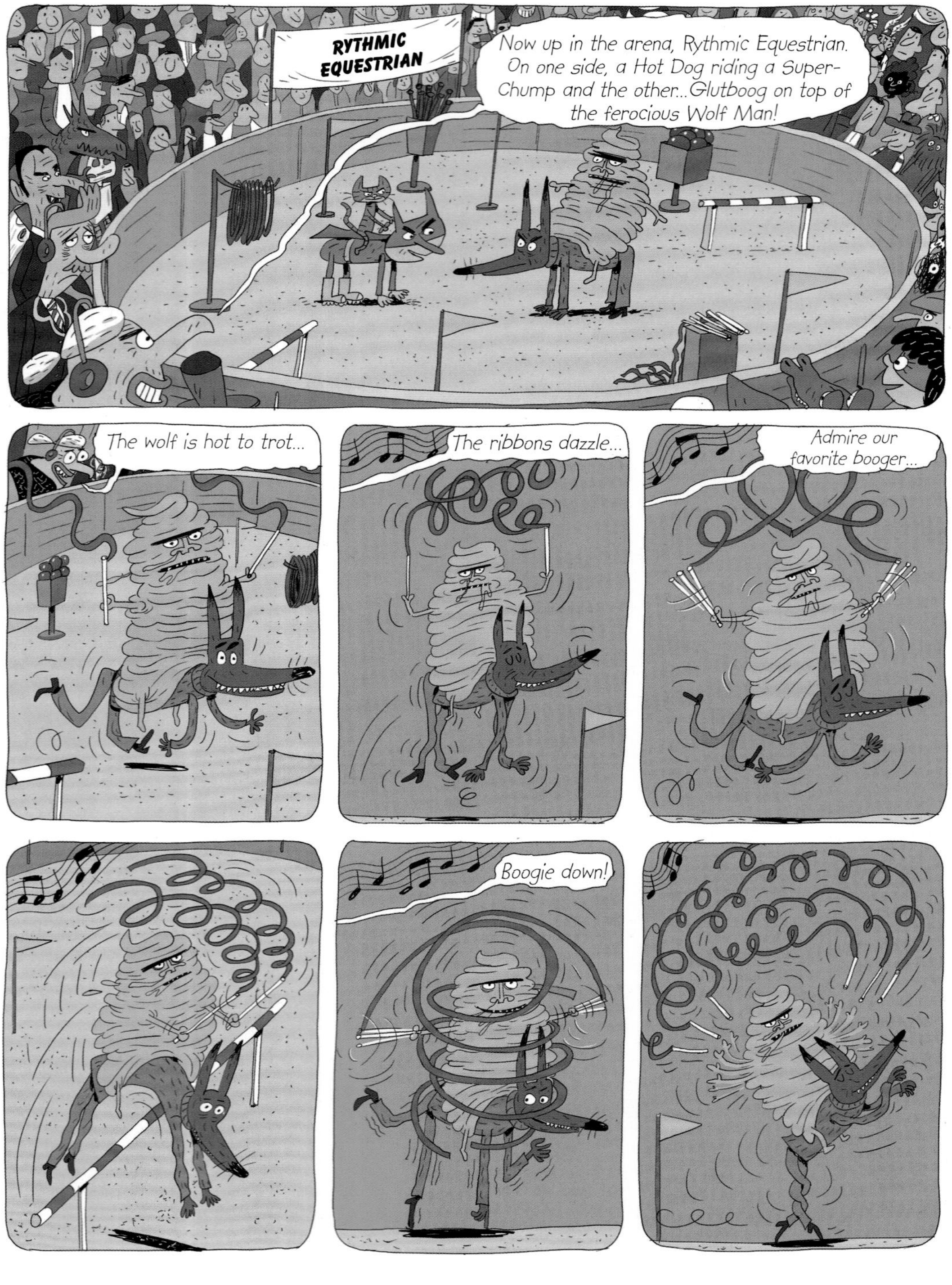
RYTHMIC EQUESTRIAN
Now up in the arena, Rythmic Equestrian. On one side, a Hot Dog riding a Super-Chump and the other...Glutboog on top of the ferocious Wolf Man!
The wolf is hot to trot...
The ribbons dazzle...
Admire our favorite booger...
Boogie down!

What's this?
Gluten hoops!
To finish, clubs!
What a show!
BRAVOOOO! MAX-I-MUM Score: 2,000!

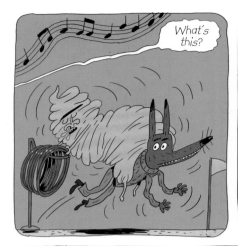

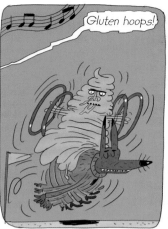

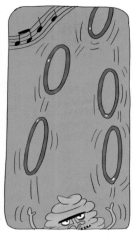

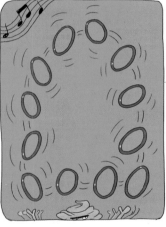

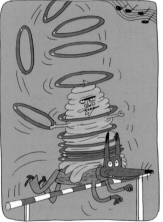

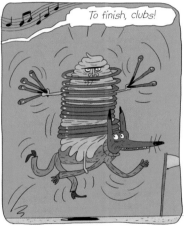

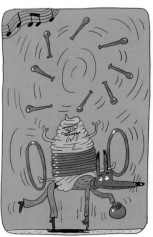

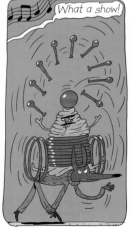

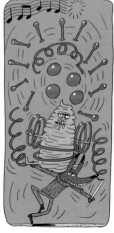

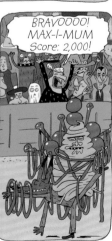

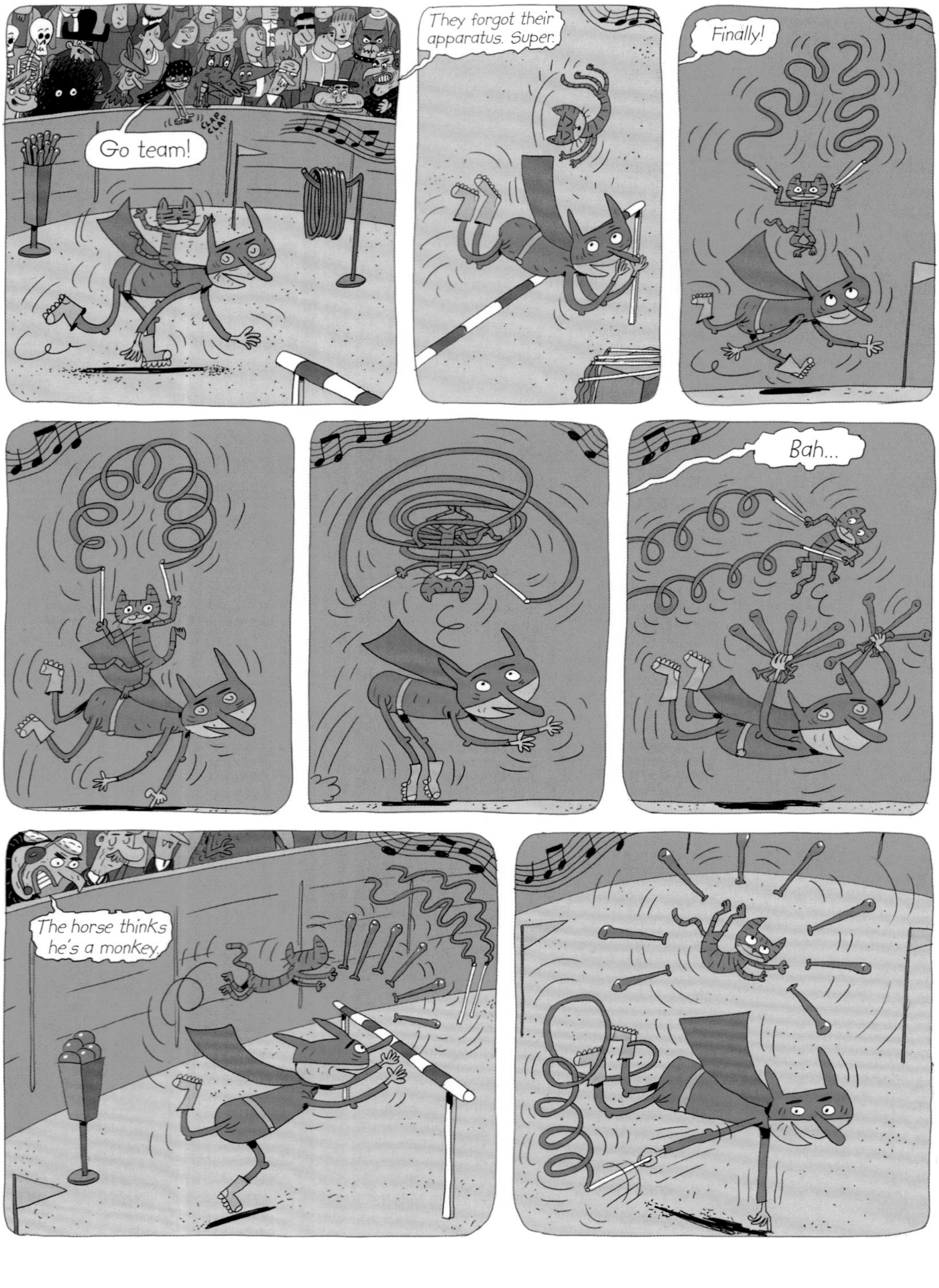
Go team!
CLAP CLAP
They forgot their apparatus. Super.
Finally!
Bah...
The horse thinks he's a monkey.

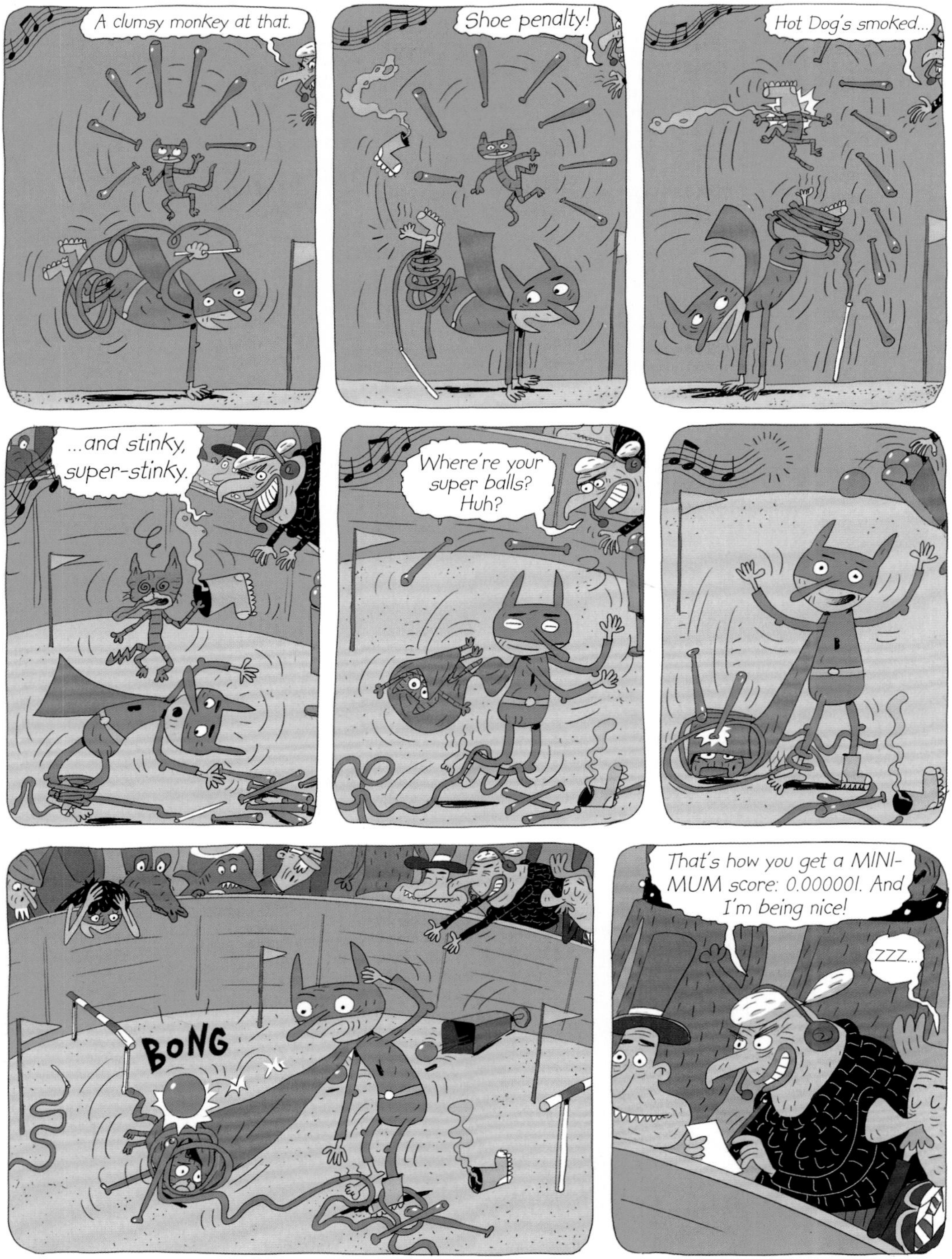
A clumsy monkey at that.
Shoe penalty!
Hot Dog's smoked...
...and stinky, super-stinky.
Where're your super balls? Huh?
BONG
That's how you get a MINI-MUM score: 0.000001. And I'm being nice!
ZZZ...

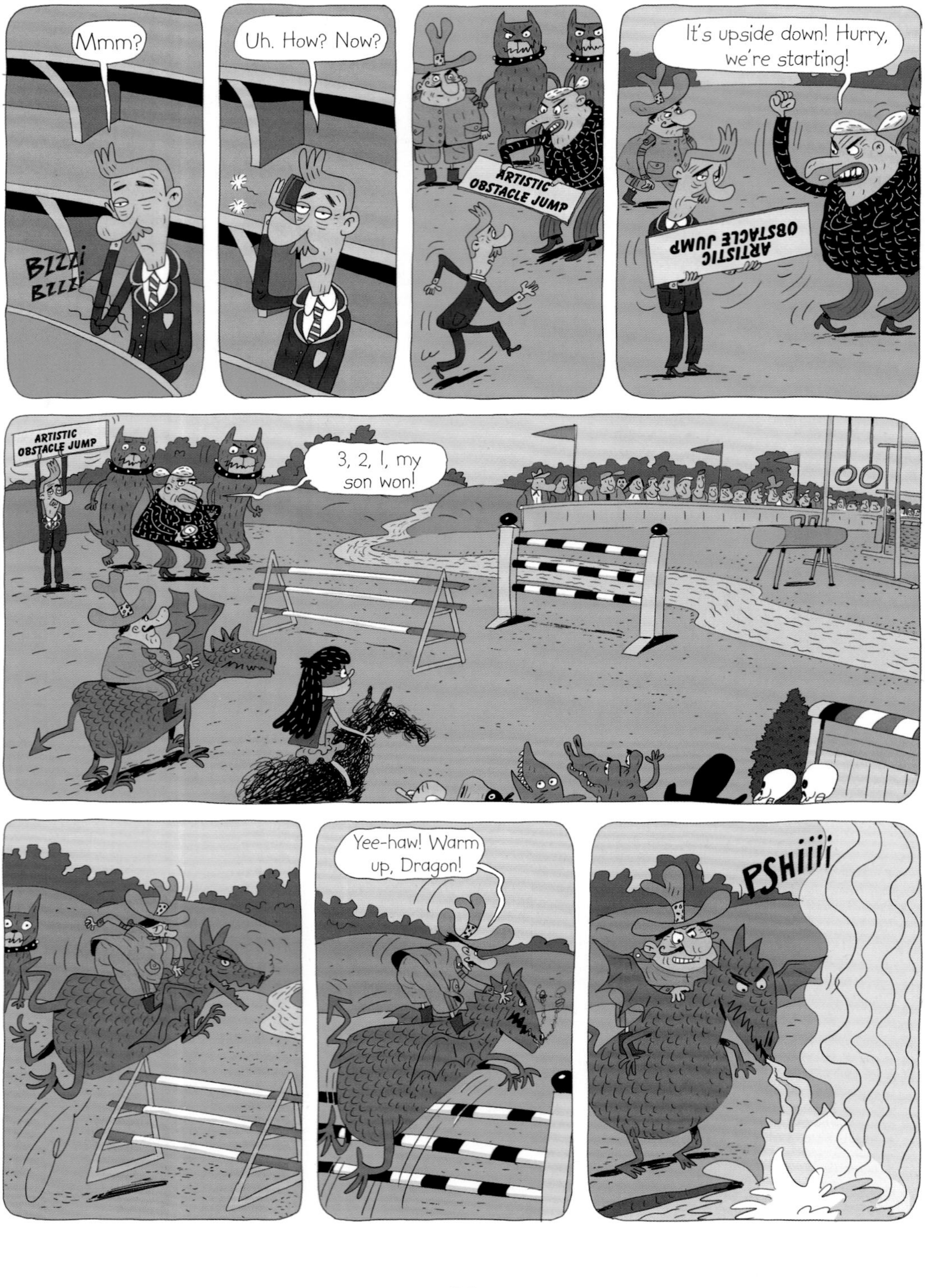

Mmm?
BZZZi BZZZi
Uh. How? Now?
ARTISTIC OBSTACLE JUMP
It's upside down! Hurry, we're starting!
ARTISTIC OBSTACLE JUMP
ARTISTIC OBSTACLE JUMP
3, 2, 1, my son won!
Yee-haw! Warm up, Dragon!
PSHiiii

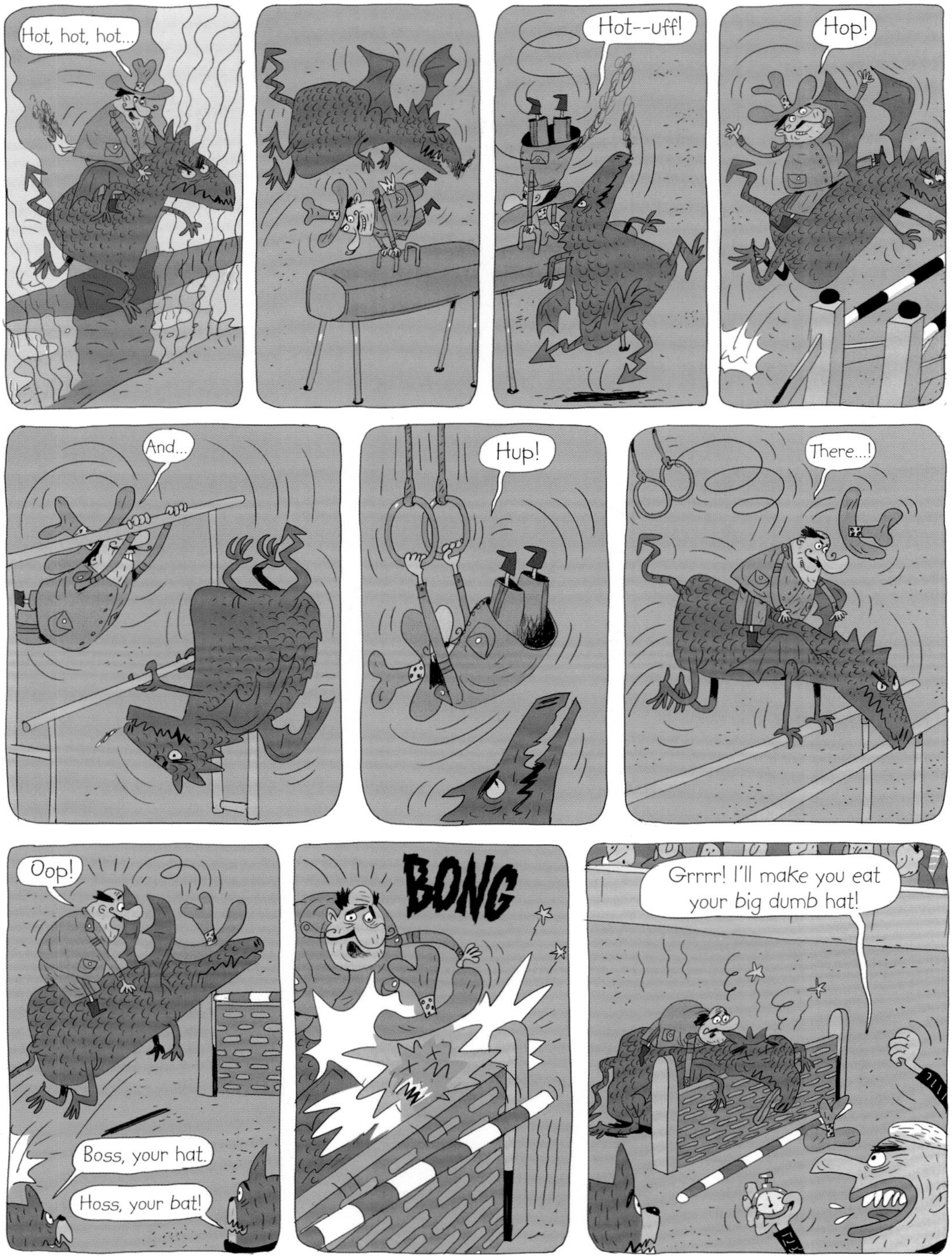
Hot, hot, hot...
Hot--uff!
Hop!
And...
Hup!
There...!
Oop!
Boss, your hat.
Hoss, your bat!
BONG
Grrrr! I'll make you eat your big dumb hat!

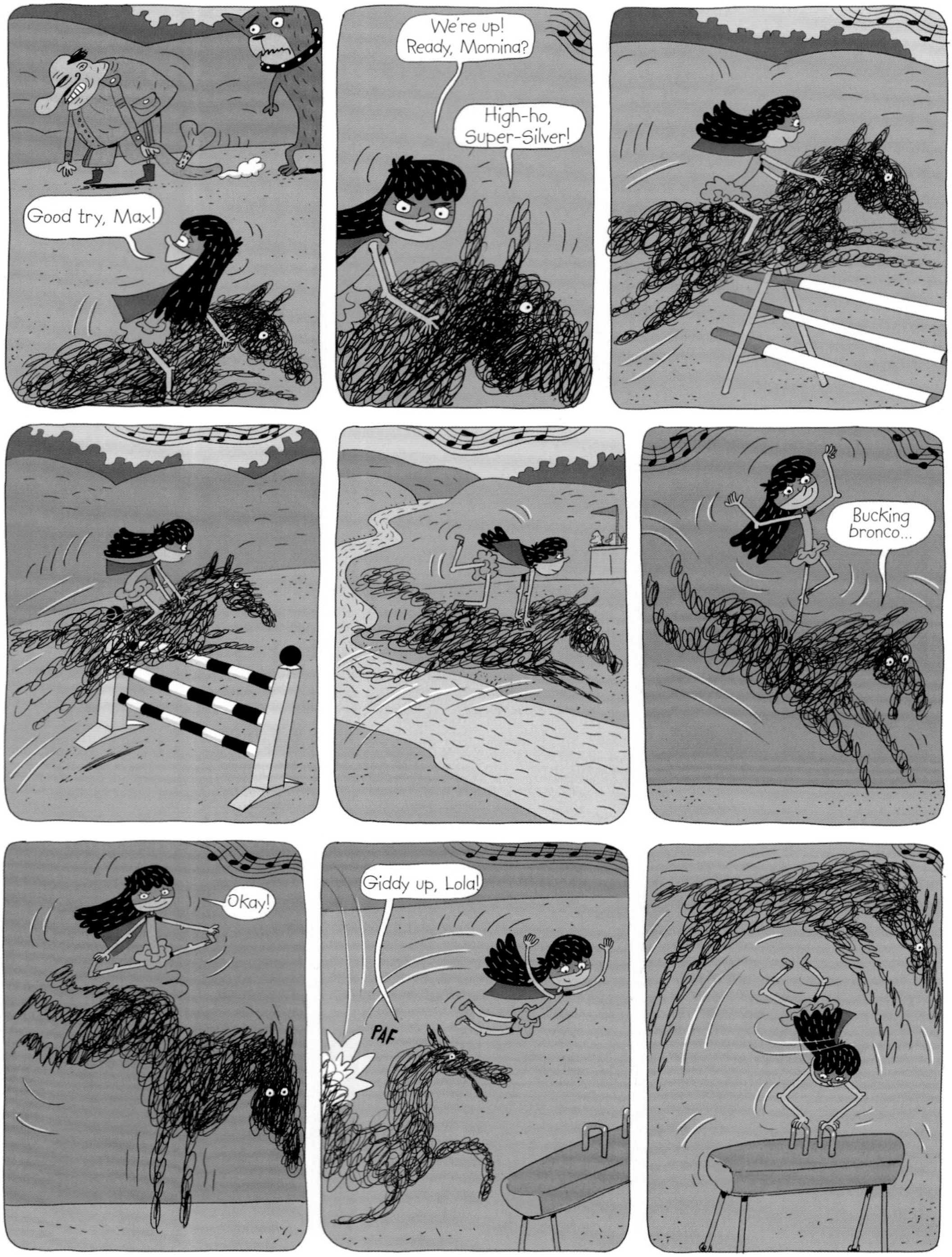
Good try, Max!
We're up! Ready, Momina?
High-ho, Super-Silver!
Bucking bronco...
Okay!
Giddy up, Lola!
PAF

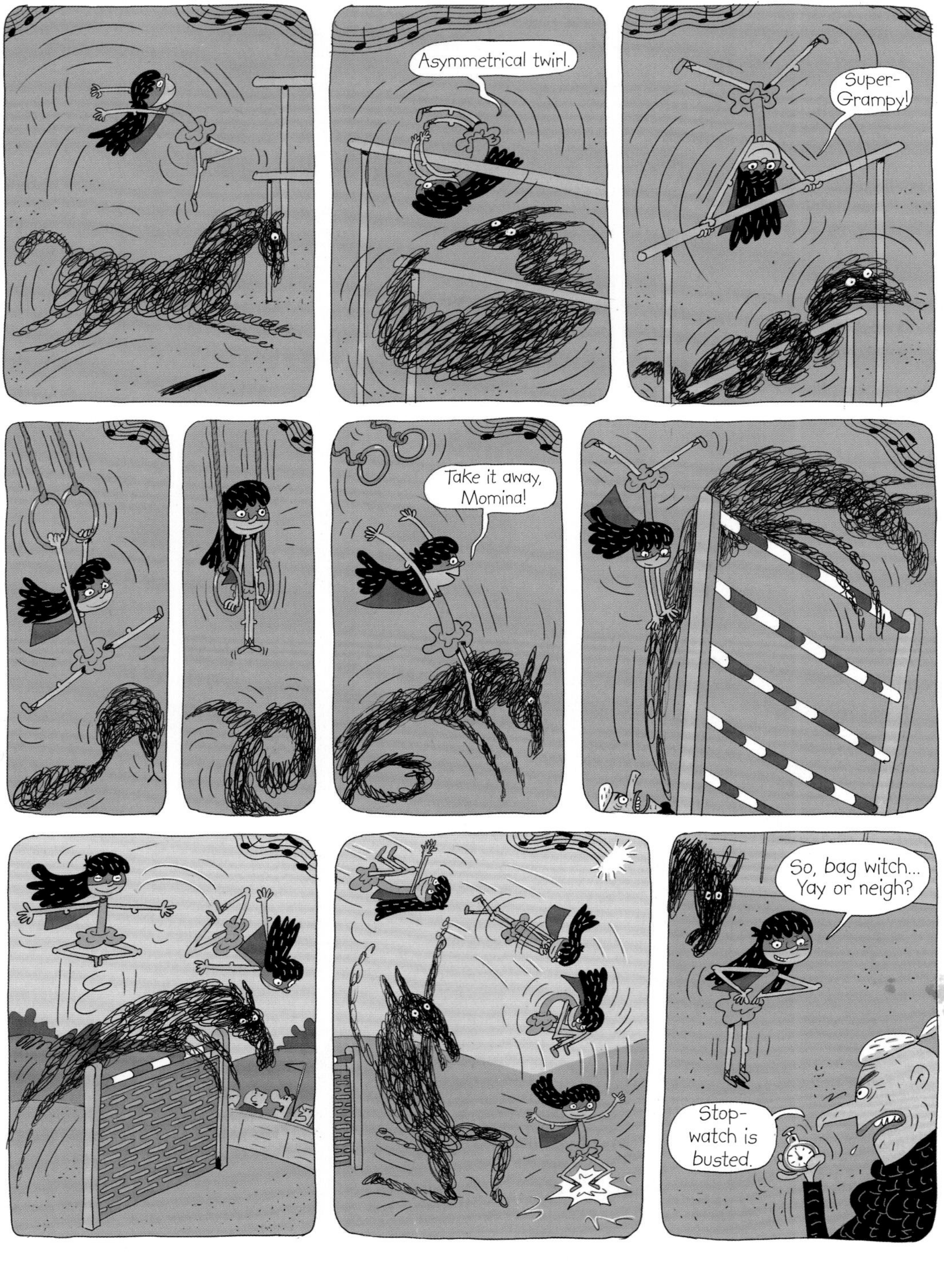
Asymmetrical twirl.
Super-Grampy!
Take it away, Momina!
So, bag witch... Yay or neigh?
Stop-watch is busted.

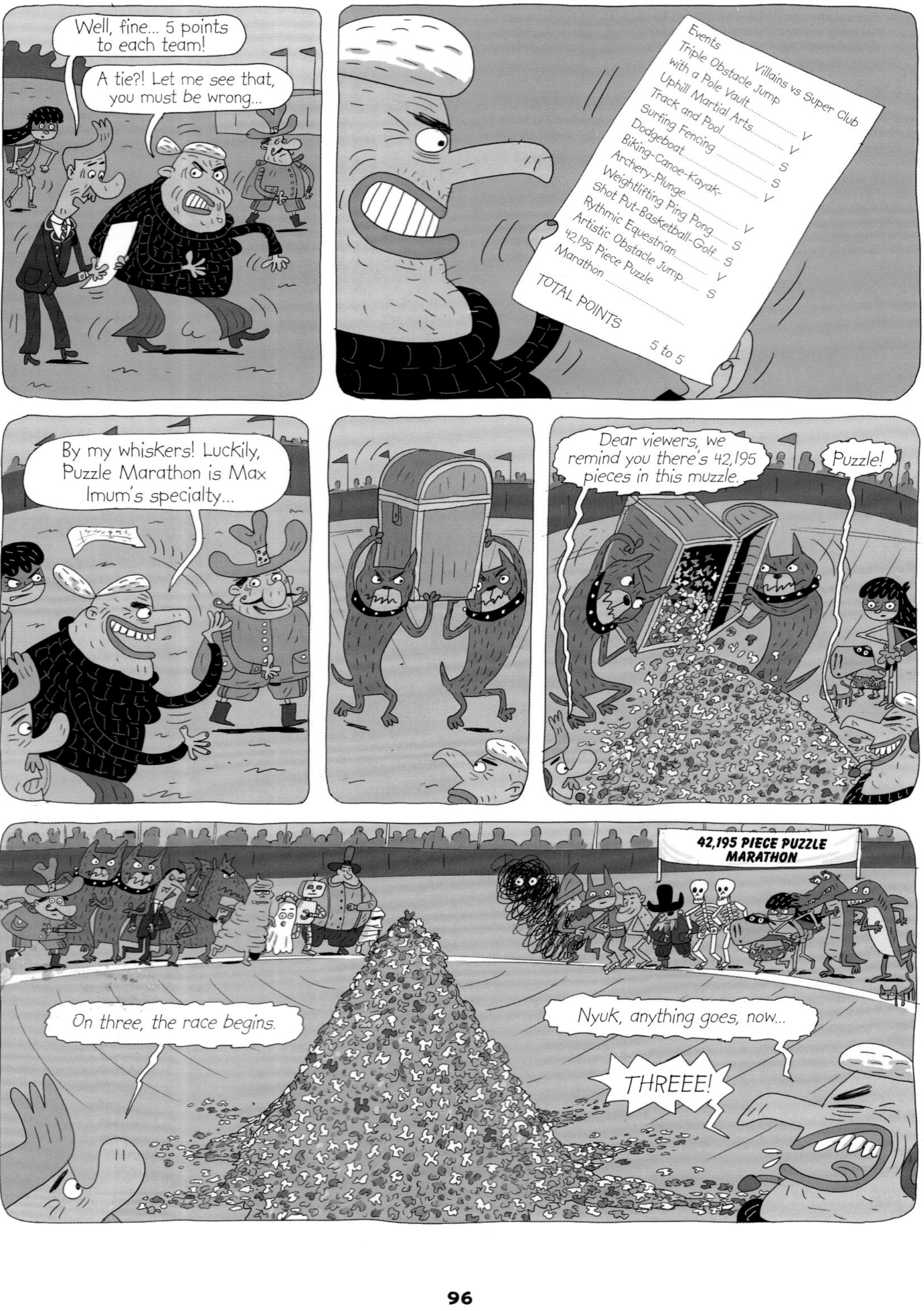
Well, fine... 5 points to each team!
A tie?! Let me see that, you must be wrong...
Events
Villains vs Super Club
Triple Obstacle Jump with a Pole Vault.......... V
Uphill Martial Arts.......... V
Track and Pool.......... S
Surfing Fencing.......... S
Dodgeboat.......... V
Biking-Canoe-Kayak-Archery-Plunge.......... V
Weightlifting Ping Pong.......... S
Shot Put-Basketball-Golf.......... S
Rythmic Equestrian.......... V
Artistic Obstacle Jump.......... S
42,195 Piece Puzzle Marathon..........
TOTAL POINTS
5 to 5
By my whiskers! Luckily, Puzzle Marathon is Max Imum's specialty...
Dear viewers, we remind you there's 42,195 pieces in this muzzle.
Puzzle!
42,195 PIECE PUZZLE MARATHON
On three, the race begins.
Nyuk, anything goes, now...
THREEE!

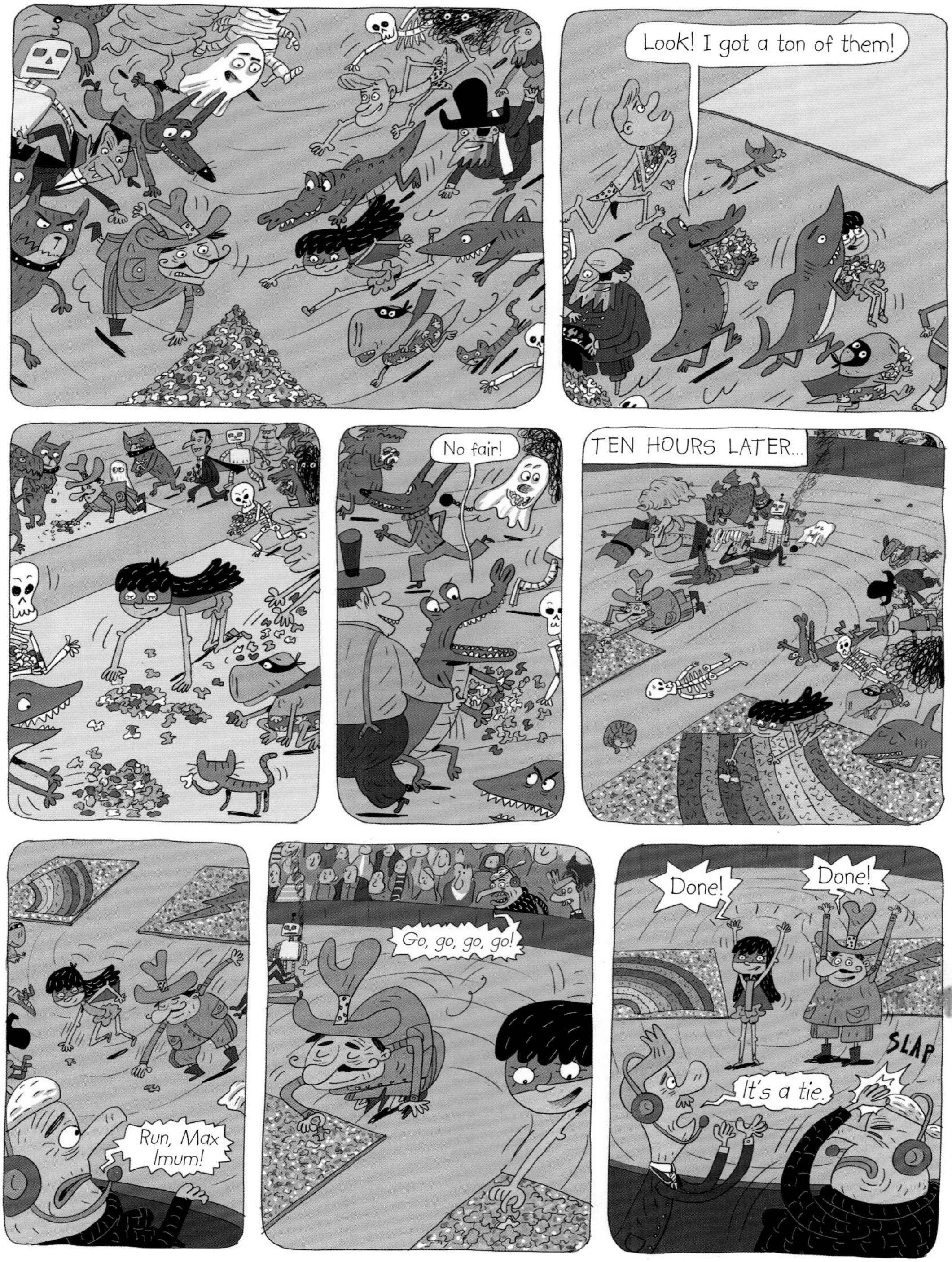
Look! I got a ton of them!
No fair!
TEN HOURS LATER...
Run, Max Imum!
Go, go, go, go!
Done!
Done!
It's a tie.
SLAP

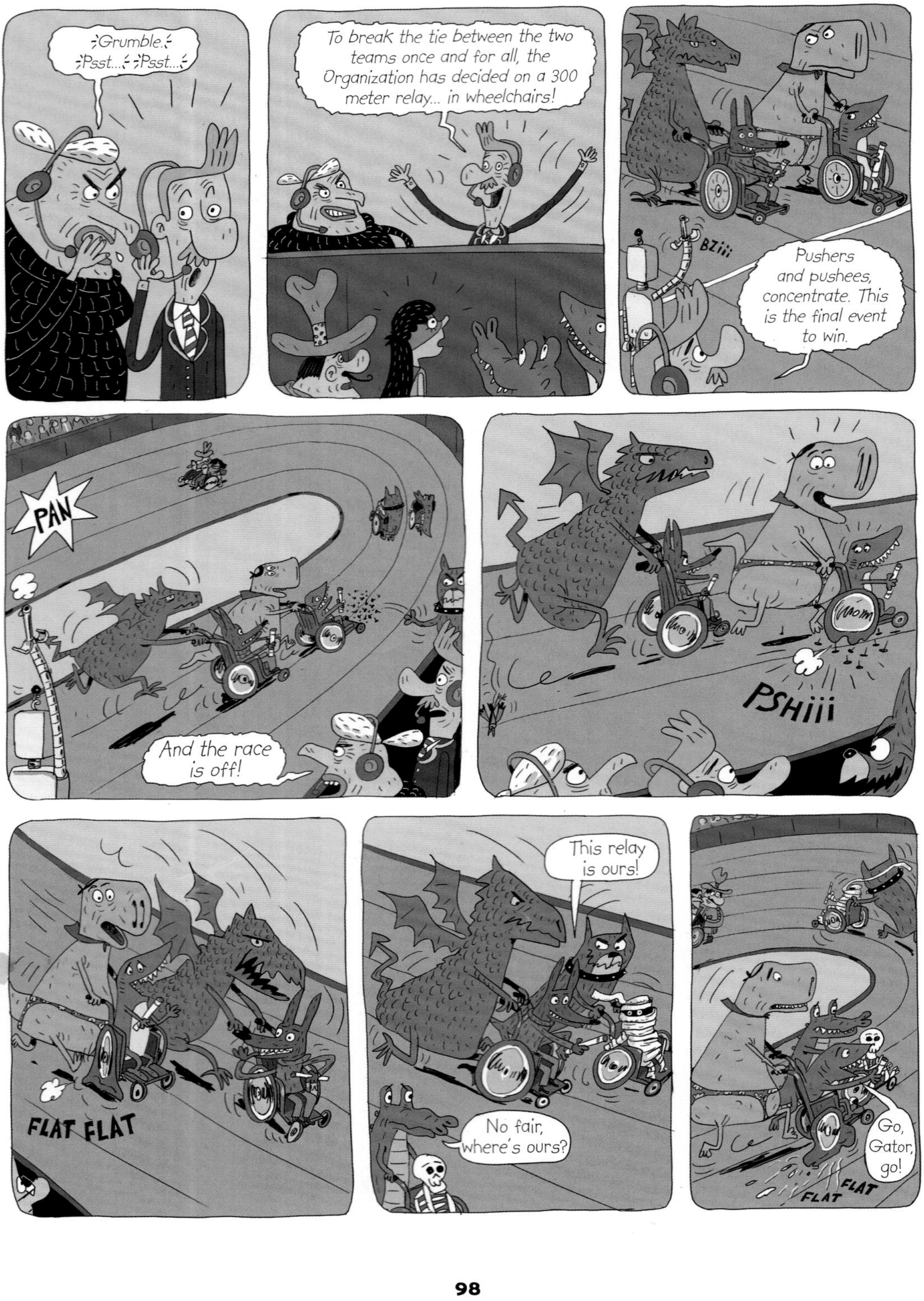
Grumble.
Psst... Psst...
To break the tie between the two teams once and for all, the Organization has decided on a 300 meter relay... in wheelchairs!
BZiii
Pushers and pushees, concentrate. This is the final event to win.
PAN
And the race is off!
PSHiii
FLAT FLAT
This relay is ours!
No fair, where's ours?
Go, Gator, go!
FLAT
FLAT

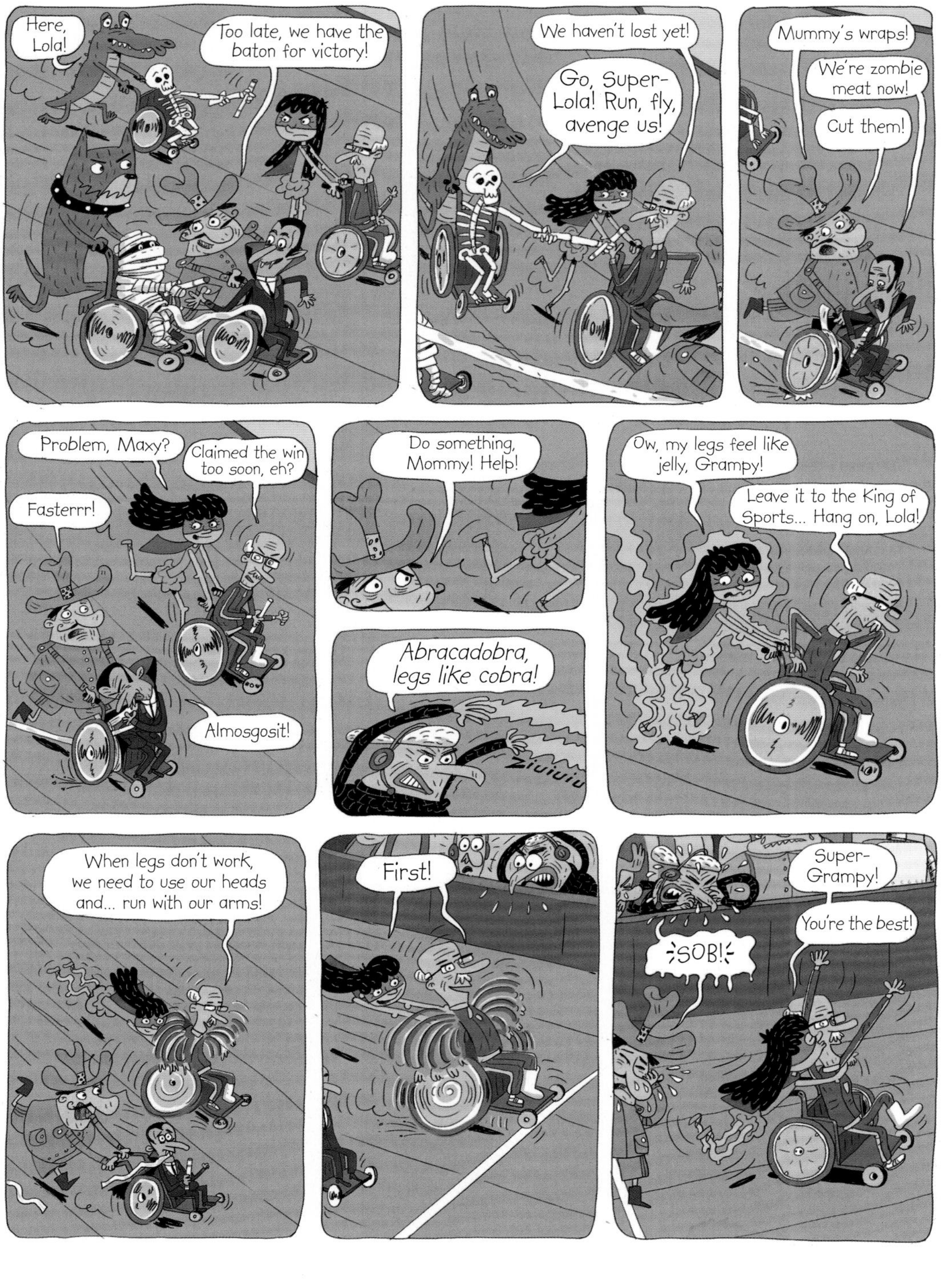

Here, Lola!
Too late, we have the baton for victory!
We haven't lost yet!
Go, Super-Lola! Run, fly, avenge us!
Mummy's wraps!
We're zombie meat now!
Cut them!
Problem, Maxy?
Claimed the win too soon, eh?
Fasterrr!
Almosgosit!
Do something, Mommy! Help!
Abracadobra, legs like cobra!
ZIUIUIU
Ow, my legs feel like jelly, Grampy!
Leave it to the King of Sports... Hang on, Lola!
When legs don't work, we need to use our heads and... run with our arms!
First!
SOB!
Super-Grampy!
You're the best!

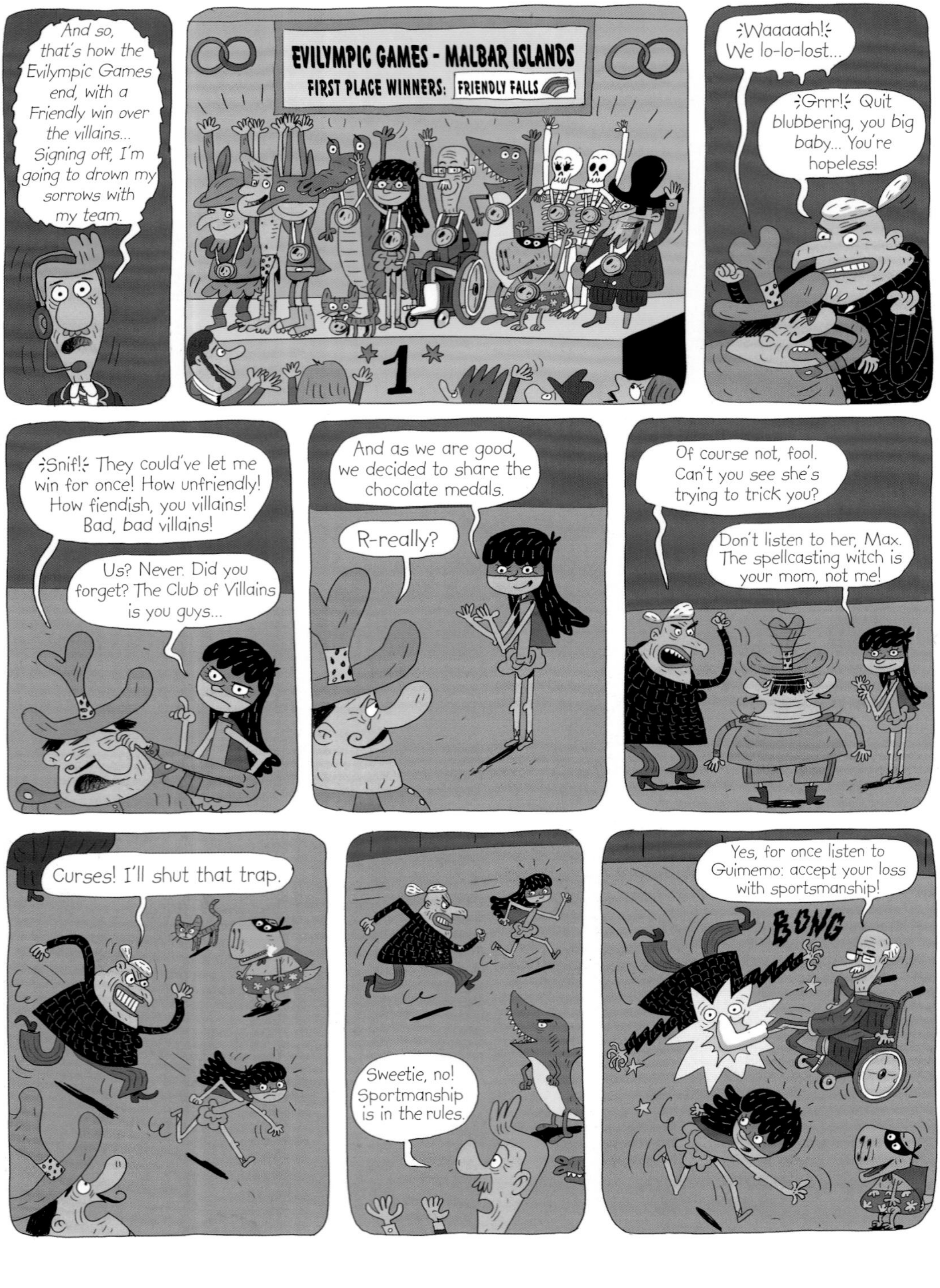
And so, that's how the Evilympic Games end, with a Friendly win over the villains... Signing off, I'm going to drown my sorrows with my team.
EVILYMPIC GAMES - MALBAR ISLANDS
FIRST PLACE WINNERS: FRIENDLY FALLS
1
Waaaaah! We lo-lo-lost...
Grrr! Quit blubbering, you big baby... You're hopeless!
Snif! They could've let me win for once! How unfriendly! How fiendish, you villains! Bad, bad villains!
Us? Never. Did you forget? The Club of Villains is you guys...
And as we are good, we decided to share the chocolate medals.
R-really?
Of course not, fool. Can't you see she's trying to trick you?
Don't listen to her, Max. The spellcasting witch is your mom, not me!
Curses! I'll shut that trap.
Sweetie, no! Sportmanship is in the rules.
Yes, for once listen to Guimemo: accept your loss with sportsmanship!
BONG

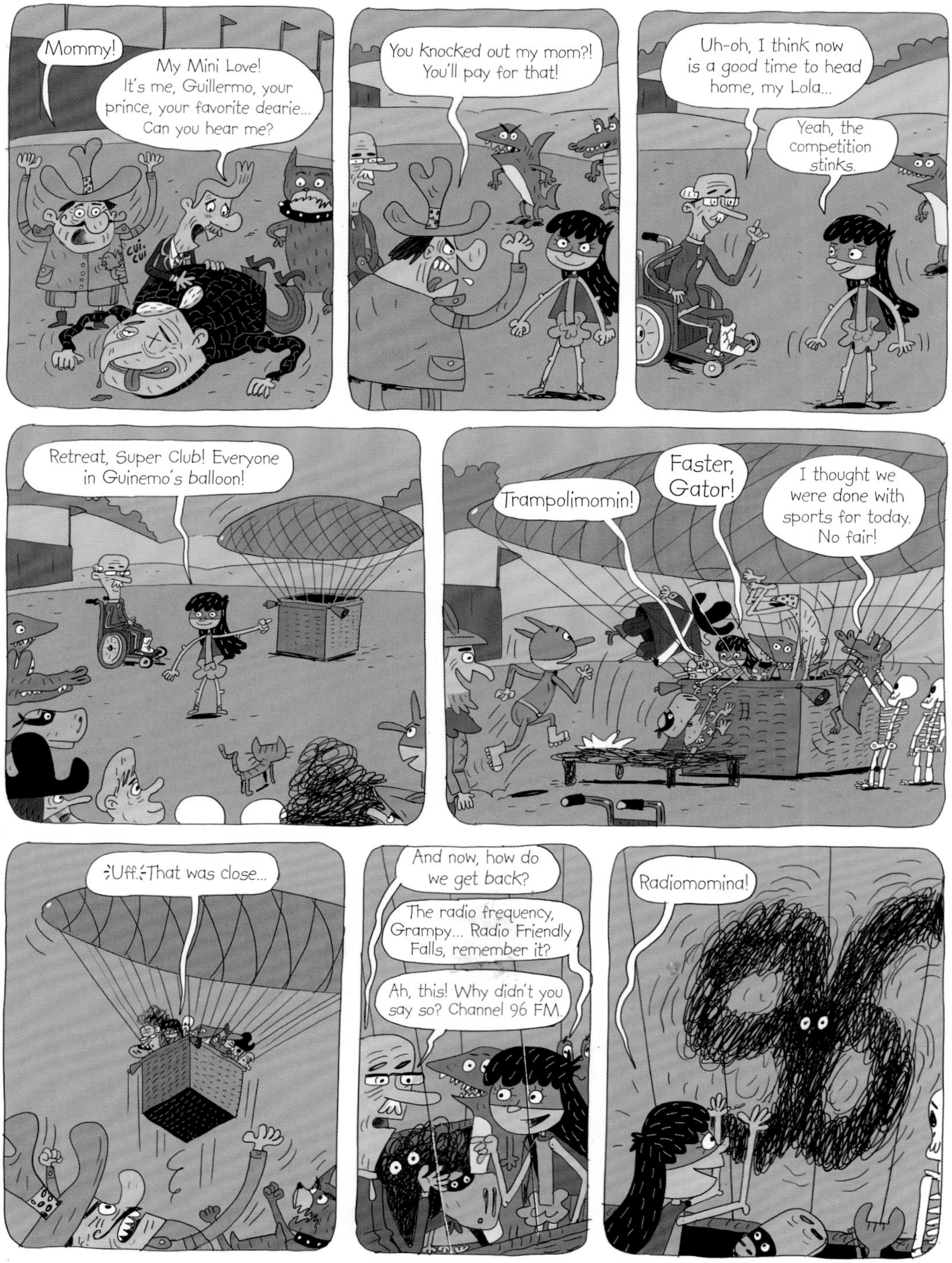
Mommy!
My Mini Love! It's me, Guillermo, your prince, your favorite dearie... Can you hear me?
CUI CUI
You knocked out my mom?! You'll pay for that!
Uh-oh, I think now is a good time to head home, my Lola...
Yeah, the competition stinks.
Retreat, Super Club! Everyone in Guinemo's balloon!
Trampolimomin!
Faster, Gator!
I thought we were done with sports for today. No fair!
Uff. That was close...
And now, how do we get back?
The radio frequency, Grampy... Radio Friendly Falls, remember it?
Ah, this! Why didn't you say so? Channel 96 FM.
Radiomomina!

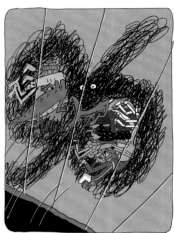

4 PM and you're listening to Radio Friendly Falls. Ah, 4, snack time!

In you go!

Time to get rolling, Mister Darkhair.

No problem, Miss. I won a gold medal in wheelchair racing...

Good one! And I'm the Queen of Friendly Falls!

You won the medal for Best Grampy in Friendly Falls and the Whole World and of All Time too!

Ah, my Lola! Friendliness is a daily event, never forget.

You got it, Grampy!

EXIT

RENE TOUILLET 2020

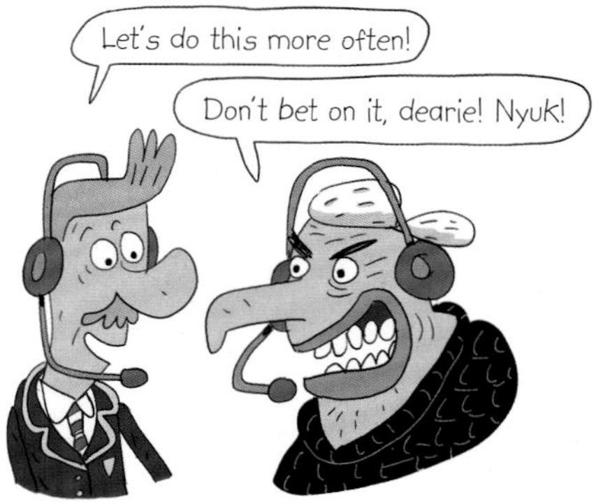
Let's do this more often!
Don't bet on it, dearie! Nyuk!

WATCH OUT FOR PAPERCUT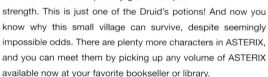

Welcome to LOLA'S SUPER CLUB #2 "My Substitute Teacher is a Witch" by Christine Beigel and Pierre Fouillet from Papercutz—those superlative sentient beings dedicated to publishing great graphic novels for all ages. I'm Jim Salicrup, the Editor-in-Chief and Max Imum's mustache consultant, here to offer some possible insights into one of the possible inspirations for some of the craziness found within this sophomoric volume of LOLA'S SUPER CLUB…

I'm beginning to suspect that LOLA'S SUPER CLUB creators are fans of ASTERIX, the classic series created by René Goscinny, writer, and Albert Uderzo, illustrator. After all, ASTERIX is one of the biggest selling comics series in the whole world, even though most Americans are still unaware of ASTERIX. Well, that's about to change because I'm proud to say that Papercutz (that's us!) has just recently become the American publisher of this classic comics property. And that's not all. It was recently announced that an animated ASTERIX limited series is being developed right now for NetFlix. It won't be available for a couple of years, but that just gives you plenty of time to read all the ASTERIX stories being collected in every volume of ASTERIX from Papercutz. By the time the animated series debuts, you'll know all about ASTERIX.

But why did I suspect the creators of LOLA'S SUPER CLUB to be fans of ASTERIX? Well, remember in LOLA'S SUPER CLUB #1 there was this: When Lola landed in 50 BC, some of you may have gotten the inside gag based on one of the best-selling comics series in the world, ASTERIX. That's the comic Lola refers to when she says, "to defeat the Romans you must drink a magic potion." And speaking of that magic potion, check out page 83 in this volume of LOLA'S SUPER CLUB, where Mini-Mum says to her partner, "Asterix has his potion and now so do you," as she hands him her cauldron of pure yuckiness.

So, who is this ASTERIX fellow that Christine and Pierre keep mentioning? To answer that we need to journey back to the year 50 BC in the ancient country of Gaul, located where France, Belgium, and the Southern Netherlands are today. All of Gaul has been conquered by the Romans… well, not all of it. One tiny village, inhabited by indomitable Gauls, resists the invaders again and again. That doesn't make it easy for the garrisons of Roman soldiers surrounding the village in fortified camps.

So, how's it possible that a small village can hold its own against the mighty Roman Empire? The answer is this guy…

This is **Asterix**. A shrewd, little warrior of keen intellect… and superhuman strength. Asterix gets his superhuman strength from a magic potion. But he's not alone.

Obelix is Asterix's inseparable friend. He too has superhuman strength. He's a menhir (tall, upright stone monuments) deliveryman, he loves eating wild boar and getting into brawls. Obelix is always ready to drop everything to go off on a new adventure with Asterix.

Panoramix, the village's venerable Druid, gathers mistletoe and prepares magic potions. His greatest success is the power potion. When a villager drinks this magical elixir he or she is temporarily granted super-strength. This is just one of the Druid's potions! And now you know why this small village can survive, despite seemingly impossible odds. There are plenty more characters in ASTERIX, and you can meet them by picking up any volume of ASTERIX available now at your favorite bookseller or library.

There's also another Papercutz super-hero we want to tell you about. His graphic novel series is just as wacky, if not more so than LOLA'S SUPER CLUB. The series is called ASTRO MOUSE AND LIGHT BULB, created by Fermín Solís, and we suspect you'll like it just as much as LOLA. Just check out the preview starting on the next page and see for yourself. Now that you have ASTERIX and ASTRO MOUSE AND LIGHT BULB to enjoy, don't forget about the next volume of LOLA'S SUPER CLUB, coming soon to that same bookseller or library that you like so much. Face it, there's never a dull moment when you're enjoying a Papercutz graphic novel—but it's no fun without you!

Thanks,

Jim

STAY IN TOUCH!

EMAIL: salicrup@papercutz.com
WEB: papercutz.com
TWITTER: @papercutzgn
INSTAGRAM: @papercutzgn
FACEBOOK: PAPERCUTZGRAPHICNOVELS
FAN MAIL: Papercutz, 160 Broadway, Suite 700, East Wing New York, NY 10038
Go to papercutz.com and sign up for the free e-newsletter!

Now, for an out of this world preview of ASTRO MOUSE AND LIGHT BULB #1

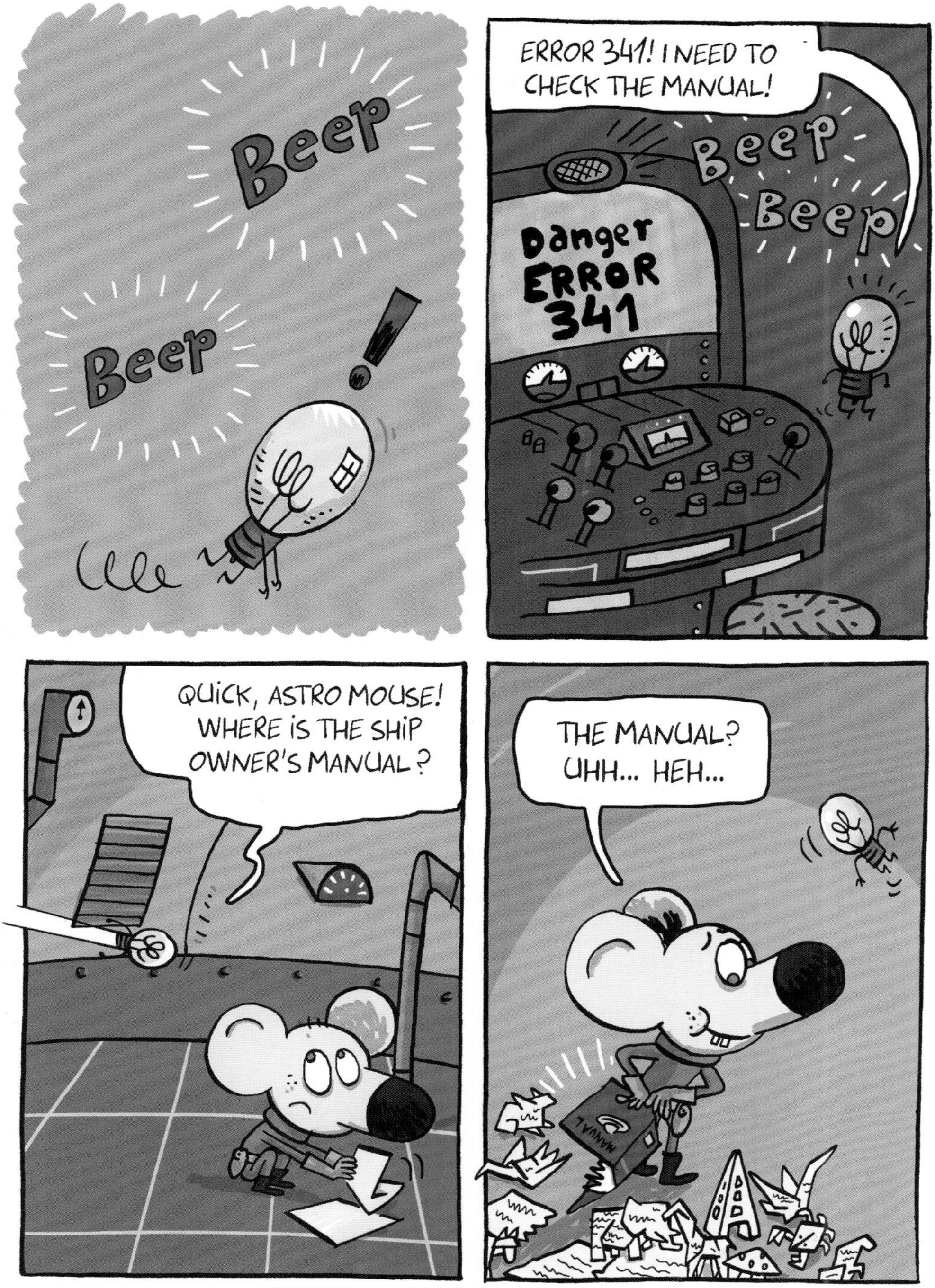

Beep
Beep
ERROR 341! I NEED TO CHECK THE MANUAL!
Beep
Beep
Danger ERROR 341
QUICK, ASTRO MOUSE! WHERE IS THE SHIP OWNER'S MANUAL?
THE MANUAL? UHH... HEH...
MANUAL

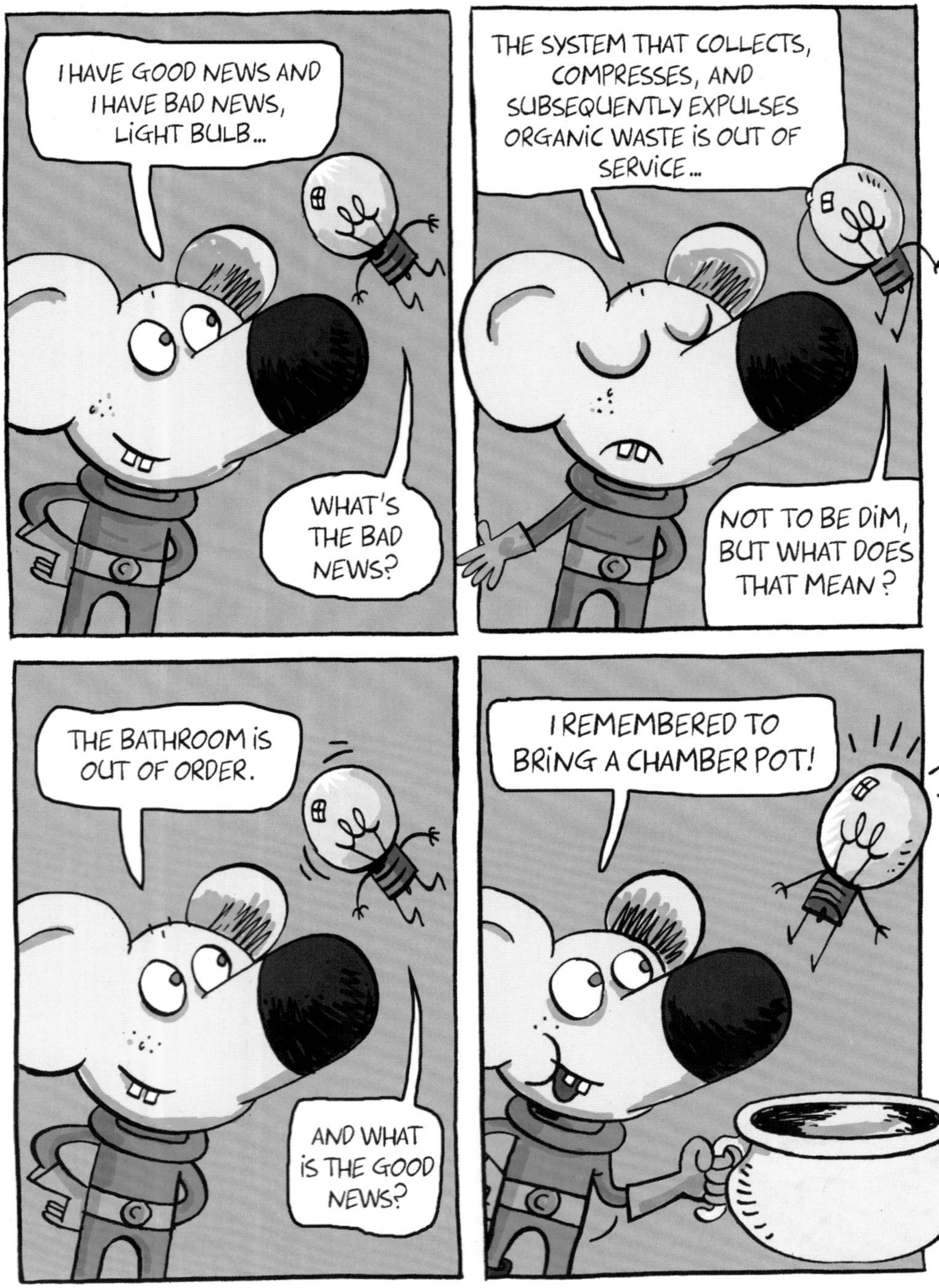
I HAVE GOOD NEWS AND I HAVE BAD NEWS, LIGHT BULB...
WHAT'S THE BAD NEWS?
THE SYSTEM THAT COLLECTS, COMPRESSES, AND SUBSEQUENTLY EXPULSES ORGANIC WASTE IS OUT OF SERVICE...
NOT TO BE DIM, BUT WHAT DOES THAT MEAN?
THE BATHROOM IS OUT OF ORDER.
AND WHAT IS THE GOOD NEWS?
I REMEMBERED TO BRING A CHAMBER POT!

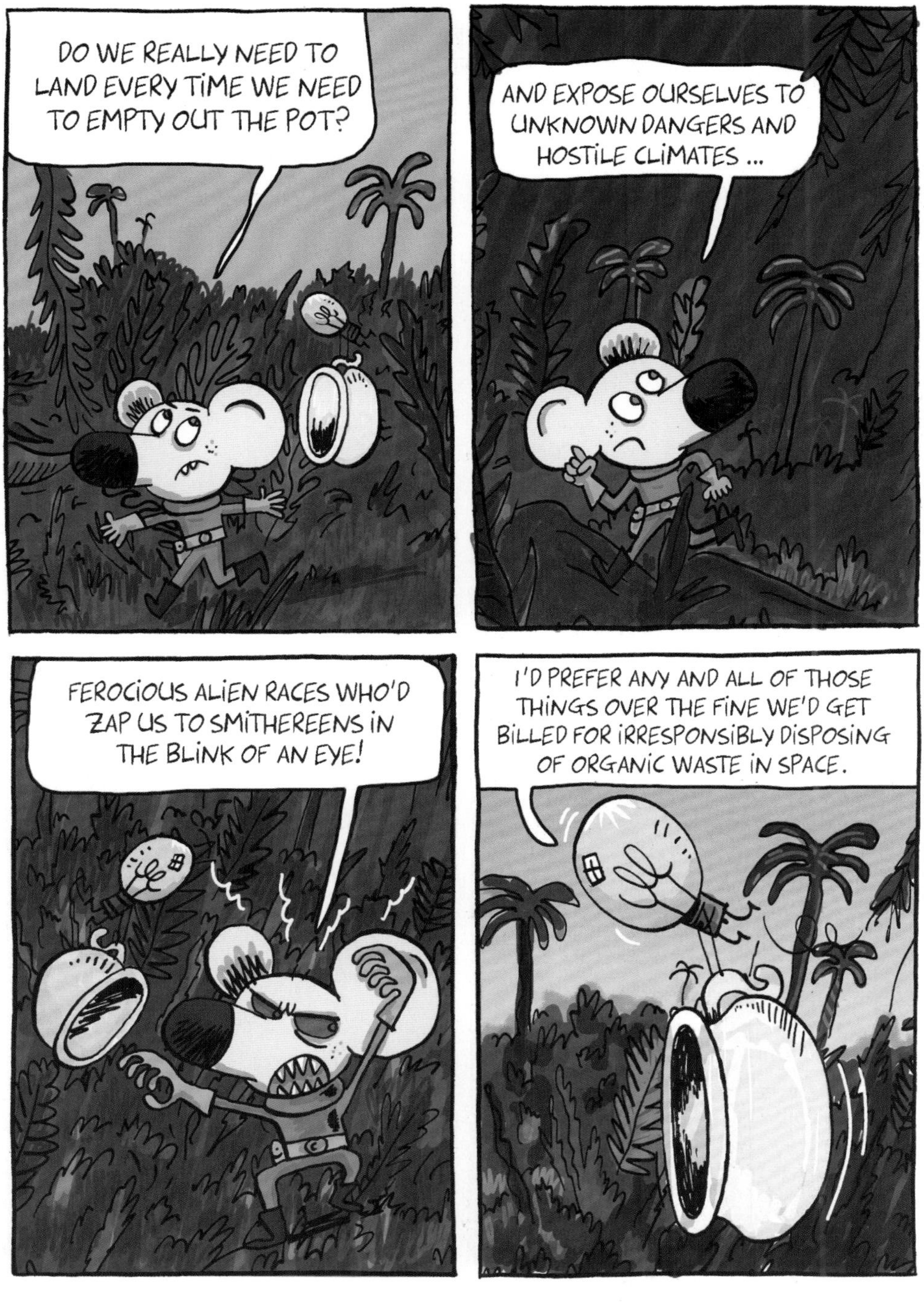
DO WE REALLY NEED TO LAND EVERY TIME WE NEED TO EMPTY OUT THE POT?
AND EXPOSE OURSELVES TO UNKNOWN DANGERS AND HOSTILE CLIMATES ...
FEROCIOUS ALIEN RACES WHO'D ZAP US TO SMITHEREENS IN THE BLINK OF AN EYE!
I'D PREFER ANY AND ALL OF THOSE THINGS OVER THE FINE WE'D GET BILLED FOR IRRESPONSIBLY DISPOSING OF ORGANIC WASTE IN SPACE.

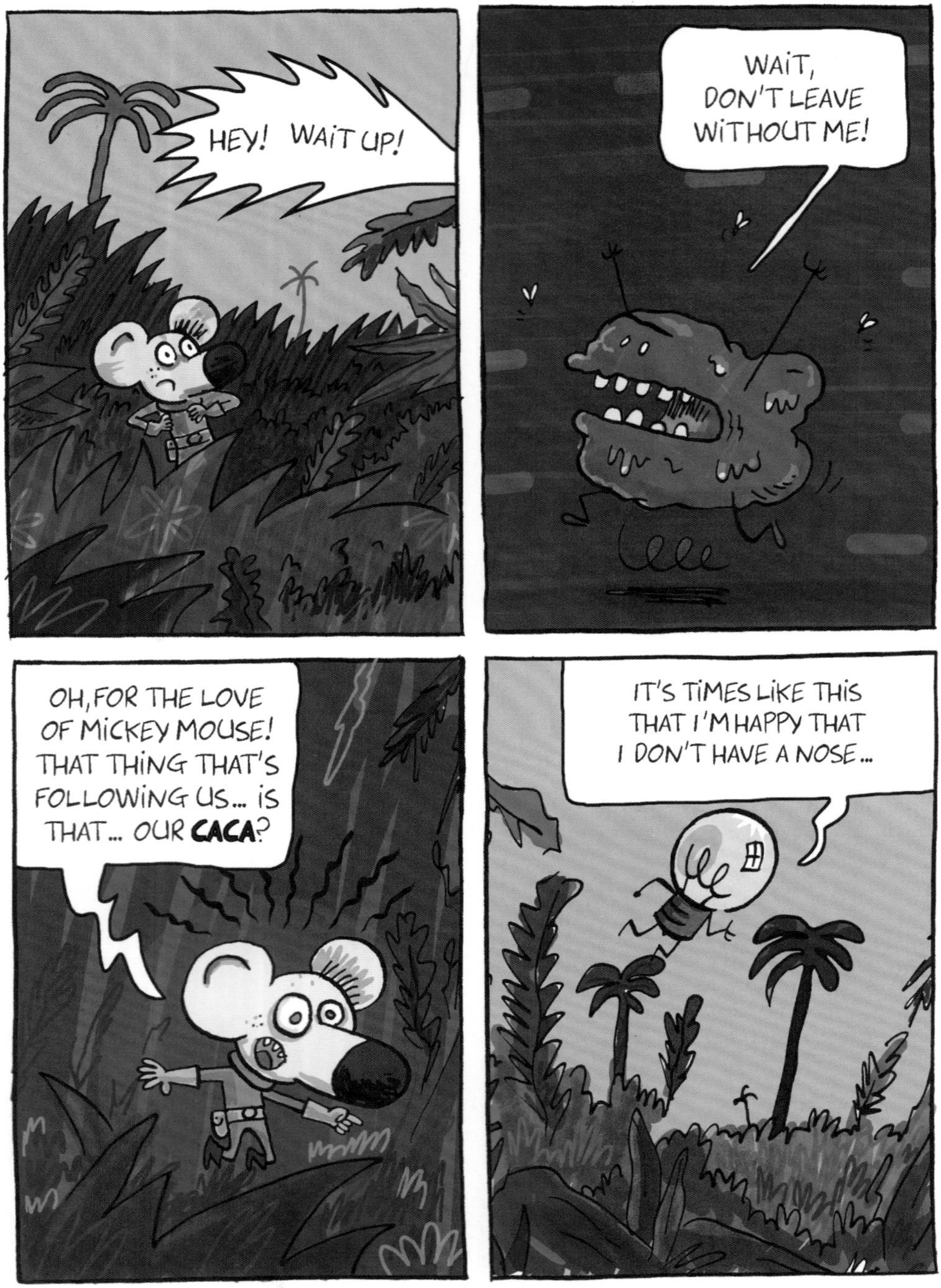
HEY! WAIT UP!
WAIT, DON'T LEAVE WITHOUT ME!
OH, FOR THE LOVE OF MICKEY MOUSE! THAT THING THAT'S FOLLOWING US... IS THAT... OUR **CACA**?
IT'S TIMES LIKE THIS THAT I'M HAPPY THAT I DON'T HAVE A NOSE...

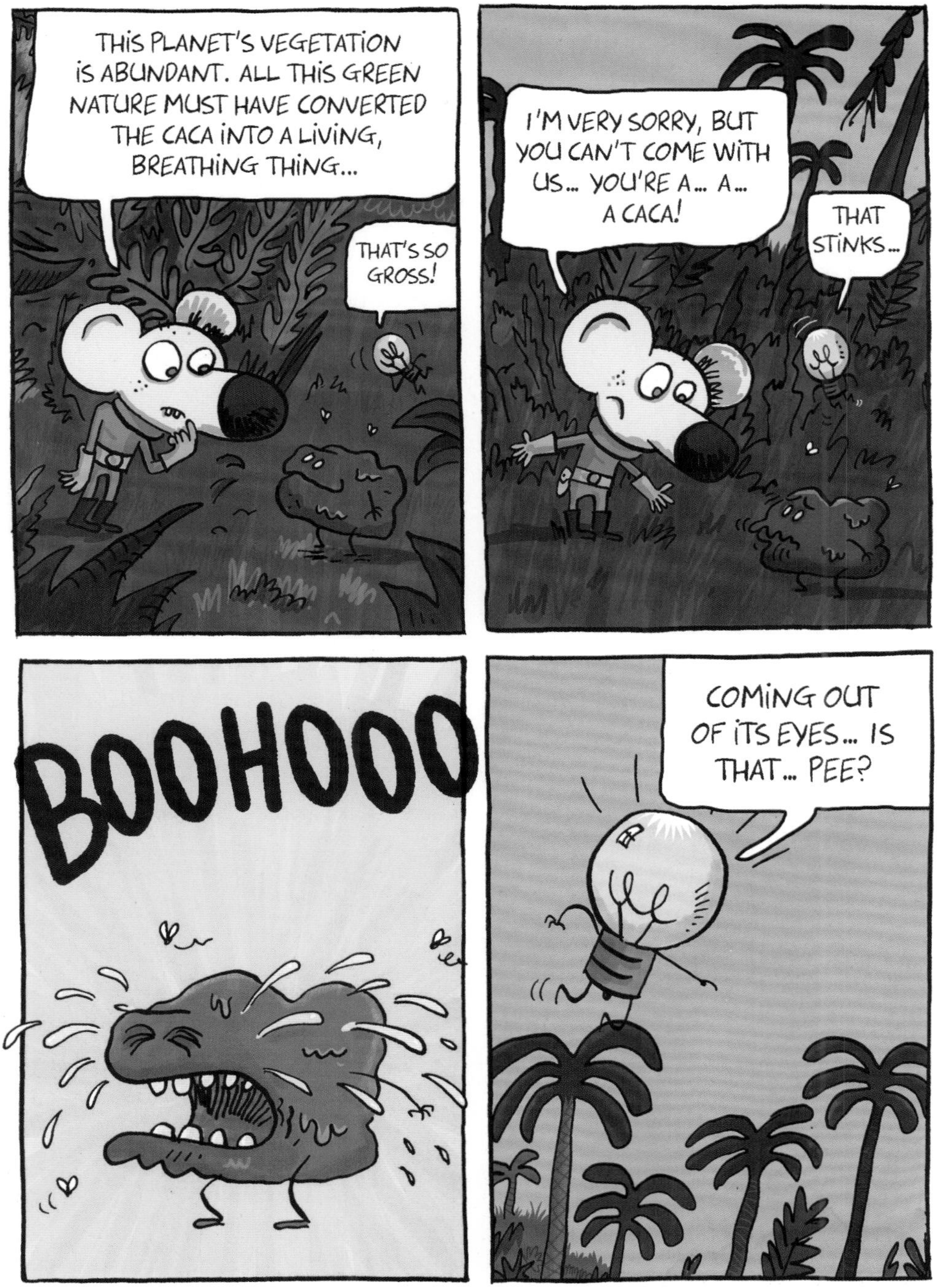
THIS PLANET'S VEGETATION IS ABUNDANT. ALL THIS GREEN NATURE MUST HAVE CONVERTED THE CACA INTO A LIVING, BREATHING THING...
THAT'S SO GROSS!
I'M VERY SORRY, BUT YOU CAN'T COME WITH US... YOU'RE A... A... A CACA!
THAT STINKS...
BOOHOOO
COMING OUT OF ITS EYES... IS THAT... PEE?

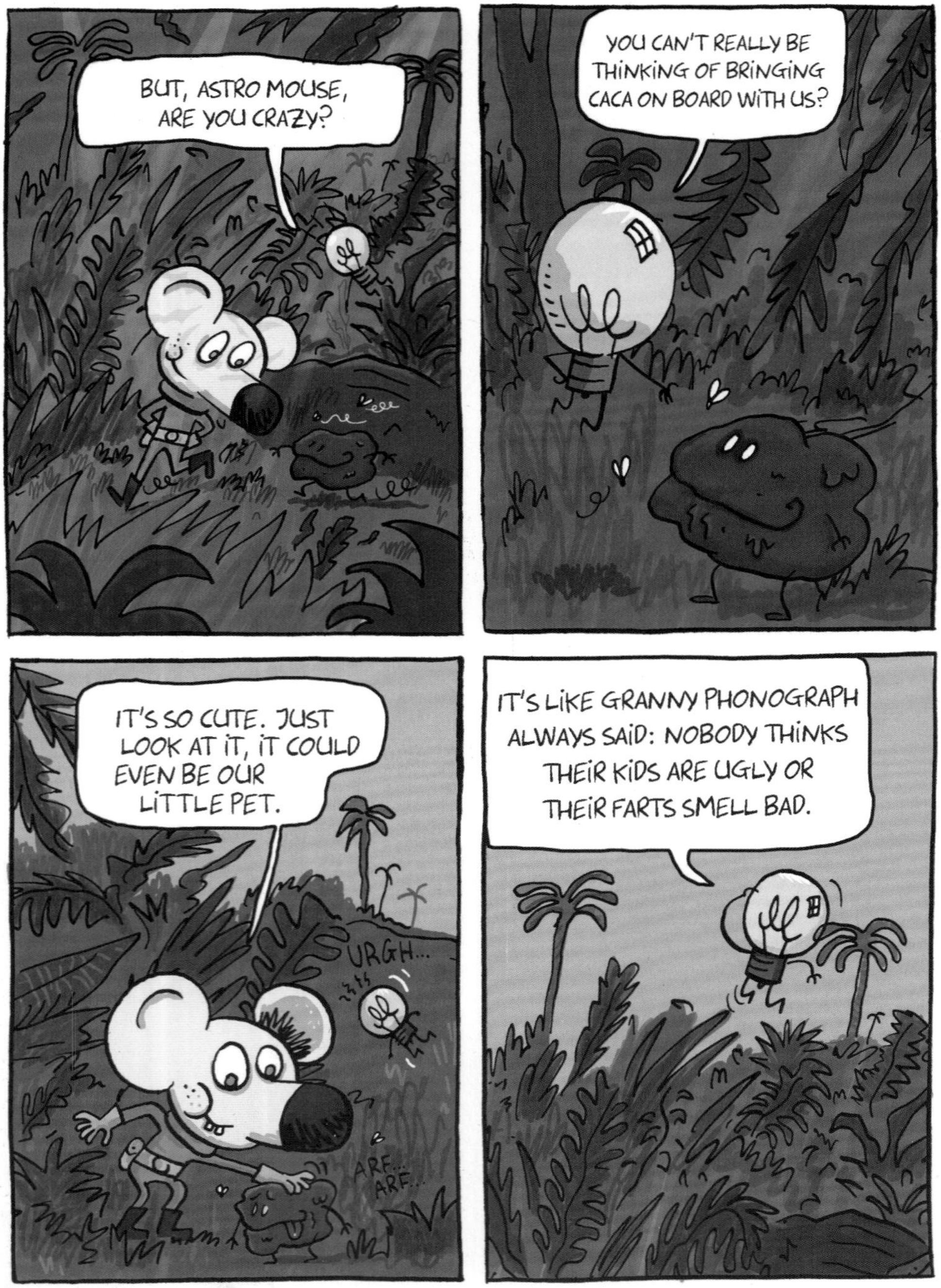
BUT, ASTRO MOUSE, ARE YOU CRAZY?
YOU CAN'T REALLY BE THINKING OF BRINGING CACA ON BOARD WITH US?
IT'S SO CUTE. JUST LOOK AT IT, IT COULD EVEN BE OUR LITTLE PET.
URGH...
ARF... ARF...
IT'S LIKE GRANNY PHONOGRAPH ALWAYS SAID: NOBODY THINKS THEIR KIDS ARE UGLY OR THEIR FARTS SMELL BAD.